PACT OF SILENCE

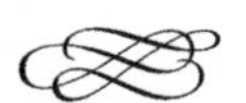

PACT OF SILENCE

LINDA HUBER

This edition produced in Great Britain in 2021

by Hobeck Books Limited, Unit 14, Sugnall Business Centre, Sugnall, Stafford, Staffordshire, ST21 6NF

www.hobeck.net

A CIP catalogue for this book is available from the British Library.

ISBN 978-1-913-793-48-7 (pbk)

ISBN 978-1-913-793-47-0 (ebook)

Cover design by Jayne Mapp Design

Printed and bound in Great Britain

❀ Created with Vellum

HOBECK ADVANCED READER TEAM

Hobeck Books has a team of dedicated advanced readers who read our books before publication (not all of them, they choose which they would like to read). Here is what they, and other independent advanced readers, said about *Pact of Silence*.

'It draws you in and keeps you turning those pages right until the last few chapters.'

'This book held on to me from the start to the end.'

'Another great book from Linda Huber!'

'What an emotional rollercoaster! Darkly addictive and packed to the rafters with secrets, I was flipping those pages, desperate to see how it unravelled.'

ARE YOU A THRILLER SEEKER?

Hobeck Books is an independent publisher of crime, thrillers and suspense fiction and we have one aim – to bring you the books you want to read.

For more details about our books, our authors and our plans, plus the chance to download free novellas, sign up for our newsletter at **www.hobeck.net**.

You can also find us on Twitter **@hobeckbooks** or on Facebook **www.facebook.com/hobeckbooks10**.

In memory of Alison, who loved books

PROLOGUE

MARIE, AGED 16

THERE WASN'T A SINGLE OTHER PERSON IN SIGHT. MARIE dropped her dad's old rucksack at her feet and stood in the scrubby grass by the roadside, apprehension pulling at her stomach. A dog was sniffing around the deserted snack van outside the petrol station further along the road, while a handful of sheep in the field opposite grazed placidly, legs wet with dew. Beyond the field was the glint of Loch Dunvegan in early-morning sunshine, misty green hills in the background completing the island scenery. Marie swallowed. This was horrible, but it was the only way. Mum and Dad wouldn't understand and they wouldn't want to, either. They wanted a good daughter, and she'd never be that now.

For the hundredth time she slid her sleeve back to see her watch. The bus was late. Marie stared towards the village, pinning the scene to her memory. Dunvegan was enveloped in the usual Sunday morning hush, old whitewashed cottages mixed in with modern dwellings and shops. She should have brought more photos; the village would soon be as lost to her as the rolling hills and craggy mountains of Skye would.

A rumble approached from the right. Thank God, the bus. Hopefully it wasn't Mr McDonald driving, or she'd be faced with a series of awkward questions before her journey began.

It wasn't Mr McDonald, and Marie heaved her rucksack right up to the back seat, where she could stare out of the rear window as childhood vanished behind her. She pulled the rucksack onto her lap and hugged it, inhaling the smell of home. Never again would she lie on her bed listening to *Sounds of the Seventies,* and she'd never curl up in the corner of the sofa to watch *Top of the Pops* again either. You had to be sixteen to leave home without the police coming after you, so she'd had her birthday, all pink candles and 'One big puff, lass,' and now she was free to go. Marie's gut cramped at the thought, and she pressed a hand against it. This was happening. Had they noticed she was gone? Would they come after her?

The island passed by the window as the sun rose into a perfect, open sky. A couple of sheep strayed onto the road, and the bus slowed down to inch round them – she wouldn't see that in Aberdeen. Marie fished for a tissue and dabbed her eyes. Half an hour more and she'd be with Euan. He'd be on his way now to meet her off the ferry at Kyle of Lochalsh, then their new life together would start with the drive to the granite city.

The bus was crossing the island now, and here was the scenery, the views the tourists came for. Dark peaks behind green hills, the odd glint from the sun on the sea, white horses topping the waves today as they sped in front of the wind. And on, and on, and tourists and cars and more tourists, and a road sign for Kyleakin. Nearly there.

The ferry was in, and Marie stood at the front of the boat for the few minutes' crossing. The wind blew her hair across her face as Kyle of Lochalsh grew closer, then the ferry jerked as it came to a stop on the other side. Marie trudged onto the slipway, where a crowd of holidaymakers was waiting to make the crossing to the most famous island in Scotland. She stopped, scanning the few buildings and the cars parked nearby. Euan wasn't here. Her stomach lurched anew and she stood still, her head swivelling from right to left. Euan, Euan, please come.

If he didn't, it would all be for nothing.

A car horn beeped, and oh, he was here and she was safe; everything was going to be all right. Her heart singing, Marie fled towards the battered Ford Escort now manoeuvring into place for a quick getaway. At the top of the slipway, she spun round for one final look. The narrow stretch of water she'd just crossed was sparkling in the sunshine, and beyond it lay her island, Skye, with its shining waters and wonderful, moving shadows and her beautiful Black Cuillin Mountains.

Today she was leaving for good – and she was taking the secret with her.

No one could ever know.

CHAPTER 1

SUNDAY, 14TH MARCH

THE BEST THING ABOUT LIVING BANG IN THE CENTRE OF YORK was that you could walk home after a meal out with an old friend. Emma Carter crossed the road and waved to Jasmin as the other woman's car passed by. They'd be able to do this more often now that Jas was living in Leeds and not London.

The floodlit towers of York Minster provided a breathtaking backdrop as Emma hurried on. She would usually stop and admire it – but not tonight. Luke would be home now, and wow, oh wow, at long last she could share the news she'd been keeping from the world since Friday. Telling your guy he was going to be a dad was definitely something you wanted to do face to face, but Luke had spent the past five days in Ralton Bridge, helping his parents after last week's storm demolished half their roof. Emma thrust her hands into her jacket pockets. It was still blustery even in town, and of course it had been a whole lot worse out in the wilds of Yorkshire where Marie and

Euan lived. But Luke had coped. He was lovely like that, her Luke. A kind person, and oh, this was going to be so good. Their baby – they'd be a family.

Emma laid a hand on her middle, fingers spreading protectively. It would be okay this time. She...

Her footsteps faltered as she rounded the corner into Aaron Street, then stopped. Glassy black windows were clearly visible in their mid-terrace home, a ground floor flat with a lovely view of the Minster from the living area. That was – odd. Luke had left Ralton Bridge over an hour ago; he'd texted her before driving off. Even in the rush hour it didn't take all this time to get here, and Sunday evening traffic was usually light. Hopefully they hadn't had a power cut or something equally disastrous. Imagine trying to get hold of an electrician at ten o'clock on Sunday evening.

Five paces on, the mystery deepened, because there was the car, parked on the street instead of in their private space behind the building. Had Luke brought his parents back for some reason? The private space was narrow and tended to be muddy underfoot, and Euan's hip made walking on slippery surfaces hard for him. Emma hurried the twenty metres to the flat, fumbling in her handbag for her keys.

Inside, she clicked the hallway light switch, and the hall table and coatstand were illuminated in the usual way. She headed straight into the main room. 'Luke – are you okay? I saw the car.'

He was standing in the kitchen area, an almost empty glass of red wine in one hand. Emma stopped dead. Here in the dimness, with the Minster floodlights throwing eerie shadows across the room, Luke looked like all the ghosts in medieval England had been chasing him down the A19. In the course of four days, he seemed to have lost his upright posture, and dark, staring eyes in a pale face completed the panda look.

He put his glass down on the kitchen island and came to meet her, enveloping her in a tight, silent hug, a pulse in his neck throbbing against Emma's cheek as if he'd been running.

It was a moment before he spoke. 'I'm fine. I just wanted to get inside quickly.'

Emma pressed her face against him, breathing in his familiar aftershave, then leaned back to see him properly. Luke might be fine, but something wasn't. She'd never seen him like this, eyes shifting all over the place and hands trembling against her back. After a few days away her husband was usually more of a 'whirl you round the room and into bed' kind of guy.

'Luke? Is something the matter with your parents?'

He kissed her forehead. 'Let's sit down. Glass of Merlot?'

Emma shook her head. By the look of things, the wine would have helped, but even the odd glass was off the menu now that a baby was on the way. She poured orange juice into a tall glass while Luke topped his up with wine.

He took a big swallow. 'It's Dad, Em. He needs another hip replacement.'

Frowning, Emma took her juice across the room to the sitting area. A second hip replacement didn't sound like a terribly big deal. Euan's first hip had been done about ten years ago, and she'd heard the story of the wound infection and subsequent long stay in hospital, but surely that wouldn't happen again?

'He'll be worried after last time, I suppose.' She let her voice trail away. Was this really about a hip replacement?

Luke joined her on the sofa, then knocked back half his

wine in two gulps. Emma removed the glass from his grasp and put it on the coffee table, then took both his hands in her own.

'Luke. I can see something's up. Just tell me.'

Silence for two beats. Then: 'We're going to swap houses with Mum and Dad.'

He stared at her, then at the floor. Emma froze, shock fizzling through her. The flat belonged to Luke; he'd bought it before they met with money he'd inherited from his grandmother, but for heaven's sake, they were married. Wasn't this something that merited a discussion, not a blunt, 'we're moving'? Ralton Bridge was a charming little place in the stretch between the North York Moors and the Yorkshire Dales and Luke had grown up there, but he'd never spoken of any wish to go back. And they'd only just finished doing up the flat.

She jerked her hands free. 'I don't… Luke, *why*?' And where had the macho announcement come from, for heaven's sake? He wasn't usually like that.

He pulled her close again. 'I'm sorry to spring it on you like this, but Mum and Dad are desperate. They can't cope with a big house any longer, and now Dad's hip's playing up and Mum's terrified he'll fall downstairs. You know how nervy she is, and with Dad being a bit older and another operation, they need a much smaller place. And preferably one without that big garden.'

His voice fell to a whisper on the last few words. Emma took a sip of juice, struggling to find the right questions.

'Okay, I can see that. But wouldn't it be better if they just sold the house and found a little bungalow? I thought you loved living here, and I certainly do.'

'I do too, but, um, Mum and Dad made a really generous offer. Financially, I mean. It's a good-sized place, Emmy, and we could make it fabulous. It's a house that could give us a future, don't you think?'

This would be the time for her news, but the joyful announcement she'd dreamed of making stuck in Emma's throat. Look at his eyes, roaming around the room, not meeting hers for more than a mini-second at a time. There was something he wasn't telling her. They'd only been married a few months and they were still discovering things about each other, which was lovely, but... you needed honesty in a relationship to feel safe. And the Luke she thought she'd known until tonight would never have agreed to such a life-changing move without discussing it with her first.

She turned away. 'Why didn't you include me in the conversation about it? I'd have come up for the weekend.'

He grabbed her hand again. 'I wanted to fetch you there, but Mum was in a real state. She insisted we sort it out right there and then. I was scared she'd lose it completely, and Dad was miserable. He feels it's all his fault.'

'I still don't understand why you agreed to swap houses. Their house would sell well, and they can do what they want now your mum's stopped working.'

He looked straight at her. 'Maybe I did let them sweep me away with their plans. But Emmy, think about it. A lovely big house, and nowadays it's only twenty minutes from York in the fast train. With the money Dad's offered me, we could do it up the way we want it, have kids, make it a real family home. We'd have a much healthier lifestyle there than here in the middle of a city.'

It was her turn to be silent. A healthy lifestyle. It was

exactly what the nurse at the GP surgery had recommended a few months ago when Emma went for advice about getting pregnant after the miscarriage she'd had at uni. Fresh air, along with a minimum of booze and caffeine and lots of vitamins was the recommended regime. According to the nurse, these very early miscarriages were usually nature's way of correcting something that had gone wrong with the pregnancy. That didn't make it any less sad, of course, and it had led to the break-up of that relationship – but in the circumstances, maybe Luke had a point.

Emma pictured the house on the edge of Ralton Bridge. A huge open plan kitchen-living room plus a pantry downstairs, four bedrooms upstairs. The possibilities were endless if you had the cash to do it up. And the garden, with a rose bed and a patch of lawn at the front, and a long, flat grassy area at the back with plenty of space for trampolines and swing sets. Hadn't she always wanted to live in a house like that, with a clutch of kids running around? Well, yes. One day. But – now? Like this?

Luke raised her hand to his cheek. 'You're okay with this, aren't you, love? I couldn't bear it if—'

For half a second, unending depths of hurt and horror flashed from his eyes, and Emma smothered a gasp. This was obviously hugely important to him. Okay, left to herself she wouldn't move quite so far from town, but this wasn't only about her now, was it? In Ralton Bridge, their child would have horses and cows on the doorstep and not a traffic jam in sight. And it was time he learned her news.

'Luke, I – I'm pregnant.'

His eyes widened, then he flung both arms around her and hugged her close. 'Oh my God. That's – amazing. A baby,

Emma!' He let her go and punched the air, a goofy grin spreading across his face. 'So you're okay about the move? That garden's perfect for a family. At least – we'll make it perfect.' Another shadow flitted across his face, then he was grinning again. 'I'm going to be a dad!'

He raised his glass and they clinked. Emma glanced outside, where the floodlit Minster stood silently, as it had for centuries. That was it, then. Soon, she'd have a different view from her living room window. There would be no wandering round quaint shops in the Shambles with the baby in its pushchair, no little feet thudding across this floor every day to look out at passers-by, no spontaneous picnics in the park. She – and her child – would live with fresh air twenty-four/seven and roses round the door. Nothing else mattered, really.

But he still hadn't said why Marie and Euan weren't just buying a bungalow.

CHAPTER 2

MONDAY, 3RD MAY

EMMA WAVED FROM THE FRONT DOOR AS LUKE REVERSED THEIR Zafira down the driveway and into Brook Lane. The car sped off towards Glenfield and the motorway to York, and oh, my, for the first time, she had a whole day alone in their new home in front of her. The move to Ralton Bridge had taken place last Thursday, just six weeks after Luke first proposed it. It was a huge amount of change in a very short time, and Emma's reservations about country life were still there, but she was determined to make a go of this, for the baby. She patted the flatness of her tummy – she still felt queasy most mornings, but it was on the wane now, and the midwife in Glenfield had assured her on Friday that everything was going perfectly. It was exactly what she wanted to hear, after last time. She'd lost that baby before she'd ever known she was pregnant, but now, at ten weeks down with thirty more to go, the danger zone was almost behind her. Bring it on.

She turned back into the hallway, which at least was free of removal boxes now. Luke had taken a few days off work last week to help get the place sorted, and the house was as organised as any house ever was the week after you moved in. They'd polished the wooden floors throughout the ground floor, and the newly installed kitchen at the back was out of this world. With French doors out to the garden as well as a smaller window at the sink, it was light and airy and ultra-modern, and Euan and Marie had paid for the entire renovation. It was gorgeous, but oh... Emma swallowed. The silence was deafening. After a lifetime with a city in the background, country quiet was going to take some getting used to.

Unaccustomed solitude seeped through her, and for a moment she slumped. It wasn't brown stuff hitting the fan, it was reality. Here she was in a new place, and okay, she had a job, but as translators spent pretty much ninety-nine per cent of their time working from home, she only had to go into the office for meetings and the like. As long as she met her deadlines, she could organise her days to suit herself. A lot of people would envy her that luxury.

She wandered across to the sink and gazed up the garden. Get a grip, woman. Moping around was no use; she needed to start putting down roots. A day off work to find her feet would be a good idea – she'd do some shopping in the village first, then she'd get started in the garden. Making a veggie plot was top of the to-do list out there. Hadn't she always dreamed of having home-grown veggies to cook?

Ten minutes later she was dusting spiders from Marie's old bike, the sun warm on her back. It was years since she'd been on a bike, but it was a skill you didn't lose, wasn't it? Hopefully. Emma pushed the bike down the driveway and along the pavement, grimacing. Typical, there was one steep hill around here, and you had to go up and over it to get anywhere at all in Ralton Bridge. Was she too young for an ebike? At least she had time to inspect the houses she was pushing the bike past, all good-sized elderly properties like theirs. And all as silent as the… Stop it, Emma.

The village centre started with the pub at the top of the hill – at least they had a pub within walking distance. From there, the road stretched downhill again, passing twin schoolhouses, the secondary school first and the smaller primary beside it.

Emma patted her middle. 'That's Daddy's old school, kiddo. You'll go there one day too.'

Now to try this bike, and yay, she could still do it! After an initial and hair-raising wobble, she caught her balance and freewheeled past a row of cottages before pulling up in the main street, where a little row of shops stood with the village hall and the library further along, and shit – even here, bang in the centre of the village, there wasn't another soul in sight. Where was everyone?

The reason for the absence of street life became clear when she approached the butcher's door and read the notice there. Oh. It didn't open until half nine on Mondays, and… she walked on a few steps. And neither did the small general store. It was the kind of thing you didn't notice when you came for an afternoon's visit with your in-laws. Actually living here was a brand-new learning curve. Oh, well, she would stroll along to the library and see what the opening times there were. It was a beautiful morning and the walk would do her good. And this was what you called whistling in the dark.

The following few minutes taught her that the library was open from three to seven Monday to Thursday and on

Saturday mornings, and there was a coffee morning in the village hall next Saturday. Good. She filled the next few minutes trying – and failing – to call Luke to ask if he wanted steak or rack of lamb for dinner. Emma stuck out her tongue at her phone. The signal in Ralton Bridge was crap. Welcome to country life… It was a relief when the church clock struck half past nine, and look, the butcher was putting one of those 'open' stands on the pavement in front of the shop. Happy face, Em – you're about to meet your first village shopkeeper.

The butcher was an older man with a bald head and one of those handlebar moustaches. His eyebrows rose when Emma went in, but he smiled as she requested mince for pasta sauce and a couple of steaks for that evening.

'Right you are, love. Haven't seen you around before.'

'We only moved here last week. I haven't met many people in the village yet.' Emma accepted the parcel of mince and waited while he weighed the steaks.

'Oh, Ralton Bridge is a great little place. Down the new estate, are you?'

'No, at the end of Brook Lane, in Marie and Euan Carter's old place.'

The butcher dropped the paper he was about to wrap the steaks in. 'The Carters have gone?'

Emma fished in her bag for her purse. 'Sort of. We did a house-swap, so they're in York now. My husband's Luke Carter, their son.'

She glanced up as she spoke. The butcher's cheeks had gone brick red, and gobsmacked would have been a good word to describe his expression. Emma hid a smile. Did no one ever leave this place?

The butcher yelled into the back shop. 'Carol! Did you know Euan and Marie Carter have moved away?'

A small woman with aggressively dyed red hair appeared, her mouth a round 'o' and her eyebrows high arches. 'Never! Kept that quiet, didn't they?' She wiped her hands on her apron, a grimace twitching across her face as she turned to Emma. 'Are you the new owner?'

The butcher spoke before Emma could open her mouth. 'Yes. She's Luke's wife.'

The butcher and Carol stared at each other while Emma smiled tentatively. What an odd couple.

After a noticeable pause, Carol met her eyes again. 'Pleased to meet you, dear. We've known Luke since he was at school with our lad. Mark's out with the van this morning.' She put a hand on her husband's arm. 'It'll be fine, Doug. Luke knows what he's doing.'

What would be fine? Emma gaped while the butcher slapped her steaks on the counter.

'Cash or card?'

Carol tutted. 'Pay no attention to him, dear. He gets nervy about new people, always has done. You'll like it here – what's your name?'

Emma supplied her name and wielded her credit card, and Carol chatted on about the spring fete, and the flea market that took place every summer on the village green, but not one word more passed Doug the butcher's lips, not even goodbye. Emma left the shop with a dozen question marks floating around in her head.

She did the rest of her shopping in the general store, which was run by a slightly younger man who spoke in monosyllables, and after the last experience, she wasn't about to attempt a conversation. So much for supporting your small local shops. If they wanted her support, they'd need to be a bit friendlier. She started back home, passing a white van parked outside the butcher's and catching a glimpse of Doug and Carol and a younger, dark-haired man in the shop. The young man looked up, but his face remained stony. Emma hurried on up the hill.

A SESSION in the kitchen filled an hour or two and transformed the mince into pasta sauce. Emma shoved the little row of tubs into the freezer and went outside, where the only thing to be heard was birdsong. A distinct aroma of freshly manured field was floating on the breeze; golly, this was a healthy lifestyle with bells on. Okay, the obvious place for her veggie patch was this strip of grass by the border fence near the back door. Emma fetched a selection of tools from the shed, and set to work. After thirty minutes' hard labour she had de-grassed a patch of ground about one metre by two, perfect for the first year's veggie plot. She swapped her spade for a garden fork and began to work the soil in earnest, trying to ignore the ache in her shoulders. Wow, you didn't need a gym membership when you had a garden, did you? The soil was streaked with thick and sticky clay that made every turn of the fork a feat of strength. When the church clock struck one, she stopped and wiped her forehead on her sleeve. Time for a shower and then lunch – she'd earned it. She'd just tidy up the edges here first. She grabbed the spade again and stabbed it into the ground, pitching forward as a jolt shuddered through her arms. A brick? She scraped soil away, and – oh, for heaven's sake, plastic got everywhere these days.

As well as a large stone, her thrust of the spade had revealed the corner of what looked like a black plastic bag. Emma pulled, but it didn't budge. It was the thick kind of bag you used to get in some clothes shops before plastic bags became taboo. She poked around with her spade, loosening the earth around the bag until up it came, dirty and clay-streaked but more or less intact, and full of something soft. What in the name of anything was this?

Dropping the spade, Emma peered into the bag. Clothes of some kind. Why would anyone—? She shook the contents onto the grass and stared.

A dark blue tracksuit and a yellow T-shirt, a smallish one, lay crumpled at her feet. They must have belonged to a woman or an older child. Emma crouched down and spread out her finds on the grass. The tracksuit top and the T-shirt were heavily stained with stiff, dark patches across the front, and the right tracksuit sleeve was torn at the shoulder. Everything was fusty and creased with age and presumably from being buried in Euan and Marie's garden for – how long? A shadow fell over the grass as the sun vanished abruptly, and Emma shivered. She stuffed the clothes back into the bag and hoisted herself to her feet. The only reason to bury something was to get it out of sight, but it was hard to imagine why anyone would want to conceal this lot, unless it was to hide those dark stains. Oil? Blood? Curry sauce? Impossible to tell.

She grinned suddenly. Of course... The whole thing had all the hallmarks of a small boy at work, in which case there was an easy way to find out, though it wasn't the sort of question she could interrupt Luke at work with. And now she'd done more than enough gardening for one day.

Whistling to cover the silence, Emma replaced the tools in the shed and went back inside. Well, country life was proving interesting, wasn't it – in a Midsomer Murders kind of way. The butcher and his family were creepy, and she'd found a bag of ominously stained gear in the depths of the veggie patch. This afternoon she'd go to the library, and fingers crossed she wouldn't end up with a trio of weird things happening in Ralton Bridge.

CHAPTER 3

LUKE, AGED 12

THE BELL RANG FOR THE END OF SCHOOL, AND LUKE STUFFED HIS English book into his rucksack. If he was quick, he'd get home in time to watch *Space Quadrant Omega* before Mum and Dad got back. He usually had to go to Alan's to watch it, because Mum and Dad said *Omega* was the biggest load of rubbish ever, and it was hard to enjoy anything with them tutting in the background all the time. But Dad was at work in York, and today Mum had gone there too to see a friend, so Luke would be home alone until half five. He slid around on his seat while Mr Aitken wittered on about homework before producing a handful of flyers from his briefcase.

'Before you go, I have a leaflet for the boys to take home. Ryan James, the trainer at Glenfield Sports Club, is starting a gymnastics group for boys aged twelve and thirteen. It's on Friday evenings in Glenfield Secondary School. Here's your chance to get fit before those exams next summer. Take one on the way out.'

Mr Aitken dumped the leaflets on the desk nearest the door and stood back. Luke grabbed his rucksack and joined the scrum to get out of the classroom. He stood in the corridor tapping his feet while Alan yakked with two other boys then trailed out reading a leaflet.

Luke shoved him in the direction of the side door. 'Get a move on. I want to watch *Omega* while I have the house to myself.'

'No way! You're home alone? I'll come too. Did you take one of these?' Alan waved the leaflet.

'No, I—'

Alan dived back into the classroom and returned with a leaflet, which he thrust into Luke's hand. 'I think it looks okay. Let's give it a go. Something to do on Friday nights.'

Luke stuffed the leaflet into his rucksack. 'Whatever. Come *on*!'

'GYMNASTICS, eh? I don't see why not. You could do with a bit of muscle on you, lad.'

Luke waited while Dad searched around his jacket pockets for a pen to fill out the form on the leaflet.

Mum kissed the top of Luke's head on her way to the dish-washer with the dirty dinner plates. 'I wouldn't have thought gymnastics was your kind of thing, darling. And I wish it was here in Ralton Bridge, not in Glenfield. You will be careful, won't you?'

Luke rolled his eyes. You'd think Glenfield was on the other side of the moon instead of five miles away, and if he had a tenner for every time Mum had told him to 'be careful', he'd be a multi-millionaire now. He accepted the leaflet from his dad and cut the form off the bottom to return to Mr Aitken. Mum was right, gymnastics wasn't his thing, but Alan was dead keen on going. And it might be fun.

Dad was shaking his head at Mum. 'Don't fuss him, Marie. Exercise is exactly what the lad needs. He spends far too much time in his room with that Game Boy. When I was his age…'

Luke stopped listening. When Dad was his age, he'd lived in Torridon right up in the north of Scotland and walked ten miles to and from school in a raging snowstorm every day. Alone. Uphill. In his wellies. You couldn't compare life in prehistoric times to modern-day Ralton Bridge, which didn't have a lot going for it, true, but at least there were other kids in the village to hang around with, even if places to go to were as rare as gold nuggets. The only other club Luke went to was the school chess club, but with just three other kids enrolled, it was pretty limp. Better than gymnastics, though.

He showed his mother the clothes list on the back of the leaflet. 'I'll need a track suit, and shorts, and indoor and outdoor training shoes.' This was beginning to sound like hard work, but he was one of the smallest in his class, so maybe Mr Aitken had the right idea. It would be awful if some of the bigger kids started bullying him because he didn't have muscles like Popeye. Luke wrinkled his nose at the leaflet. He wasn't soft, not really, but he wasn't sporty either. A few more muscles wouldn't hurt.

THE FIRST GYM club session was the following Friday, and Alan and his dad, Keith, picked Luke up on the way to Glenfield.

Keith chortled as they drove up Glenfield High Street. 'Reckon I've got a couple of Olympic champs in training in the car with me, eh, lads?'

Luke grimaced at Alan, who was rolling his eyes. Keith had no idea. He was a farmer, so Alan had to help with the stock in his free time, which would be why he was so wiry and probably why he was keen to join the gym club and get away from home more, too. Luke took a moment to be glad his own dad was a music teacher and didn't need help with his job all the time. It nearly made up for him being ten times older than everyone else's dad. But at least Keith was dropping them off and not coming in with them like Sid's dad was going to. That would've been totally embarrassing.

Glenfield Secondary was larger than Ralton Bridge Sec. The changing room was vaguely smelly, and with sixteen boys and five dads it was squashed for space, too. Luke pulled on his blue gym shorts and yellow T-shirt, then stared around the other boys. He knew about half of them, and judging by the big smiles they were all happy to be here. Two were flabbier than he was – great. The dads were all in a good mood too; a lot of joking was going on. Maybe this wouldn't be so bad.

The training team was waiting in the gym: a youngish man who must be Mr James, and two older boys, all wearing navy trackie bottoms and white T-shirts. The dads sat on the benches at the side of the hall while the boys huddled together on the floor. Luke crossed his arms in front of his chest. Just hopeful he'd be able to do this.

Mr James stepped forward and introduced the training team. Luke caught Alan's eye and they made a funny face at each other. Their coach had won ten county medals for floor gymnastics, and he'd run several marathons, too. That was pretty impressive. He wasn't a big man, but you could tell he had loads of muscles. He was younger than most of the dads, too, but he looked kind of old-fashioned with his black hair in a short back and sides cut, a bit like the guy who'd been the first James Bond yonks ago. Mr James soon had all the dads onside, anyway, talking about discipline and team spirit and all that stuff.

'Okay, boys – I'm sure you all want to know what we'll be doing over the next ten weeks to Christmas.'

Luke jerked to attention and nodded along with the others. Mr James, who they were supposed to call Ryan as this was a club and not school, was grinning down at them. It was a nice grin, but Luke's apprehension was tight in his gut. Why had he ever agreed to this? It was all Alan's fault, but he'd have to go through with it because Mum and Dad had spent all that money on his gear.

Ryan held up his index finger. 'The first aim: gradually increase your fitness level, and the important word there is *gradually*.' He swung round to the dads. 'This isn't the army. The boys are still growing. They should finish training feeling they could still do more.'

He turned back to the boys on the floor, and Luke held his breath.

'Second aim: have you all running at least three kilometres by Christmas.'

Gasps came from the boys, and nausea rolled right through Luke. Three kilometres! That didn't sound like gradual training.

'Bring your outdoor kit every week, and if the weather's respectable we'll be outside for half the session. Third aim: to get acquainted with some of the apparatus. Ready to get started?'

'Getting started' meant doing a whole load of core exercises, which were really just tummy and back stuff, then watching Harry, one of the two older boys, demonstrate a run up to a star jump, then straight into a forward roll and finishing up standing, feet together and arms outstretched. They split into three groups to practise that, and it wasn't as easy as it looked. Luke and Alan were in Ryan's group, and the trainer stood beside the end mat ready to grab them after the roll and shove them into position.

'Chest back, head up, don't stick your behind out, Luke.'

Firm hands pushed against Luke's chest and then his backside. Gawd, this was getting a bit personal, wasn't it? But at least he didn't fall over like some kids. At the end of the session, Ryan clapped his shoulder – in fact he clapped everyone's shoulder – with a hearty 'Well done!'

Luke shook himself as they gathered round at the end. He hadn't really done well, but it was nice of Ryan to say it to everyone.

'Bring your outdoor gear next week, lads, and we'll run to the top of the woods and back!'

Luke closed his eyes; this was getting better and better. It was miles up through Glenfield woods. Outside, Dad was waiting to collect them, and Luke sat in the back with Alan, and oh, man, his legs were complaining already. Ryan was okay, but... This was going to be hard work, and he wasn't sure he wanted to do it.

CHAPTER 4

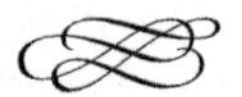

MONDAY, 3RD MAY

THE LIBRARY WAS OPEN WHEN EMMA ARRIVED AT HALF PAST three, showered and fed and having left the mysterious track-suit and T-shirt in the garden shed. A post-lunch phone call from her father in Jerusalem had cheered her up – he was so pleased about the prospect of being a grandad, and maybe the baby would help them regain the closeness they'd had when Emma was small. They'd lost that when she was a stroppy teenager, and with Dad remarried in Jerusalem now, things remained stilted between them. The baby would help fix that, but right now, she was going to find some like-minded human beings to interact with in real life.

She pushed her way through two sets of double doors into a long, high room with floor to head-height bookshelves around the walls and across the centre space. No one was behind the desk, but a woman was up at the far end with a trolley, slotting books into shelves.

The woman glanced up, then came to meet her. 'Hello! A new customer! I'm Kate Johnson.'

She thrust out a hand and Emma shook. At last, a real person around her own age, and she looked nice, too. Emma introduced herself, and Kate abandoned the book trolley to print out a library card.

She tapped Emma's address into the computer. 'I'm not sure there are any other non-retired people on your side of the village, you know. We live in the Vale – that's the new estate across the river, and most of our younger library visitors do too. We're extending the children's section after the holidays. At the moment they have a mere three shelves, poor things, but my husband and a couple of others are going to convert the old pantry into a separate kids' room. They'll love it. You got kids?'

Emma grimaced. That was another thing. They'd agreed to wait until twelve weeks before telling the world in general about the baby, but surely Marie and Euan should know? Yet Luke was holding out for not straining his mother's nerves in the meantime. It was ridiculous – she'd told Dad and her grandparents right at the start, and wouldn't Marie and Euan be thrilled at the prospect of their first grandchild too? Keeping them in the dark like this seemed heartless, and not at all like Luke. It would be so good to tell people about the baby, share the excitement and happy anticipation, but... Oh, well. Another two weeks would have them at the twelve-week scan, and then it would be all systems go.

She accepted a library card and smiled at Kate. 'Future music. But a kids' library's a fab idea. Is there a book club in the village?'

'I'm hoping to get one started after the summer hols. Jo Rivers and I took over here at Easter when Marge Simmons moved into sheltered housing, and we've big plans to bring the whole service right into the current century. I'll put you on the book club list, shall I?'

Emma agreed enthusiastically. This was great, just how she'd imagined village life would be. Kate showed her round the shelves, then went on to tell her about the Women's Group and the Hiking Club, which organised monthly hikes in the Yorkshire Dales or North York Moors.

'Ralton Bridge is tiny, but it's a good little place to live,' she finished up. 'What do you do?'

'I'm a translator – English to German, and the other way around too.'

'Wow! You must speak really good German.'

'I lived with my grandparents in Germany all through secondary school. Mum was German, but we lost her when I was just a kid. Dad's a diplomat, and he was sent to the Middle East at that time, so it seemed best for me to stay with Oma.' Emma blinked, hugging the books she'd chosen to her chest. With Dad and Wendy in Jerusalem and Oma and Opa in Friedrichshafen in the south of Germany, family was a bit scarce in her life. It didn't normally bother her, but… must be the pregnancy hormones.

Kate put a hand on her arm. 'How about a cuppa? Come into the staffroom.'

Over tea they discussed their upbringings and careers, with Kate running into the library a couple of times to deal with customers. Emma felt more at home by the minute. This was brilliant; she was making friends.

Kate finished the story about getting the library job and waved her hand at the window overlooking the hills to the west of Ralton Bridge. 'I haven't been here long either, though my husband's lived in the area most of his life. He works on his dad's farm and he'll take over the running in a few years.'

Emma took her mug to the sink. 'I wonder if our guys know each other. Luke grew up here too. What's your husband's name?'

'Alan. Let's find out – and we can organise a get-together either way, can't we?'

Three people came in and Emma left, a selection of books in her basket. She'd found a friend – how amazing was that? And hallelujah, Luke would be home in less than an hour.

HE ARRIVED PUNCTUALLY, and poured a glass of beer and one of juice while Emma told him about Marie's bike and going to the library.

Luke nodded, leaning on the work surface. 'I was thinking, I'll go to work by train sometimes. I can bike to the station in Glenfield, or if it's wet you could drive me. That would let you get out of the village more easily. You won't find much here.'

'Good idea – we can organise it as and when. By the way, do you know an Alan Johnson? The librarian's his wife, and she said he'd grown up here too.'

Luke cursed as beer sloshed over his wrist. 'Hell. Alan Johnson, yes, we were at school together here before I went to York, if it's the same bloke. Haven't seen him for years, though. Let's get those steaks on the go, huh? I'll get changed and light the grill.'

He about-turned and left Emma gaping after him. Had that been just a little abrupt?

Five minutes later Luke was striding back across the kitchen en route for the garden.

Emma followed on. 'I started to dig a veggie patch this afternoon. I thought we could go to the garden centre and—'

Luke stepped through the back door and stopped so suddenly she bumped into his back.

He swivelled round. 'Oh no, Emmy, you can't make a veggie patch there.'

'Why ever not?'

'It's, um, bad drainage at that side. Mum had hers there for a while, then she changed it because of that.' His eyes slid away and he gestured across the back garden. 'Anyway, I'm thinking we could get a big patio made all the way across here, with one of those automatic sun roof things that go in and out. We'd have the grill there and get a pizza oven, maybe, and it would be nice and flat for entertaining and, um, prams and so on.

He strode over to the gas grill parked under the eaves, and Emma stared at his back. He didn't want the veggie patch where she'd started it, that was clear. It didn't matter where the veggies were grown, and possibly she should have discussed it with him before leaping in with a spade, but his reaction was jarring, after all the 'Whatever you'd prefer, darling' she'd heard over the past several weeks. Still – a patio was a good idea.

She shrugged. 'No problem. The veggies can go further back.'

Luke blew her a kiss. 'I'll do the heavy digging, and a trip to the garden centre's a fab idea. Shall we plan what we want to grow tonight, and go there tomorrow? Yum, these steaks look good.'

Emma opened her mouth to tell him about the bag of

clothes she'd dug up, then closed it again as Luke's phone rang. He spoke briefly to a workmate, then bustled around the grill, pulling it into a better position and looking very busy. She watched as he lit the gas burners, his face pale. Was it her imagination, or was there something a little odd about all this?

CHAPTER 5

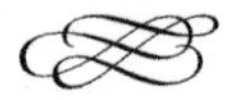

TUESDAY, 4TH MAY

THE DECISION WAS MADE. AFTER YESTERDAY EVENING'S SKYPE call with Oma and Opa in Friedrichshafen and seeing how happy they were about becoming great-grandparents – Oma had an impressive selection of baby cardies knitted already – Luke had agreed to tell Marie and Euan about the baby. He didn't want to go out for a special celebratory meal and give his parents the happy news there, like Emma suggested, but they were going to call tonight and let Marie and Euan know. It couldn't come soon enough for Emma – Marie was going to be overjoyed. Emma hugged herself. It was lovely to feel she'd be getting closer to Luke's family as well as her own. Now they'd all be able to bond over the new family member. Visions of everyone round the Christmas tree floated through her head – and they could visit Oma and Opa every summer.

She spent the morning with the usual vague nausea, but scrolling through baby furniture websites was a good distraction, though they weren't planning to buy much just yet. Apart from the master bedroom, the upstairs rooms still needed redecorating, and anyway, the baby would be in with them for the first few months. Imagine a little cot by the bed, or one of those attachments you could get to let the baby sleep right beside you. This was going to be so good…

Emma patted at her still-flat middle. 'I can't wait for your first ultrasound pic, baby. We'll show it to the family abroad, and your grandma and grandpa in York. Your daddy's all worried about his mum worrying about you, you know.' What a crazy family she'd married into, but at least they cared.

Luke had gone in early that morning for a meeting, so he was home by four, the perfect time to call Marie and Euan with such lovely family news. They settled down on the sofa, Emma's anticipation fizzing. Luke, Marie and Euan were all only children, so the Carters were a tiny family. Hopefully she and Luke would add a few more names to the family tree. She clasped her hands as Luke tapped on his phone then put it on speaker and held it between them. Marie didn't do FaceTime, unfortunately, so they wouldn't be able to see her and Euan's reaction.

'Hi, Mum. How's things?' Luke winked at Emma.

'Luke, darling, how are you?'

Emma smiled. It was the start of every conversation with her mother-in-law.

'I'm fine. Mum, put your phone on speaker, and get Dad. Emma's here too, and guess what?'

'Dad's right beside me. What is it? Has something happened with the house?'

Emma kept tight hold of her happy, excited feeling. Why did Marie always anticipate the worst?

Luke rolled his eyes at her. 'Nope. It's a family thing.'

'You've found some old photos in the attic?'

Emma laughed. 'Nothing like that. You can start knitting, Marie. You'll be a grandma by Christmas!'

A gasp came from Marie, then Euan spoke first. 'Congratulations, both of you – that's wonderful news.'

When Marie's voice came, it was three octaves higher than usual, and Luke held the phone further away.

'Oh, my goodness, Emma – are you all right? You'll have to look after yourself.'

Marie sounded more terrified than delighted, and Emma rushed to reassure her. 'I'm absolutely fine. Still feel a bit ropey in the mornings, but that's normal. I can't wait, and Luke's going to be a great dad.'

'Have you seen a doctor? What tests do they do nowadays?'

'We have a scan in Glenfield in two weeks. We'll send you any photos we get of the baby – and they might do a DVD later on as well. I'll probably go to the midwife unit in Glenfield to give birth.'

'A hospital would be better, Emma, then you have experts on hand if anything goes wrong. Luke, tell her.'

Marie's voice was trembling, and Emma clenched her fists on her lap. Marie didn't know about the baby she'd lost, and thank heavens for that or she'd be even more nervous. Where was the 'Oh, such lovely news, darling' kind of response she'd had from her own family? Was Marie going to jitter her way through the entire pregnancy? And heaven knows what she'd be like when the baby was born and she had a real live child to worry about. Thank goodness they weren't doing this in a restaurant; Luke had been right about that.

It took all the reassurance she and Luke could muster to

end the call with Marie sounding happy about the baby. Or maybe happy-ish would be a better description. Emma flopped back in the sofa.

Luke grinned at her. 'Told you she'd hit the roof. But that's the deed done, and she has another six months to get used to the idea. Come on, let's get going. It's almost five now, and those plants won't buy themselves.'

Emma rose to her feet, not knowing whether to laugh or cry. Hopefully the baby wouldn't inherit its paternal grandmother's nerves, that was all. She grabbed her bag and went through to the kitchen area for the list they'd made last night.

THE GARDEN CENTRE was on the far side of Glenfield, and Emma scrolled down the website on her iPad while Luke drove. As well as buying plants they meant to compare decking and tiles of some kind for the patio-to-be. Luke had suggested paving stones, but Emma was leaning towards wood. Imagine little feet pattering over the deck... Neither of them had a clue about making patios, though, so an info session with someone who knew what they were talking about would be a good start.

She glanced up as they turned into the main road to Glenfield. 'I wish your mum was more pleased.' The thought was out before her brain engaged, and Emma winced as Luke's face fell.

He pulled out to overtake a tractor. 'She won't worry so much when she's used to the idea. She's always been nervous, especially about medical stuff, but I'm sure she'll be thrilled inside.'

Emma laughed when he told her about the time Marie had taken him to A&E with a bashed elbow and then fainted while the doctor was examining him. Poor Marie – but her heart was in the right place.

Luke nodded towards the iPad, still open at the DIY store website. 'Okay, what have we decided about this patio?'

Emma put Marie's nerves to one side. 'Whatever we go for, it would be easiest to have someone in to do it for us.'

'If we get paving slabs, yes, but you might be right about wood being best. Tiles would be massively more expensive, and it's a big area. We could lay wooden decking ourselves quite easily. I had a look on YouTube at lunchtime.'

Emma pulled a face. The good thing about this move was Euan and Marie's generosity. The money they'd received from Luke's parents had paid for a whole load of extras they wouldn't normally have had, like the ensuite in the bedroom and the addition of a downstairs loo in what used to be the hall cupboard. 'Too expensive' was a concept she hadn't come across in combination with their new home – until today.

'Oh, Luke, we don't want to spend every waking minute for the next few weeks laying decking.'

'It could be our summer project. Don't worry, I'd do all the heavy stuff.'

He was taking the first two weeks in July off, but they weren't going away this summer, so they'd be stuck at home with wood and mess everywhere for heaven knows how long if they did it themselves. Emma stared out at the passing countryside. Slabs were sounding more attractive by the minute.

A farmer's market in Glenfield was packing up by the time they arrived in the town, and Emma made a mental note to come again next week. It would be ages before their veggie patch was producing anything edible, and they should support the local traders now they were living in the country. She said this to Luke.

He grimaced. 'Ye – es, though you won't find much in Ralton Bridge. That butcher must be the most expensive ever. We should suss out the minimarket in the Vale, and of course there's a huge Tesco's here in Glenfield.'

He pointed out the supermarket as they drove through town, and Emma nodded. She could take her time finding her favourite shops in the area, but this was a decent start. Luke swung into the surprisingly busy DIY store car park, and Emma went for a trolley. No matter what they decided about the patio, she wanted a selection of instant flowers for Marie's tubs – their tubs, now – at the front door. Some window boxes with geraniums would be nice too, though she'd need to read up on how to look after everything. She should have taken more notice of Oma's window boxes when she was a teenager.

They wandered around the outside area first, looking at different paving stones before going on to the wooden decks. Emma peered at the prices, doing sums in her head. Luke was right – decking was a lot less expensive, and maybe laying it themselves would be fun. She was about to suggest finding someone to talk to when her name was called from behind, and Emma spun round to see Kate from the library hurrying towards them. A tall, dark-haired man was pushing a trolley in her wake, a frown on his good-looking face. Luke gave a little jerk.

'Hi Emma! Well met. This is my husband Alan, and I'm guessing you're Luke?' Kate beamed at Luke, then turned to Emma. 'Have you started *The Blood Doctor* yet?'

Emma had, and opened her mouth to enthuse about it, then glanced uneasily at the two men. Both were standing with forced smiles on their faces, listening to her and Kate. What had happened to 'Great to see you again, mate'? The pair of them were acting as if they'd be best pleased if they didn't see each other for another twenty years or however long it had been. Emma aimed a discreet kick at Luke's ankle, and he mumbled at Alan.

'How's life in Ralton Bridge, then?'

Alan's reply was another mutter, but at least they were talking. Emma went back to her conversation with Kate. 'The book's fab. Are you here for plants too?'

Kate edged them both a few steps away. She smiled at Emma, two dimples appearing in her cheeks.

'We are.' She lowered her voice. 'Do you get the impression these two weren't exactly bosom buddies at school?'

Emma inched round to see behind her. The men were at least two metres apart and seemed to be having a conversation about wood. Alan was hefting a piece of decking and talking, and Luke was nodding and frowning, both hands stuffed into the pockets of his jeans. Neither man was looking at the other.

Emma's heart sank. 'An unresolved issue in the playground, you think?' For heaven's sake, they were grown men now. They couldn't still be arch-enemies, even if they had been back in the day. It would be so great if she and Luke could make friends with this couple. Kate was lovely, and she'd be able to introduce them to other people, too.

'Hm. Alan didn't say much when I told him about you, now I think of it. Let's find out.' Kate moved back to the two men. 'When was the last time you two saw each other, then?'

Silence for a beat, then Alan spoke. 'We'd be teenagers, I suppose. Luke went on to a different school in York, and we lost touch after that. I had a lot of work on the farm with Dad, and I guess I didn't have much time for socialising.'

The silence stretched uncomfortably. Luke's smile was going nowhere near his eyes, and Emma took his arm. No matter what had happened back then, this was no place to start a post-mortem into why the friendship had broken down. She would find out more at home.

She met Kate's eyes. 'Any ideas about patios? We can't decide between wood and slabs.'

Kate leapt into the breach. 'We put down a wooden one when we moved in, but if we had the cash, I'd prefer...'

She chatted on about the pros and cons of wooden decking, Emma chipping in with a few questions while the men stood like trees beside them. A message pinging into her phone gave Emma the opportunity to break things up.

'We'd better get a move on. I'll come into the library tomorrow, Kate, if you're there?'

Kate gave her a knowing look. 'I'll be there from three onwards. We can get you set up to borrow ebooks too, if you like.'

Emma followed on as Luke manoeuvred their trolley back to the paving slabs, where a store employee was unloading sacks of something from a trolley. Thank goodness, Luke was looking more normal now they'd left the other couple. She listened as the store guy waxed lyrical about natural slate paving while Luke nodded enthusiastically by her side. The store assistant produced a handful of leaflets and left them to look for themselves.

Luke rolled the leaflets up and stuffed them into his inside pocket. 'Let's think about it at home. We can get estimates in for both stone and wood, and take it from there. Okay – plants for the tubs.'

Emma loaded a mixture of geraniums, petunias and begonias into the trolley while Luke hefted in some compost for them, and they left the store. Kate and Alan were at the far end of the car park, but Luke either didn't notice or didn't comment, and Emma didn't either. It was a conversation to have at home.

She broached the subject when they were unloading the plants.

'Going to school in York must have been a bit of a journey for you in those days, and a wrench leaving Alan and your other friends behind.'

Luke went pink. 'Sorry about that, in the garden centre. Alan and I were friends when we were kids, but we didn't get on when we were older. Mum and Dad thought I'd get a better education in York, so they sent me there when I was thirteen. I suppose they wanted the best for me. I always felt a bit out of things, here in the village. Dad was so much older than everyone else's dad, and he wasn't friendly with any of the other dads. Stuff like that matters to kids at that age. I was glad to go to York, and they were right – it was a better school.'

Frowning, Emma put her tray of begonias into the shed while she digested this long – overlong? – explanation. 'I wonder if any of your other old schoolmates are still around? It would be nice to know more people here.'

Luke took her arm as they walked back to the house. 'Ralton Bridge is the kind of place most kids can't wait to get out of when they're old enough. We don't need to lose our York friends, Emmy. Don't forget how close it is by train. We can go to as many pub crawls as you like in downtown York.'

This was true, except she was off the booze for the foreseeable, but it was no reason not to make friends in the local community, was it? Emma put the subject to bed for the moment and pouted at the grey stone container that had stood by the back door for as long as she'd known Marie. It was odd, inheriting stuff like this. The pot wasn't her taste, but it was a handsome piece and there was no reason to throw it out, was there?

Maybe Luke was right and they should go back to York for evenings out. And chumming up with people was possibly more of a girl thing, so she'd do her best and see where it took them. They strolled round the garden, planning fruit trees and swing sets and sandpits for later. Luke's ideas for the baby made up for Marie's lack of joyful enthusiasm, and it wasn't until he was snoring beside her in bed that a thought struck Emma.

Luke hadn't told her why he and Alan had stopped getting on. She rolled on her side, pulling the duvet tight round her neck. Men weren't half complicated sometimes.

CHAPTER 6

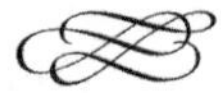

LUKE, AGED 12

THIRD GYM CLASS, HERE THEY CAME. LUKE STUFFED HIS FRESHLY ironed kit into the new sports bag Dad had bought him. Dad was one hundred per cent onside about the gym club now. He went around saying things like 'It'll make a man of you, son,' and 'No pain no gain.' Ryan James' ex-girlfriend was Dad's bank manager's daughter, and she was away now doing voluntary service in India, and Dad said the world needed more people like that. Mum said she didn't want Luke to go to India, but it showed you what good, community-spirited people they had around here, because Ryan worked in the animal shelter in Glenfield in his spare time. Luke sniffed. In other words, he was stuck with the gym club for the duration. At least Alan's dad was letting the two of them do their running practice in the long barn at the farm if it was raining.

Last Friday had been wet, so the first official gym club run in the woods had been put off until tonight. Luke was dreading it. He was always the first out of puff when they played footie at school. Hopefully they wouldn't have half the town out ogling them tonight, that was all. Alan was dead keen to get going on the apparatus training afterwards, too, because all they'd done last week was floor work. Luke shrugged into his jacket. What he needed was some of his friend's enthusiasm.

Dad was dropping them off tonight, and Alan's dad would pick them up at the end. The doorbell bing-bonged, and Luke grabbed his bag and ran. That would be Alan; he'd said he was going to walk down to the village as a kind of warm-up. Talk about over-keen... Mum had the front door open before Luke made it downstairs, and Alan was yakking to her on the step.

'I did forty sit-ups this morning. I'm going to get fit as fast as I can.'

Luke pulled a face when Alan wasn't watching. He'd heard nothing else all week. But at least Mum was on his side.

'Make sure you don't overdo it, lovvies. Remember you're still growing.' She fussed at the collar of Luke's jacket and kissed him before he managed to escape, and Alan stuck his tongue out at him.

Luke led the way round to the car, Alan blah-blahing in his ear all the time. What a waste of an evening, scampering around in the woods getting all hot and sweaty, then jumping over boxes and stuff in the gym. But the sooner they got to Glenfield, the sooner they'd be coming home again.

Fourteen boys were messing about in the changing room this week. The other two had apparently decided gym club wasn't for them. 'Losers' was the general opinion, and Luke sighed. If it was left up to him, he wouldn't be here either, but he wanted more muscles, didn't he? He fixed on a happy expression and laced up his outdoor trainers. Glenfield Wood, get ready for action. Whoopee.

Ryan was waiting in the gym with Harry and Jason. 'We'll warm up all together in here, then Harry will set the pace through the woods. Jason, you stay mid-group, and I'll bring up the rear. Boys – no talking, no taking short cuts. Stick to your own walk-run rhythm. Don't try to keep up with your mate if he's faster. This is not a race. Ready?'

Mumbles of 'yes'.

'I didn't hear that. Are we ready?'

'Yes!'

Alan was bobbing up and down on his toes, all keen to get going, and Luke shuffled to the middle of the group. They marched briskly round the gym hall for a few minutes, doing arm swings and twists, then Harry blew his whistle and set off outside. Luke trotted along, Alan beside him with a big stupid grin stretching from ear to ear, and actually it wasn't too bad – they were going pretty slowly. They cut across the playground and tramped along a scrubby path behind the school before heading up into the woods and - oh, man. A gentle slope was a mountain when you were running.

Luke fixed his eyes on the track ahead as his legs screamed in protest. Glenfield Wood stretched all the way up and down the valley. They'd come here sometimes to look for leaves and conkers and stuff when he was a little kid in the Beaver Scouts, and what wouldn't he give to be safe in the Beavers tonight? He should have stuck to the scouts; they were on Friday nights too, and oh, no, the others were all overtaking him and he couldn't go faster, he was going to—

A hand thudded on Luke's back as Ryan appeared behind

him and literally shoved him up the track. 'Nearly there! You're at the top! Walk now.' He rubbed Luke on the head and went back to give Mark, the butcher's son from Ralton Bridge, a shove uphill too.

The walking pace was slower this time and Luke caught up with a couple of the others, but he was still winded when he had to run again. His legs had gone all pink and shaky. The dank smell of woodland after this morning's rain was all around them and the trees were bobbing up and down as he ran, and oh, he couldn't do this. He was going to be sick. Two more boys passed him, and Alan had vanished into the distance. This was the pits.

'Nice and slow, lad. You'll be fine.' Ryan was beside him, with Mark stumbling along behind. Mark was a big, sturdy boy – his voice was breaking already – in the same year as Luke, but right this minute he looked almost as bad as Luke felt.

'Keep to your walk-run, but make it slow.' Ryan's hand was on Luke's back, rubbing across his shoulders as they walked. 'Five minutes, and we'll be back.'

The track flattened out then tipped downhill, and Luke chugged along, glad of the encouraging words and glad of the hand across his shoulders as they went. Mark was managing better now too, but they were the last – bummer, the others were right out of sight.

Ryan grinned at them. 'Ready for a quicker bit? On we go.'

The pace lifted, and Luke set his teeth. He had to keep up with Mark at the very least or Alan would never let him hear the end of it.

Ryan's hand was pushing again, propelling Luke forward. 'Okay, we're going to catch them up. Go!'

The pace increased again, and Luke gripped the front of his T-shirt. His heart was going boom-boom-boom under there; was that healthy? Ryan's hand slid down until he was shoving him along right down at his bum, heck. Luke tried to twitch away, but the hand stayed on his backside, hard fingers pushing him forward. Oh man, this was seriously weird…

Luke pulled out reserves he didn't know he had, forcing his legs on and on along the track, and Ryan let go. Relief flooded through Luke. They rounded a bend, and yay, he was catching up! Mark was there with the last of the others already, and thank God, they were back in the group.

Elation filled Luke as they trundled out of the woods and back to the playground, where Ryan shot ahead and pulled the group around him so that no one could see who was first and who was last. He was good like that, Ryan. Glenfield Sec had a clock above the main door, and Luke glanced up while he was trying to get his breath back. Holy cow, they'd been out for less than half an hour. It felt like several centuries.

Ryan high-fived them each in turn. 'Well done, team. We'll have a break and a quick shower if you want one, and we'll meet back in the gym at ten past. I'm proud of you!'

Alan was pink and you'd think he'd just finished the Great North Run, the way he was going on about being fourth out of the woods. Luke flopped down on the hard bench in the smelly changing room and sipped his water. Some of the others had disappeared into the showers, but he didn't have the energy and he'd only have to shower again later anyway. He massaged his blotchy pink thighs. This had better be worth it in the end. Good job Ryan wasn't one of those sergeant-major types of coach. He gave you a hand when you needed it, even if… Luke pushed the uncomfortable feeling away. It was all right; nothing had happened.

After the break, they went into the gym, where they had to turn some benches over, leaving the narrow bar along the base uppermost.

Ryan clapped his hands. 'Balance work now, two to three boys per bench. You want to practise slow walking along the bar, forwards and backwards.'

Luke joined Alan and Mark and led the way walking along the bar, which was actually more difficult when you were trying to go slowly. He said this to Alan.

Alan snorted. 'That so? Better go super-slow, then. That'll make it even harder, won't it?'

He started doing an exaggerated slow-motion walk along the bar, stretching his arms to the side and making out he was going to fall any second. Mark sniggered, and Alan turned his head to say something and promptly pitched off the bench, grabbing Luke as he fell. They both ended up on their bums on the floor.

'Hey! What did we say the first rule of gymnastics is?' Ryan towered above them, thick black eyebrows knitted together.

Luke scrambled up. 'Be safe.' Everyone was gawping at them now.

'I wasn't asking you. You weren't being unsafe. The first rule, Alan, is…?'

Alan got to his feet too, grimacing. 'Be safe.'

'Don't do that again. What hurts?'

'Stubbed me toe.'

Ryan examined the toe and sent Alan to sit out for five minutes. 'No harm done.'

The class ended with them all cross-legged on the floor

while Ryan talked about different runs he'd done. He even told them a funny story about how he'd ignored instructions on his first ever run when he was their age, and ended up with a sprained ankle.

'And the lesson we learn from that?' He raised his eyebrows at the boys.

'Do what you're told?' Luke spoke before his brain engaged. Glory, Alan would kill him.

'Correct. Discipline.' Ryan ruffled Alan's hair. 'We'll make that stubbed toe the first and last non-discipline accident, huh? You have potential, mate – use it.'

The last sentence was to Alan, and Luke rolled his eyes as his friend went bright red. Potential! He'd never hear the end of that.

Ryan was waiting when they came out of the changing room after class. 'Who's picking you up, Alan?'

'My dad.'

'Good. I'll come out with you and mention your stubbed toe – and that it wasn't your fault, of course.'

Ryan winked at Alan, and Luke grinned at his friend's face.

'Aw, no, Ryan.'

'Aw, yes, Alan. Got to show the parents I'm trustworthy, huh?'

Ryan walked with them to the car, and explained to Keith that Alan had stubbed a toe but there shouldn't be any ill-effects and boys will be boys and so on. By the end of that, Alan's dad was laughing and Alan was too – the 'p' word had come up again.

Keith winked at Alan while they were waiting for the traffic lights at Glenfield market place. 'Potential, eh? Might see you on the telly one day.'

The thought crossed Luke's mind that his dad was unlikely to hear that word – or not in connection with the gym club, anyway. He rubbed his thighs again. They were aching already; tomorrow was going to be murder. Ryan had told them to have at least one rest day now. He'd be disciplined as you liked about that.

CHAPTER 7

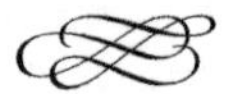

THURSDAY, 6TH MAY

EMMA WAVED AS THE TRAIN PULLED AWAY FROM THE PLATFORM. It was a long time since she'd been out and about so early, but today she'd brought Luke into Glenfield to catch the ten past six train. He was on his way to London for a two-day course, leaving Emma with the car, and all of Thursday and Friday to fill. She trudged back to the deserted car park, loneliness spreading through her gut already. Thank heavens the morning sickness had faded to almost nothing now. She plonked into the driving seat, planning. She'd go home now – not much else she could do, at this time in the morning. Later, she would drive back to Glenfield and see what they had in the way of veggie plants at the garden centre. A pair of wellies would be good, too, and some gardening gloves that fitted her. Then this afternoon when the garden was drier, she'd grab the chance to get the new veggie plot started. Luke was kicking his heels about that.

Determinedly cheerful, she drove along the deserted country road to Ralton Bridge. Two days home alone wasn't much of a prospect, although the lovely evening she and Luke had spent in York yesterday had gone a long way towards making her feel better about the removal. She'd picked him up at his office after work, and they'd met a couple of friends for a meal in a vegetarian restaurant followed by a visit to their favourite pub. It was brilliant to be out in town again. Luke was right – nights out in York were perfectly possible even when you lived in Ralton Bridge. Happy thought for the day.

Home again, Emma made a mug of orange rooibos tea and sat down for a couple of hours' work on the crime novel she was translating. It was pretty gory, which wasn't really her thing, but by half past ten she'd managed two more chapters. Pat on the back, Emma. And this was a good time to head to the garden centre. She would pop into the café while she was there, and see if they had something gooey and luscious she could buy to indulge in tonight, when she was planning on watching *E.T.* for the millionth time. Not so bad after all, this being alone, was it?

She saved her document, hearing the clunk of the letter box. Snail mail? They didn't often get any. Sure enough, a white envelope was lying on the doormat. Emma scooped it up.

The envelope was flimsy and unaddressed with no stamp, so it hadn't come by post. An advertisement? Emma put her head outside, but whoever it was had gone. Back in the hallway, she ripped the envelope open then sank onto the stairs, her heart thudding wildly. *Mind your own business or else* was printed in a weird, thick black font on a sheet of A4, and there was no signature. Dry-mouthed, Emma stared at the paper shaking in her hand, her initial fright turning to anger. How disgusting, an anonymous letter. And a threat, too. Cowards. And 'mind your own business'? About what? She shoved the letter back into the envelope and stuffed it into the drawer under the hall table before going into the downstairs loo to wash her hands. She felt tainted, after that. Welcome to Ralton Bridge... Homesickness for York and city life welled up all over again, and she wiped her eyes. Good job she hadn't put on any mascara yet. Have a glass of water, Emmy, and pull yourself together.

She sipped, then held the coolness of the glass to her forehead, still struggling to regain her composure. Even when you were more angry than shocked, an anonymous letter was still a vile thing to get. Someone was trying to scare her, and she was damn well going to show them, in case they were watching – which was the worst thought ever – that they hadn't succeeded. She allowed herself one of the expensive pralines a London friend had sent as a 'new home' present a couple of weeks ago, and was still savouring it when a new thought struck. That letter wasn't addressed. Was it intended for her or for Luke? Or for them both? This was getting odder and odder, but there was nothing to be done until she could talk to Luke about it. Emma grabbed her handbag and the car key and left the house, whistling as jauntily as she could and trying hard to suppress the thought of a weirdo anonymous letter writer peeking at her from behind a newspaper in one of the parked cars up and down the street. Stuff like that only happened in films – didn't it?

Ten minutes' drive brought her to the outskirts of Glenfield without seeing a single car behind her on the narrow country road. Good. And thank heavens the garden centre had a café.

Tears rose in Emma's eyes as she sat down at a corner table with a coffee and a Danish pastry as a treat. Comfort food, except it wasn't going to be comforting, and now that she'd had time to think about it without her gut chiming in, that letter was dodgy as hell. Should she call the police? She'd never had an anonymous letter; she didn't know what you were supposed to do. Emma rummaged for her phone. It was eleven o'clock and Luke would be in the middle of his course, but he could call back. She tapped out a short message, and a moment or two later, her phone rang.

'Emmy – are you all right? That's horrendous. What does it say, exactly?'

Emma repeated the contents of the letter in a low voice. Thankfully, Thursday morning wasn't a busy time in the garden centre coffee shop. It was healing, talking to Luke. Anger and indignation spluttered down the phone as he talked.

'That's unbelievable. I think you should go to Mum and Dad tonight. I don't like to think of you alone in the house.'

Emma hesitated. Marie would insist she stayed until Luke arrived home again, and she didn't want that. 'I'll be fine. Anonymous letter writers are cowards – everyone says that. I wondered about going to the police, though?'

She could almost hear Luke's brain ticking in the short pause that followed.

'Wait until I'm home. I think I might know who it was. I'll do some digging online, and I'll see if I can get an earlier train tomorrow. I can miss the post-course aperitif. But go to Mum's, sweetheart.'

'*You think you know who—?*' Emma swallowed her incredulity. No point ranting at Luke; this wasn't his fault. 'I'll see how I feel later. Don't say anything to Marie, huh, in case I don't go.' And she wasn't going to, that was clear already.

'Okay. I'll call you tonight. Love you.'

The connection broke as he finished speaking, and Emma bit into her pastry. Who in all the world among Luke's acquaintances did he think had sent an anonymous letter? That he thought he knew was almost as gobsmacking as the letter itself. But she would put it behind her for the moment – or try to, at least. She finished her pastry and wandered round the garden centre shop, choosing a pair of swish pink wellies with yellow hearts and two pairs of flowery gardening gloves, as a kind of gardening equivalent to comfort food. Now to grab a trolley and get some veggie plants. Halfway to the trolley park, she stopped. No. She didn't want to plant stuff now, did she? Not today, not any more. Misery swelled in her throat.

EMMA LIMPED out to the hallway – she'd been translating on the sofa with her feet tucked beneath her, and her left leg had gone to sleep. It was almost three, and a brisk walk was what she needed now. She'd had no exercise today and she had to look after herself and the baby. If she went up the hill and down to the village, she could pop into the library and see if Kate had time for a chat. Apart from Luke and the woman in the garden centre café, she hadn't spoken to a soul all day. Get going, Emma. Find some people to talk to.

She glanced up at the house next door as she passed. It was identical to their own, and occupied by a seventy-something lady whose husband had died when Luke was still a boy. They should invite Mrs Alderson for dinner, now they were settled in. Or – better idea – they could wait until after next week's scan, and then they could tell her about the baby.

At the top of the hill she came to the pub, and Emma's sense of humour kicked back in. Had they put The Black Bull here so that it was downhill all the way home for the punters, no matter which side of the village they lived on? The pub was in an old, old building, and was aggressively olde-worlde. Grey stone walls were topped by a red slate roof, and the outside window ledges were crammed with cheerful geraniums in long terracotta window boxes. Emma stopped to admire them – hopefully her tubs would be blooming like this in a week or two.

The brow of the hill behind her, she stared down at the old village centre. And – well. Ralton Bridge. Lovely old cottages, a village green, a pond. A quintessential English country village. And there wasn't a soul in sight. It was just a moment in time, of course, but still... Unexpected tears welled up, and Emma rummaged for a tissue. This was nothing but hormones. And loneliness in a place where she – whisper it – hadn't really wanted to live, had she? Not to mention being targeted by a disgusting cowardly anonymous letter writer. But she was better than this and she was bloody well going to make this move work. For the baby.

A few steps on, a bell rang in the secondary school, and chattering voices floated through the open windows as the kids changed classes. And look, two women were coming out of one of the shops further down the hill, too. This was better. Emma marched on. A white van sped past and pulled up outside the butcher's shop, and the dark-haired young man she'd seen before emerged and went round to open the back doors. Carol the butcher's wife appeared from inside the shop and started a conversation with him. She was patting the young man's shoulder very chummily – could this be her son, the one who'd been at school with Luke?

The pair had their backs to her, so Emma walked past then turned to say hello.

Carol wasn't looking happy. 'Oh, hello, dear – Emma, isn't it? Mark, this is Luke Carter's wife I was telling you about.'

Emma blinked up. Mark was one of the tallest people she'd ever met, a big, strapping man whose build matched his height.

He nodded at Emma without smiling. 'Luke's done well for himself. An accountant, I think?'

It was hard not to feel intimidated; those thick black eyebrows were drawn together above eyes that were so dark blue they were almost black. Emma swallowed. 'Yes. You were at school with him, weren't you?'

Another grim nod. 'He was a bit of a swot in those days. Tell him—' He pulled a crate of something from the back of the van and balanced it on one hip. 'Tell him I was asking after him.' He strode into the shop without saying goodbye.

Carol slammed the van door, her face troubled. 'He's worried, we all are. With supermarkets springing up all over the place, village shops are losing out. We can't compete on price or variety, and quality isn't what people are after, these days. Doug's been depressed for years, with the stress of it all and – everything. Mark's future's here, but what kind of a future can he build with a shop that's—? Oh, I'm sorry, dear. You don't want to hear my moans. Have a good day.' She swung round and went into the shop without a backward glance.

Emma was left with an unsaid goodbye on her lips. She wandered on towards the village green and the library. Carol seemed pretty certain that Mark would stay in Ralton Bridge, but it didn't sound as if they were making much of a living here. No wonder he looked dour, but that was no reason to be so sniffy about Luke, was it?

A little group of three and four-year-olds ran into the library as Emma approached, followed by a man and two women. The story club? Emma stood on the pavement outside. Kate would have enough to do without chatting to her, and a conversation about anonymous letters was best held in a less public place, anyway. She walked round the duckpond then headed back uphill, passing the butcher's, but there was no sign of life in the shop. Emma thought guiltily about the supermarket meat she'd put in the freezer at the weekend; oh, dear, maybe they could get more steaks from the butcher soon. Not that two steaks would make much difference to Mark's livelihood.

The white van sped past her again near the top of the hill, Mark hunched over the wheel. He must have seen her, but he didn't wave or hoot. Emma trudged on. She'd met two of Luke's old school friends now, though the word 'friend' didn't seem to apply to either man. Mark had been dour bordering on rude, and his parents were a little strange too, so perhaps that was just the way the butcher family was. But Alan must be a nice person, because Kate was lovely. Why hadn't these two men been more welcoming? And Luke had been no better at the garden centre on Monday. Emma frowned. Kids argued and fell out a lot, of course, but these guys were all adults now. It was all just odd, and it wasn't a good feeling.

CHAPTER 8

FRIDAY, 7TH MAY

A METALLIC BANG IN THE CHEERLESS GREY LIGHT FROM OUTSIDE woke Emma from a restless doze, and she rushed to the window. The bin lorry was meandering down the road, and help, it was after eight; she should get up. She put a hand on her middle. Was the nausea here today? Not really, good. Hopefully that part of the pregnancy was behind her.

Alone at the kitchen table, she ate her usual toast, staring glumly at rain-spattered windows. Luke had texted to say he'd be arriving in Glenfield about six, so she had nine hours to kill, and with gardening off the menu, the choice was going somewhere in the rain, or staying at home and getting on with the blood-thirsty translation. Emma loaded her plate and mug into the dishwasher, forcing back the bleakness dragging through her gut. Chin up, woman.

A couple of chapters of translation work later, the sun was struggling through, and Emma stood up and stretched. It was almost eleven and she'd had no exercise today yet. A breath of fresh air would do both her and the baby good.

The gardening gloves and wellies she'd bought the day before were waiting by the back door, and she pushed her feet into the boots. Time for the maiden voyage...

The grass was sodden, and Emma congratulated herself on a very necessary purchase as she trekked up the garden. She deposited the gloves on the workbench in the shed, then crossed the grass to the side path to find a good spot for the next attempt at a veggie plot. The border all along the fence was lovely; no point uprooting the phlox to grow broccoli. Right at the back was another idea, but that was where they'd planned the fruit trees, and it was furthest from the kitchen, too. On the sunny side of the shed? It was the best place left, and at least it would be handy for trowels and so on.

Emma approached her new site and prodded the soft ground with her foot. The ground seemed even wetter here than it was nearer the house, in spite of what Luke had said. It was too wet to start digging this morning, anyway. Oh, well. She pouted at the ground, wrapping her arms around her middle. That letter... it had made her feel – fragile. But that was the solitude, and yes, the loneliness here talking. She was better than that; she and Luke would talk it through tonight and decide how to deal with it. Emma thrust her chin in the air and stepped across to close the shed door. The plastic bag of clothes she'd dug up last week was still on the shelf where she'd left it, and heavens, she'd never found the time to ask Luke about them. Who'd have thought life in the country would be so complicated?

Back inside, she made beans on toast for lunch, then wandered around the ground floor. There was still plenty to be done inside, too; she could reorganise the cubbyhole under the stairs, for a start. In the short time they'd been here, it had turned into the place where everything was shoved out of sight in the meantime.

She was on hands and knees tidying the little cupboard when the letter box rattled and the doorbell rang. Bent over a box of cleaning materials, Emma straightened up so quickly she banged her head on the shelf above, and swore. She backed out into the hallway, where a flyer for a new Chinese Restaurant in Glenfield and an envelope addressed in Dad's scrawly handwriting were lying on the mat. But why had the postman rung the doorbell?

She opened the front door to find a parcel the size of a shoe box sitting on the edge of the stone tub beside the begonias. Gawd. Was this a country custom, leaving stuff in full view for anyone to nick? The post person hadn't even pretended to hide it, and judging by the handwriting on the label, this was from Marie. Emma took everything through to the kitchen. Dad's letter was a card, with *Welcome to your new home!* printed in rainbow lettering above a picture of a sweet country cottage with a flowery garden. Inside, Dad had written *All the very best, looking forward to a visit asap, love from Dad and Wendy xx.*

Emma stood it on the work surface, regret pricking through her. All the way from Jerusalem, but they wouldn't be coming asap or anything like it, would they? The couple had visited last year, and that would be it until the baby was well and truly here. Emma stroked her middle where her bump would soon be. Baby, you have a lot of family-bonding to oversee. But babies were good at that, weren't they?

Now for Marie's parcel. Emma pulled off the paper. A little card was sitting on the box lid: *I bought these for you in the health shop – look after yourself, and the baby. Marie xx* The box contained a selection of vitamin pills, stretchmark oil that smelled of weed, and a packet of powders that claimed to ensure both mother and baby had healthy bones. And loads of pamphlets and a book about eating in pregnancy. It was kind of Marie, but what was in those pills and powders, exactly?

Emma tapped on her phone. 'Hi, Marie. Your parcel's come, thank you so much. It's lovely of you to take such good care of us.'

'I'm glad it's arrived safely. All I want is to keep you and the baby safe. Babies are so precious and so fragile, especially when their mothers are a little older.'

Emma swallowed as annoyance flared. Older? She was twenty-eight, for heaven's sake. Luke always talked about Euan being older, but Marie wasn't even in her mid-sixties and she often behaved like a hundred-and-ten-year-old.

'I'm fine, Marie, honestly. Weren't you about the same age as me when Luke was born? You didn't have problems, did you?'

'I was thirty, actually, and although I had no problems with the pregnancy, we'd wanted a baby for oh, so many years. I'd given up when I fell pregnant with Luke. You shouldn't take anything for granted, Emma. I'm in the health shop at least once a week, so I'll keep an eye out for more things for you.'

Yikes. How to stop that without mortally offending her mother-in-law?

'That's so kind, but with all these things here, and the stuff the midwife gave me, I think I'll have enough for now. How about if I let you know when I run out of anything?'

'Well – make sure you do, Emma. The most important thing is to stay well and grow a beautiful healthy baby.'

Golly, Marie was nearly in tears now. Emma gripped the phone hard. It was wrong to feel impatient with Marie, who only meant well, but… time to change the subject. As far as the older woman was concerned, looking on the bright side simply wasn't a concept.

'I will. How's Euan?'

'Still in a lot of pain, but I found him some oil to rub on his hip, so we're going to try that. I do hope he gets his operation soon.'

Emma chatted for a few more minutes, then rang off to a list of instructions about what she should and shouldn't do. It was nice to think she and Luke's mum were getting closer, but thank heavens – oh, how horrible she was, but thank heavens Marie didn't live next door.

BY MID-AFTERNOON, the hall cubbyhole was organised, the tall kitchen cupboards likewise, and Emma was trying hard not to look at the clock every five minutes. This was pathetic; she should have gone to York and stayed with a friend while Luke was away. But that was pathetic too. Cup of tea? She was waiting for the kettle to boil when the doorbell chimed again and she jumped in fright, then shook herself angrily. Was she going to bang her head on the ceiling every time the doorbell went for the rest of her life? Damn that letter-writer to hell. And this had better not be a cold caller; she was in just the right mood now to give them an earful. Emma marched down the hallway to the door.

It was Mrs Alderson next door. 'I made some ginger biscuits. Would you like to come over for a cup of something and a chat?'

She was rescued. Emma grabbed her bag and key, and followed her neighbour to the house next door. It was the twin of their own place, and she hadn't been inside it yet. Mrs Alderson led her into the spacious ground floor room, and Emma looked around curiously. Like them, the Aldersons had knocked through their kitchen and living room, though the floor in the living area here was carpeted and there were no French doors out to the back garden. What Mrs Alderson did have, though, was a beautiful old cast iron fireplace, shiny black with green and flowery tiles up and down both sides. Emma sat down on the sofa and accepted a cup of lemon and ginger tea and a biscuit.

Mrs Alderson took the armchair. 'The fireplace? It's lovely, isn't it? Edwardian. I had it brought down from the spare bedroom when the renovation was done eight years ago. It seemed a pity to have it in a room that's so seldom used.'

'It's gorgeous. I guess any fireplace that used to be in our house was removed years ago, more's the pity.'

'You should ask Marie. It may simply have been boarded over. No one considered them fashionable thirty-odd years ago.'

'I'll do that. Any other antiques I might uncover?'

They chatted for over an hour, and Emma went home much happier. Her neighbour might be two generations older, but that wasn't going to stop them being friends. And look at the time – Luke's train would be steaming into Glenfield soon. She dived upstairs to redo her lippie.

LUKE STRODE from the train and wrapped Emma in a bear hug that left her warmed through. The aggro about the letter diminished as soon as there was someone to share it with, and they chatted about his course while she drove back to Ralton Bridge.

The house felt more like home with Luke here too. He dumped his briefcase on the stairs and held out a hand.

'Let's have this letter, then.'

'Who do you think sent it?' Emma handed over the letter, and Luke's brow furrowed as he read.

'What a bugger. Let's sit down.' He pulled her through to the sofa, and sat with his arm around her. 'I don't know, but I have a feeling it might have been a guy I used to know at school. He went into property and he always said if Mum and Dad ever left this house, he'd like to buy it. He owns a couple of other places in the area, and I wouldn't put it past him to try and scare us into selling up here.'

Emma screwed up her nose. Yet another ex-schoolmate from Luke's past who seemed to have it in for him? But it was no more way-out than being sent an anonymous letter in the first place. The whole thing was beginning to sound like an Agatha Christie novel.

She rubbed his knee beside her on the sofa. 'How despicable. What's his name?'

'Sid something. Don't give this another thought, Emmy. You opened the letter, but it was aimed at me and I'll deal with it right now.' He ripped both letter and envelope into small pieces, balled them together and took them through to the bin.

That evening, they strolled round the garden, planning fruit trees at the far end and a swing set in the middle. Emma pointed out the place by the shed where she'd wondered about having the new veggie patch, and Luke nodded approvingly.

'Good plan. I'll make a start at the weekend. And next week

I'll get someone in to make an estimate for the patio. We can order the slabs from them, too.'

Sudden annoyance prickled through Emma. Was this another decision she had no part in?

She poked his arm. 'Have we decided about decking versus slabs, then?'

Luke's eyebrows rose. 'Well... no. We can get an estimate for both.'

Emma nodded. Fair enough, but he shouldn't need reminding that she was an equal partner in the decision-making, even though the house had been in his family for decades. Which reminded her...

'Was there ever a fireplace in one of the upstairs rooms? Mrs Alderson has a lovely one.'

Luke stared into space. 'There was, now you mention it, but it was boarded up. I don't think it was a proper one. Not sure if the fireplace itself is still there, or just the hole.'

That didn't sound promising, but they could check, couldn't they? Emma turned back to the garden, and the words bubbled out before she had time to think. 'By the way, I found something in the old veggie patch when I was digging last week. It gave me quite a turn. I put it in the shed.'

'You *what?*' Sheet-white, Luke leapt two steps back, his eyes wild. For a moment, he was motionless, a white-knuckled hand clutching at his shirt. Then he fled inside.

CHAPTER 9

THE BACK DOOR SLAMMED SHUT BEHIND LUKE, AND EMMA stared after him. What on earth was going through the man's head? She told him she'd dug something up, and his immediate response was to storm off. What in the name of anything did he imagine she'd found? Well, she wasn't about to go after him – he could have his tantrum all by himself, and then come back and apologise. Exasperated, she strode into the shed, pulled the plastic bag down from the shelf and tipped the clothes onto the workbench. The answer to why anyone would bury these was no more obvious than it had been when she dug them up.

Luke calling her name made her jump. Good, his temper hadn't lasted long. Maybe he was just tired, after his course.

'I'm in here!' Emma put the bag down and waited. Tired or not, this was where he could explain what was going on here.

He began talking before he arrived in the shed. 'I know it looks awful, Emmy, but there's a good—'

He stopped dead in the doorway, gaping at the clothes on the workbench. His face blanched, then flushed as his eyes swivelled from the plastic bag to Emma and back again. He gave a short bark of laughter, then leaned forward and lifted the stained T-shirt.

'Is this what you meant? I thought... It's only clothes, Emma. Jeez...' He dropped the T-shirt again and passed a shaking hand over his mouth and chin, his Adam's apple bobbing as he swallowed loudly.

Was that relief in his eyes? And what had he thought? Was there something else buried in the garden? A family pet? That might explain his reaction, actually.

Emma folded her arms. 'I can see it's clothes. What would be interesting to know is why they were buried in the garden.'

He perched on the edge of an ancient wooden barrel. 'It – they were mine, as you saw.'

No, she hadn't, not for sure, anyway. Emma waited in silence.

'It was a prank. We were kids, messing around on the farm, and we, ah, we broke a piece of machinery and got, um, oil, muck, I don't know, all over the place. I was hiding these from Mum and Dad.'

'Who's 'we'?'

'Alan and I. Afterwards, his dad thought one of the cows was to blame, so, I, um, buried the evidence, so to speak.'

Emma pictured a small boy frantically burying a bag of clothes. He'd dug quite a deep hole for them, and it seemed like a lot of bother to go to. 'Why didn't you chuck them out? Or burn them?'

'I was scared Mum or someone would find them. And it's not so easy to burn stuff when you're that age. We were only about twelve.'

Emma turned back to the clothes on the wooden worktop. Something here still wasn't adding up.

Luke put a hand on her arm. 'Don't make a big deal of this, huh? It's a twenty-year-old prank, that's all.'

Emma gave up. 'Well, I'll leave you to sort out whatever you want to do with them. Anything else buried here I should watch out for? Cats? Dogs?'

Luke coughed violently. 'No, no. We had a budgie at one point, but it's not buried here, don't worry. Emmy, leave the digging to me, huh? I'm going for a shower. Why don't you make a cuppa and we'll have one of those yummy chocs Jane sent?'

He gave her a fierce hug and jogged back down the garden, leaving the clothes still on the work bench. Emma folded them roughly and laid them on top of the plastic bag on the shelf. Not her problem.

THEY GOT up to torrential rain on Saturday, and Luke went upstairs straight after breakfast to start stripping the wallpaper in the smallest of the three bedrooms. Emma tidied around in the kitchen, then sat down to answer the call coming into her phone. It was Kate.

'Hi Emma, I'm at the library. I put *A Dark-Adapted Eye* to the side for you. Do you want it?'

'Ooh, yes! I've seen it on DVD but I've never read the book. I'll be with you in five.' Emma grabbed the car key, called to Luke where she was going, and drove uphill and down.

Kate was talking to a man searching for something in the leaflet stand by the side of the desk, and Emma waited until she was free. The library was pretty quiet today.

Kate handed over the book. 'Here you go. Doing anything nice this weekend?'

'Just stuff around the house – and garden, if the weather improves.'

Two women came in and headed for the crime fiction section, and Kate lowered her voice. 'Has your other half recovered from meeting his old pal in the garden centre?'

Emma laughed. 'I'm not sure they were pals, you know. But maybe we can change that. They've grown up since then.'

'As much as men ever do,' said Kate darkly. 'Alan said they were BFFs for a while, so I guess they had a big falling out. I think we should get them together over a glass of something and see if we can't rekindle their friendship. I can invite you and a few other couples for drinks.'

Emma put her book into her bag. A get-to-know-you party sounded fun, but healing old wounds might be best done in a less public setting, initially, at least. And Luke wasn't what you'd call a party animal.

'Lovely, but let's try something more, um, private first, to test the waters. How about we meet you and Alan at the pub sometime? Coincidentally, of course.'

'You're on, and no time like the present, if you're around tonight? We can see what's going on later, and text if we can make it. Oh, that reminds me – one of my neighbours is trying to get a group together for fitness training, starting after summer. It'll be in the school gym. Would you be interested?'

She pointed to a poster on the wall behind Emma.

Emma hesitated. But the scan was a week on Monday; there couldn't be any harm telling her friends now, could there? 'Um – theoretically yes, but can I get back to you on that? I should check with the midwife first.'

She patted her middle, and Kate's eyes rounded.

'Wow! Congratulations! You must be over the moon!' Kate fished up a list attached to a clipboard. 'Add your name and email address anyway. That way, you'll get the info when anything's decided. When's the baby due?'

Emma filled in her details and stood chatting until a group of elderly ladies arrived and claimed Kate. Back at home, Luke was still stripping wallpaper and whistling along with the radio. Emma cuddled into the corner of the sofa with her library book. It was the weekend, wasn't it? She was allowed to blob.

Her phone vibrated on the coffee table before she'd finished the first chapter, and Emma opened a message from Kate. *Have persuaded Alan to go to the Black Bull tonight. Join us?* Emma shrugged mentally. Her new friend was a quick worker. She hadn't even mentioned the pub to Luke yet, but an evening at the village pub was a perfectly normal thing to do on a Saturday, wasn't it? She tapped: *I'll do my best. Wish me luck!*

'Hey!' She tried her best cheerful voice when Luke came downstairs. 'A woman in the village was recommending the pub here. How about giving it a go tonight?'

Luke brightened immediately. 'Good idea, it's a great pub. Mum and Dad used to...'

Emma sat back, satisfied. Mission accomplished.

LATE SPRING SUNSHINE was casting long shadows across the street as they walked uphill to the Black Bull that evening. Emma hugged herself. Was this the start of proper socialising for them in Ralton Bridge? They'd had a couple of lunches here with Marie and Euan in the past, but this was her first evening visit. The ten or so tables in the garden to the side of the pub were busy, mostly with young families, the parents enjoying a glass of something while the kids were tumbling around on the swing and slide set. Kate and Alan were nowhere to be seen, and Emma ducked inside while Luke held the heavy wooden door open. Heavens, the pub was dim after the sunshine outside.

The decor in the bar was dark wood with artistically illuminated bottles all over the place and horse brasses round the leaded glass windows. A convivial buzz of chatter filled the air, and Emma led the way to a table near the door. This was where she had to be a little bit coy.

'Your round. I'll have tonic, please. With ice and lemon.' She gave Luke a big smile, and he joined the crowd waiting for bar service.

Emma whipped out her mobile and messaged Kate under the table. *Am near door. Luke at bar.*

Her phone was barely back in her bag when Kate's exclamation rang across the room.

'Luke! Good to see you again! Is Emma here too?'

The two of them arrived at the table a few moments later, Luke clutching two glasses and Kate with a couple of bags of peanuts, which she tossed onto the table.

'I'll bring Alan over.' She rushed off to the back of the pub.

Luke glared after her, then hissed at Emma. 'Did you know they were here?'

The arrival of the other two saved her from answering. Kate slid onto the bench beside Emma and started talking about patios and gardens while the two men sat silently on separate stools. Emma hardly dared look at them. Alan was bent over his glass on the table, staring at the beer in much the same way you'd stare at your mobile while you were waiting for a message to arrive. Luke's lips were thin, and the lines stretching downwards from the corners of his mouth reminded her suddenly of Euan. Heck. Getting these two together wasn't going to be a quick fix. Emma's stomach lurched – was this a mistake? People did outgrow friendships.

'I don't remember you at school, Luke.' Kate was frowning across the table.

Emma started. 'Were you at school with them? I didn't realise.'

'Yes and no. I was here for about a year, living with my granny while my parents were back and forward to the children's hospital in Manchester with my sister, who needed a whole series of operations after an accident when she was five. I was a couple of years below the guys, too. I didn't know them then, but I remember Alan being in the gymnastics team that won medals at one point. Were you in it too, Luke?'

Luke shook his head. 'Not the team. Alan was better than I was. I don't remember you, either.'

Kate laughed. 'My most vivid memory of that school is the nativity play where I was a sheep. We had a live donkey, and the wretched creature peed on my feet while we were gathered round the manger. I had hysterics and the music teacher went ballistic; it was more like an episode of *Fawlty Towers* than a nativity play.' She dimpled at Alan. 'That play was the first thing I thought about when I spotted Alan across a crowded room a couple of years back.'

Another jolt of surprise struck Emma. She'd got that wrong too; the couple hadn't been together for ages. And this tonic was going straight through her. She gazed around the rapidly filling pub.

'Where are the loos?'

Kate stood up. 'I'll come too.' She led the way to the back of the pub, Emma following on. She glanced back as they went round the bar. Luke and Alan were hunched on their stools, and it didn't look as if they were talking.

Kate was fixing her mascara when Emma came out of the loo. She rinsed her hands and patted hot cheeks with cold fingers. 'Where did you and Alan meet, then?'

'In a nightclub in Leeds. It was your original love at second sight, and we were married less than a year later. Alan had been working for a farm machinery company, but we came back here to help when his dad had flu last winter, and somehow, here we still are, and no prospect of leaving. I miss city life.'

'Me too.' Emma lifted her handbag. 'Shall we do the shops in York sometime?'

'You're on.'

Emma threaded her way back through the pub, then stopped short as Kate grabbed her arm. Luke and Alan were standing at the bar now and they were arguing, that was plain. Emma watched, horrified, as Luke's fist thumped on the wooden bar top and Alan poked him with a vicious, stiff finger while two other men strode up and pushed between them. One was Mark, the butcher's son; he was towering over Luke, his face livid. The barman, a thickset man who must have been in his fifties, rushed up flapping a towel, and Emma's heart plummeted. She pulled Kate through the crowd to the little circle of men surrounding Luke and Alan.

Alan was poking Luke again, spit flying from his mouth as he hissed, his face inches from Luke's. 'It was all your fault. You should have kept your bloody mouth zipped.'

The barman flapped again, leaning forward. 'Shut it, Alan! You know whose fault it was. Now for God's sake leave it there.'

Luke swept Alan's arm away. 'You didn't tell me anything!'

'We were kids. None—'

To Emma's horror, Alan grabbed a handful of Luke's pullover and practically lifted him off his feet.

'None of it would have happened if you hadn't shoved your stupid little bloody nose in where it wasn't wanted.'

Kate pulled Emma a few steps back, and Luke wrestled himself free.

'If you believe that, you're a bigger prat than I thought you were.' He stood there, panting.

Emma pushed forward to grab Luke's arm, and held on. 'What's going on?'

He was shaking, but she couldn't tell if it was anger or distress. Another man came forward – another schoolmate? He was the right age, and he was almost as tall as Mark. He put a hand on Luke and Alan's shoulders and pushed them further apart.

'Guys. This isn't doing anything, and we can't change what happened. Let it go.'

The barman leaned over the bar. 'Be careful, Luke. I think you should go home. You need to calm down.'

'Don't worry. I will. Come on, Emma.' Luke lifted an almost-full pint glass, chucked the contents over Alan, and strode from the pub, Emma hanging onto his arm for dear life.

He marched on down the hill, and Emma let go and stopped. 'Luke – what's wrong? What happened back there?'

Luke wheeled round to face her, his mouth working and his face pale. 'He was blaming me for something none of us had any control over because we were kids. It's nothing, Emmy, a playground scuffle from twenty years ago. Forget it, because I had. I'm remembering why I didn't keep in touch with him, though.'

A scuffle? Jeez, it must have been some scuffle. Emma took his arm again, and they walked on in silence. Luke poured a large whisky as soon as he entered the house, and Emma went to make tea. That was the end of going out with Kate and Alan, then. She and Kate would need to work out what to do with their budding friendship after this.

Her phone vibrated, and she pulled it out, squinting at Luke, now wandering around the darkening garden with his whisky.

It was a message from Kate. *Not sure what happened there or what went on in the past. You ok?*

Emma tapped: *I'm good. Not sure either. See you next week.*

A thumbs up came in reply.

CHAPTER 10

LUKE, AGED 12

ALAN WAS BOUNCING UP AND DOWN ON THE BACK SEAT AS KEITH drove them to Glenfield Secondary. 'I hope we get to do jumps off the vaulting horse again. Dad, Ryan said I'm one of the best!'

Keith chuckled. 'You've mentioned that before, lad. No need to get swollen-headed about it, eh?'

Luke heaved a sigh. He hadn't been at gym club last Friday because he'd had a tooth filled on the Thursday and it went a bit wonky, and the dentist only had a free appointment late on Friday afternoon. He didn't know which was worse, gym club after a week away, or the extra visit to the dentist. The good thing about tonight was the weather. Autumn was here, and it had rained like the second flood all week. The sky was still chucking it down, so a jog through the woods would be off the menu. He hoped.

Ryan wasn't there at the start of the class, but Harry and

Jason got them all running round and round the gym, which was better than outside because it wasn't uphill, so you didn't get nearly so out of breath. Luke trotted up the long side, along the top, down the other side and across the bottom. Wow, he was managing all right here; all the training he'd done in Keith's barn over the past couple of weeks was paying off. He'd never be a gymnast, but he was one of the okay runners now. It was even quite fun tonight.

Ryan arrived with a fair-haired boy as the half hour was up. He stood by the finishing line and did a round of high-fives. 'Good work, team. Boys, this is Noel. He's staying in Ralton Bridge for a few months, so he'll be going to school with some of you, and he's joining us in the gym club too.'

He dropped a hand on Noel's shoulder, smiling down on him, and behind Luke, Mark gave a sudden hiss. Luke turned round and stared. Mark's face was like he'd just drunk an entire bottle of vinegar. He scowled at Luke and shuffled his feet.

Ryan didn't notice. 'Right, lads. Vaulting horses. Jumps and landings again, and this week I want to see perfection. Luke, come with me and Noel and I'll show you what you missed last week.'

The others started to carry out the two big vaulting horses. They were the pyramid-shaped kind with wooden sides, and you could use them at full height, or take off the bottom levels to lower the vaulting surface. Luke was glad to see that the lowest level was off. Good, he'd never be able to land steadily from full height. He followed Ryan into a corner, where he and Noel stood side by side on a bench while Ryan explained about jumping off with bent legs then straightening them mid-jump, bending again on landing, and no side-stepping as you straightened up again. Luke watched the demonstration, then had first go while Ryan stood to one side.

'Not bad. Okay, this time I'll help you with the landing position.'

Luke jumped and landed, then his heart thudded in shock as Ryan grabbed him the moment his feet touched the ground. Bloody hell, was the man an octopus? This was worse than the run in the woods. A hand pushed against his bum, then another shoved his chest back as he straightened, then his shoulders were gripped and pushed back. He couldn't have taken a side step on landing even if he'd wanted to; Ryan was right there in his face.

'Better. Have another go, and concentrate mainly on your shoulders when you land.'

At least he knew what to expect this time. Luke stood on the bench, fixing the jump in his mind: take off, straighten, land and bend, straighten again and don't forget the shoulders. He jumped.

The same hand on his bum, but this time it was his tummy that was given the shove-into-place treatment. Ryan's fingers spread downwards, and – bloody hell. A shrill yelp escaped before Luke could choke it back. He twisted away from Ryan to land on his backside on the mat, his heart thundering almost as hard as it had on the run in the woods. Heat flashed through his middle as deathly silence fell in the gym. Everyone was staring at him, and quite a few of them were sniggering, too.

Ryan grabbed his arm and helped him up. 'Okay, lads, show's over. Nothing happened.' He turned his back on the others and spoke quietly to Luke. 'Sorry about that, Luke. You landed a bit further forward than I'd anticipated and my hand slipped. Are you all right?'

Luke put a hand up to his hot cheeks. His face was still flaming. He squinted sideways, but the others had gone back to setting up the vaulting horses.

'I'm fine. I'm sorry.' Why was he apologising? He'd done nothing wrong. Jeez, this was dire. He'd never hear the end of it at school if the others realised what had happened. Luke risked a glance at Noel. The other boy was standing a few steps away, his face thoughtful.

Ryan was still for a few seconds, then he clapped Luke's shoulder and grinned. 'On we go! Let's have one more by yourself before you join the others.'

His heart still hammering, Luke performed the jump, Ryan's eyes following his every move.

'Well done. You'll be doing it from higher up on the horse in a moment, but it's the same jump. On you go to the others while I help Noel.'

Luke fled to the group where Alan was, not daring to look round to see if Noel was getting the same treatment. Trainers had to touch you, of course they did, but that had been a bit too close to home. Luke took his turn to trot up the bench to the top of the horse, stand for half a second at the top, then jump off. Thankfully, Ryan ignored him for the rest of the session, though two or three of the others came in for the push and shove treatment as they landed.

'Ryan's great, isn't he?' Alan came to stand beside Luke as they waited for their turn. 'He sees exactly what you need to do to make a perfect jump.'

Luke sniffed. Was he the only one who didn't like being grabbed and shoved around? At the end of the class Ryan called them together and they sat in a circle on the floor.

'You're shaping up well, lads. For the next couple of weeks, you'll be working in two groups. One group will be in here with me while the other's out in the woods with Harry and Jason, then we'll swap at half-time. If it's too wet to be outside, the running will be along the corridors here. I can see you're all training well at home, too. Not much like the group of flabby kids that started out, are you?'

Mark put his hand up. 'Who'll be in which group?'

Ryan smiled. 'You'll be with me. And Noel, Kev, Alan, Sid, Jon and—' His eyes swept round the group. 'And Luke.'

Luke trailed across the gym as the others jostled out to the changing room. Ryan stopped him, stepping a few yards away from the last two boys. 'All okay, Luke? Do you want me to come out with you and explain to your dad how you fell?'

Luke nearly died. That would be the worst, the absolute worst thing that could happen. Imagine Ryan telling Dad about grabbing Luke in an embarrassing place and Luke shrieking his head off…

'No-no-no. No. I'm fine.'

'No sore bits or anything?'

'None at all. Honest, Ryan.'

'Okay. On you go, then.'

A hand landed heavily on Luke's shoulder before he could escape. Please, please, don't let the others tease him about this – had anyone seen how Ryan had grabbed him? Noel had been nearest, and he'd been watching, too. Crap.

Luke trailed into the changing room, where Alan and Mark were congratulating themselves on being in Ryan's group. Was he pleased too? No, he definitely wasn't. He would never like gymnastics. Fortunately, the others ignored him, and Luke and Alan left the changing room behind a gaggle of Glenfield boys, and went out into the darkness of a cold October night.

The car was in its usual place, and Dad got out when he saw them. 'You'll need to squash up, boys. Your mum and I went to the garden centre while we were here, Luke, and we bought some of that cut-price garden furniture I was talking about at dinner.'

Luke peered into the back of the car, where two folding chairs were belted into the seat at the far side.

His dad opened the boot, which was also full. 'We'll squeeze your gear in here, then you'll have more space in behind.' He took Alan's bag and shoved it in, then reached for Luke's.

'There's not much weight to this, son. Have you got everything?'

Luke unzipped the bag and rummaged. Bummer, after all that aggro he'd forgotten his trainers. He ran back inside. Hopefully there was still someone here, because the changing rooms were locked at night. The corridor to the gym was spooky and dim, but a thin strip of light was shining under the changing room door. Good. Luke pushed it open.

The locker room was empty, but water was running in the showers at the back. Luke grabbed his shoes from under the bench and was about to leave when a deep cough came from the showers. Luke stood still. Was that Ryan? Why wasn't he in the teachers' shower room?

Taking tiny silent steps, Luke crept across to the doorway and peeked round. The showers were communal – one reason he always waited until he was home, though the water wasn't too warm here either. It was steamy enough tonight, though. Ryan was standing with his back to Luke, but no one else was there, unless they'd gone into the bogs. Ryan stretched his arms up as the water rained down, and the muscles in his back rippled. Luke held his breath. Wow. Ryan was like one of those pictures you saw of weightlifters, with a shiny wet triangle-shaped back above a round tight bum. Luke inched back as Ryan stood there, arms stretched up, his hips circling around as if he was dancing. Shit… This was weird; he had to get out of here. He crossed the changing room on tiptoe, almost tripping over Mark's blue Adidas bag on the floor.

The shower stopped running, and Luke pulled the changing room door open. Into the corridor, don't let the door slam, outside, quick as you can.

Panting, he flopped into the back of the car with his trainers.

Dad started the engine. 'You took your time. Find them okay?'

Mum swivelled round in her seat. 'Seat belts on, boys?'

It was Mum's contribution to the start of every journey they made in the car. Luke stared out into the darkness.

Mum wasn't finished, though. 'Are you all right, Luke, lovey? You look a bit pale.'

'I'm fine.' He wasn't really, but how could he explain?

Dad stuck the key into the ignition. 'It's those street lights. They make everyone look peely-wally.'

Luke hugged his trainers, relaxing back into the seat. It was probably true about the street lights, because Alan didn't look right either. Luke nudged him with his elbow, glad when the answering nudge came. They always did that when a parent had been embarrassing. It was a kind of wordless support thing.

When they'd unloaded Alan at the farm, Luke spread out in the back, zipping his jacket right up to make up for the chill of no warm body squashed against him as they drove home through the foggy night. It was good to be safely back in his everyday life, here in the car with Mum and Dad and everything where it should be.

They pulled up at home, and Luke helped Dad unload the garden furniture while Mum went in to put the kettle on.

'Thanks, lad.' Dad clapped Luke's shoulder.

The sensation of Ryan's hand landing on his shoulder slid into Luke's gut. He closed his eyes to keep the tears in, pushing away the memory of that jump and Ryan's fingers and everyone staring at him when he landed on the floor. That had made him feel… crappy. And – why had Ryan been in the kids' showers? The feeling of being caught up in something he didn't understand made Luke's gut cramp suddenly. But no way could he talk to Mum and Dad about it. Misery welled up inside him. They never talked about stuff like that at home.

CHAPTER 11

MONDAY, 10TH MAY

ONCE STARTED, THE PLAN FOR THE PATIO MOVED FORWARD quickly. Emma lifted the sample piece of slate they'd been given when they went back to the garden centre on Sunday. The way the colours changed when light hit it from different angles was amazing; she'd never have guessed slate was so decorative. They'd arranged for a garden construction company in Glenfield to come and estimate costs for wooden decking as well as the slate slabs, but unless the slabs were going to be horrendously expensive, slate it would be. It would last them a lifetime.

The landscape gardener was due at nine that morning, and Luke had arranged to start work later, so he'd be here to talk to the man too.

Emma wasn't sure if she was insulted or not. 'Scared I'll organise something you don't approve of?' It was only an estimate, and they knew what they wanted. But then, it was a lot of money and probably it *was* best if they were both here to ask questions. She shouldn't be so touchy.

She glanced out to where the patio would be. All Luke's talk since their disastrous visit to the Black Bull on Saturday had been about the baby and the house and garden; he'd refused point-blank to discuss the scene at the pub or whatever had happened when he and Alan were kids.

'It wasn't worth worrying about then, and it certainly isn't now,' was the only answer he gave Emma when she tried to bring it up. So that was that. She would have to trust him on this one, and it did seem ridiculous that Alan was still hung up on a decades-old schoolboy feud.

The man from the gardener's turned out to be a woman, and Emma laughed out loud at Luke's expression when he saw 'the patio bloke' emerge from the company car. They took Cherie, a forty-something blonde with green streaks – how appropriate for a gardener – round to the back of the house.

Luke waved his hand from one side of the garden to the other. 'We'd like the paved area to extend all the way across the breadth of the plot. Then we'll have plenty of space for socialising and so on.'

Cherie screwed up her eyes, gazing from side to side then up and down the garden. 'That's a pretty wide patio, and it would make a very abrupt border when you walk round from the front of the house. My suggestion would be to make it narrower, maybe a shade more than the width of the house, and leave a strip of shrubbery down the sides. You could increase the patio area by making it a couple of metres longer, which would suit the proportions of the garden better. You have plenty of space here.'

Luke was wearing his most stubborn expression. 'We really wanted a wide patio. Could you cost up both variations for us?'

Emma shot him a look. If they'd discussed wide versus long patios, she'd slept through it.

Cherie was tapping madly into her tablet. 'No problem. And you want which stones?'

Emma showed her the brochure and the sample from the garden centre. 'These ones.'

The next few minutes were taken up with chat about various edging possibilities and the superiority of slate over wooden decking, then Cherie took some measurements.

'I think that's everything. I'll email the estimates later today, and we can take it from there.'

Emma walked round to Cherie's car with her. 'How soon would you be able to start?'

'Pretty much straightaway. There's not much call for patio laying this year, though we did several for the folk up at The Vale when the estate was new.'

Emma said goodbye, then went inside, where Luke was having a quick coffee before he left for work. She put the kettle on and fished for a tea bag. 'I'll mark out the suggestions Cherie made about size, and we can discuss it tonight.'

'Nothing to discuss. There's no reason not to go for a nice wide patio.' Luke drained his mug and pecked her cheek. 'See you later.'

Emma pecked back and took her mug out to the proposed patio area, where they'd put up Marie and Euan's old garden furniture in the meantime. She leaned back in the elderly chair, trying to imagine how the garden would look this time next year, with fruit trees at the back and a lovely patio with a baby asleep in its pram. A real family home, just like she'd always wanted. She'd be used to this living in the country lark by that time. Emma smiled, massaging her middle. Their first scan was a week today; it would be totally magical to see the baby at last.

The church clock striking half past ten jerked her back to Monday morning. Okay, there was a ball of garden string in the shed. She would mark out the patio sizes right now.

She jogged up the garden for the string, and set to work. Cherie had suggested a length of four metres if the patio was stretched across the entire plot, and five if it was the width of the house. Emma marked out both variations, then scowled at the side sections. Cherie was right; the fence-to-fence option would look distinctly squat. Surely it was better to stick to the longer, narrower one, and that way she'd be able to have her veggie patch here at the side where she'd started it in the first place. Emma stuck her chin in the air. More often than not, she was head cook and the one who'd be needing veggies from the garden. And whatever it had been in the past, nowadays the soil at the side seemed no damper than the rest of the garden. There. She had made an executive decision. The patio would be long and not wide, and the veggie patch could go where she'd wanted it. And as there were no more buried bags of old clothes waiting to surprise her, she could start digging straightaway.

She whacked off a quick message to Luke. *Long patio much more elegant, let's go for that.* Her phone remained mute, though the double blue tick showed her he'd seen the message. Okay – she would take silence as consent.

She changed into what had become her gardening trousers, and wow, these were getting tight round the waist. It would be lovely to buy maternity clothes – maybe she and Kate could do that York trip they'd talked about soon. Emma smiled dreamily. Okay, she would do a metre's worth on the veggie plot now, then this afternoon she'd go to the library for a chat with Kate, and get some lettuce plants from the hardware store in the village. Emma whistled as she worked.

THE POST ARRIVING while she was making her lunchtime sandwich didn't immediately have her heart leaping into overdrive today, but the sight of the plain white envelope lying on the mat soon changed that. Emma whipped the front door open, and the postman gave her a cheery wave as he strode further up Brook Lane. She turned back to lift the letter on the mat. Oh. This one was stamped, and addressed to Luke. Apart from that, its appearance was exactly the same as the anonymous letter's. Emma frowned – they should have kept the first for comparison. Letter in hand, she took her mobile out to the garden.

The slap of Luke's hand against his desk vibrated all the way down the phone. 'Stick it in our bedroom. I'll see to it when I'm home, but chances are it's a circular.'

Emma shook her head, but there was no point arguing about who opened a potentially dodgy letter. Had anything come of the message he'd sent his suspect schoolmate Sid?

Luke wasn't finished. 'Oh, and about the patio. Cherie's sent the estimates already, and the long version is actually more expensive as it needs more of the border tiles, so we'll go with the wide one. I called them, and they're starting the groundwork tomorrow.'

He ended the call, and Emma went back inside, frustration fizzing through her middle. Luke should have discussed the estimates with her before he made arrangements – why hadn't he? After everything she'd said about him arranging the move here in the first place, too. She pouted, then grinned shamefacedly. When you thought about it, she was just as bad. She'd decided on the long version without consulting him this morning. Heck, was the shape of the patio worth getting annoyed about? Emma went back to her sandwich. The size of the patio wasn't important. The non-communication thing was, and they were each as bad as the other. They would need to talk about this.

Her phone rang while she was finishing her lunch. Marie, help – it wasn't like her mother-in-law to call like this. Marie always called Luke. But then, Luke wasn't pregnant with Marie's grandchild, was he?

The call was nothing to do with the baby, though. Marie's voice trembled down the phone.

'I didn't want to disturb Luke because he'll be at work, but Euan was at the doctor this morning, and they've brought his operation forward. It's on Thursday.'

'Goodness. Has his hip got worse?'

'The pain has. He's in agony with every step. I don't know what to do to help him.'

By the sound of things, Euan wasn't the only one needing support. Emma rushed to comfort Marie. 'I guess it's better to have the op sooner rather than later, isn't it?'

'Oh dear, I hope so. We've decided he should have it done privately. The NHS is so over-worked, and those waiting lists are dreadful when you're in constant pain. It was the specialist we saw today, and he gave Euan stronger painkillers, but it's all so frightening for him.'

Emma made comforting noises. She wasn't in favour of private medicine, but what Marie said was true, and her parents-in-law weren't short of a bob or two. And Marie was the nervous type at the best of times. A long wait with Euan in pain would have her exploding.

'Try not to worry, Marie. I'm sure he'll feel better now he knows the op will soon be over. And it's very routine these days.' Gawd, that wasn't going to comfort someone whose nearest and dearest was about to go under the knife, was it? Emma planned on her feet. 'Tell you what. Why don't we fetch you and Euan here for a day or two? That way, he'll be distracted from the operation, and we can keep an eye on him together.' And it would be an opportunity to cement her relationship with her parents-in-law, too.

'Oh! Are you sure? I didn't mean to drop hints.'

'You didn't. Luke and I were saying the other day we'd need to have you here soon, to see what we're doing with the place. You can help us keep an eye on the gardeners making the new patio. I'll call Luke in a bit when he'll be on his break—' No way would Marie agree to her calling him when he was supposed to be working, '—and one of us will get back to you.'

She ended the call and tapped to connect to Luke again. His phone was switched off, so she sent a quick email outlining her plan. It was a pity he had the car today; she could have whizzed straight down to York to collect Marie and Euan. The solution was easy, though. She would go to York on the train, collect the car, and drive Marie and Euan back to Ralton Bridge, leaving Luke to come home by train.

Happier, Emma rushed out to catch the bus to Glenfield station. How lovely – she had a whole afternoon with plenty to do and people to do it with.

. . .

'EMMA, the new kitchen's gorgeous. And the floor's just perfect. I don't know why we didn't have it polished years ago.'

Marie was wandering around the kitchen, peering approvingly at the new fittings.

Emma put a hand on the older woman's arm. 'We have you and Euan to thank for most of it. We really appreciate it, Marie.'

Marie flushed, and Emma switched on the coffee machine, glancing out to the garden table where Euan had settled down with a book. 'I hope Euan'll be okay on the stairs? I didn't think of that when I suggested this.'

'I'm sure he will. He'll only need to go up in the evening and down in the morning, and we can help him with that. The stronger painkillers are making a difference already.'

Emma balanced the garden centre brochure on top of the coffee tray and led the way outside.

'Coffee! What do you think of the new patio idea, Euan? Look, we're having these slabs here. They're slate.' Emma put a mug beside Euan and handed him the brochure.

'Looks good. How big will the patio be?'

Emma pointed out the proportions, and Euan nodded approvingly.

Marie beamed, and relaxed back in her chair. '*Excellent*. I'm all for a nice wide patio.'

Emma sipped. This got the prize for best idea of the week, but oh, the letter waiting in the bedroom, possibly another anonymous one... that was hard to ignore. She wouldn't be happy until she knew what was in it. As soon as she'd finished her coffee, Emma ran upstairs and put the letter in her handbag – she and Luke could look at it in the privacy of the car when she collected him at Glenfield that evening. An hour and a half to go…

The York train was on time for once, and Emma was waiting at the station entrance when Luke came striding through the ticket hall. She held up her face for their usual hello kiss, but his lips barely brushed her cheek.

He flopped into the passenger seat and twisted round to face her. 'Did you bring that letter?'

Emma handed it over, and he ripped it open. *Stop digging or else* was all it said. Emma stared. Stop digging the patio? The garden? How stupid; this was only meant to scare them. Anyone with anything real to say would say it straight out.

Anger swelled in her chest. 'What buggers they are. I still think we should go to the police.'

'Nah. They'll get tired of it soon enough.'

Why was he being so blasé about this? Emma opened her mouth to object, but Luke was finished with the letter.

'Emma, I wish you'd leave Mum and Dad to cope for themselves. They like being independent, and I'm not at all sure it's a good idea having them back in the house, when they had to leave it like that.'

Emma could only gape at him. What on earth was that supposed to mean? Marie and Euan had given every indication of being delighted to be back in Ralton Bridge. And hadn't they been the ones who'd wanted to move in the first place? She pressed her lips together and turned the key in the ignition. With Marie and Euan waiting at home, she should postpone the argument until later.

A thought chilled through her as they were driving into Ralton Bridge. Did that letter mean, stop digging up the past?

CHAPTER 12

TUESDAY, 11TH MAY

EMMA WAS HALFWAY THROUGH HER CORNFLAKES THE FOLLOWING morning when a car door slammed outside, and then another. The gardeners were here, and golly, if Euan and Marie were still asleep upstairs, they soon wouldn't be, with the racket those guys were making. Emma wiped her chin and went out to say hello.

The patio team was made up of three gardeners and Cherie the landscape architect, who would get them started then leave them to it. Luke had taken the day off to help and was outside already, his grumpiness of last night thankfully forgotten.

Cherie gave the others a series of instructions, most of which could have been in Chinese as far as Emma was concerned, and left. Emma retreated inside, and a few minutes later Luke joined her in the kitchen.

'They'll start at this side—' He waved across to where the one-time veggie patch had nearly been. '—and level out the ground first. We're not supposed to go in and out the French doors until it's finished.'

That wouldn't be a problem; they normally used the back door anyway. The French doors wouldn't come into their own until they led onto a patio instead of an invariably muddy patch of grass. Emma winced as loud bangs outside accompanied the arrival of some kind of electric presser. She watched a small digger being driven into position, then the team started unloading the slabs, which they piled up on the grass. Marie called from upstairs, and Luke went to help his dad while Emma cleared the table and reset it for Marie and Euan. The rattle of the letter flap set her heart thumping, and she cursed that letter-writer yet again. Luke had messaged his ex-classmate again yesterday, but so far hadn't had a reply.

Emma trailed out to the hallway – not to get the post, no, snail mail was rarely interesting. She was going to *check* the post, wasn't she? In case there was another plain white envelope. And this time she'd dispose of it unread, like you did with those emails that came after someone's account had been hacked and the sender wanted you to click on a link to a shedload of malware.

A flyer for the new fitness classes in the village hall was lying behind the front door, and how horrible it was that she should be so relieved about a stupid flyer. Emma slapped it onto the hall table as the digger spluttered into action outside. She went to watch at the kitchen window.

Luke and his parents came in, and Marie and Euan settled down at the table.

'Breakfast coming up, guys.' Luke started the coffee machine.

Emma sat down with Marie and Euan. Hopefully the team

out there would get the noisy part done quickly. Even with the windows shut, the drone of the digger as it moved back and forwards shifting the hard-packed earth wasn't what you'd call conducive to comfortable conversation.

Luke was standing at the French doors now, watching closely, and Marie took her cup over to join him. For a moment no one spoke, then Marie's voice quavered.

'Luke darling, don't you think—?'

'Shit! They're going way too deep. They can't—'

Hand over her mouth, Marie wheeled round to lock eyes with Euan, who was sitting there with his mouth hanging open. Luke left the house via the forbidden French doors, and Emma gaped. What was all this about? The gardeners had made hundreds of patios; they must know what they were doing. She joined Marie and stared out. Luke was talking to the digger driver, waving his hands about. The rest of the team gathered round, and an animated conversation took place.

Marie was wringing her hands. 'Oh, Euan...'

Emma turned round. Euan was hunched in his chair, the fingers of one hand plucking his other sleeve and his eyes roaming from right to left and back. He looked like an animal caught in a trap.

He cleared his throat, his face flushed. 'Hush, lass. It'll be all right. Don't worry.'

A moment later, Luke was back. 'Um. Change of plan. We're going for the narrower patio after all.'

Emma rolled her eyes, biting back a sweary retort. She was getting sick of the patio and the endless 'this way, no, that way'.

'But what does it matter if they dig deep? You were dead set on the wide one before.'

'I was, but...' He cleared his throat. 'They'd have to dig even deeper than I'd thought, to get the ground levelled and the base put in. They might damage the roots of Mrs Alderson's quince tree. Don't want aggro with the neighbours already, do we?'

'I think that sounds very sensible, don't you, Euan dear?'

Marie the peacemaker, and Euan's head was going like one of those retro noddy dogs you saw in cars sometimes.

Emma gave up. 'Fine by me. The narrow patio, I mean. So I can have my veggie plot where I'd originally wanted it, then?'

Luke's hands flapped around before he clasped them together. 'Ah. Yes.'

He came over and wrapped his arms around her from behind, patting where her bump would be. In spite of everything, Emma smiled. Wow. Their baby.

Luke kissed her ear. 'As soon as the patio's finished, I'll dig the veggie patch and get it ready for you. You can leave it all to me.'

'Okay. Thanks.' No reason to pass on an offer like that, was there? And Marie was beaming now, and Euan was still nodding, and they were all happy families together. Emma went back to her Earl Grey, irritating little thoughts prodding away in her head.

First she'd found that plastic bag of clothes. Then Luke didn't want the veggie patch at the side near to the house. Then the patio had to cover the entire area. Now the gardeners were digging too deep so they were back to the narrower patio. And Luke was going to dig the veggie patch.

Was there something else buried there he didn't want found? She'd wondered that already, hadn't she? And if there was, did Marie and Euan know about it?

. . .

EMMA'S MOBILE rang when she was loading the dishwasher after breakfast. Ah! Kate. The first contact since the pub fight on Saturday. She took her phone into the garden to talk.

'Hi, Kate – good you've called. I've been meaning to get in touch too.'

'Oh, I'm so glad. I didn't know if you still wanted to be friends.'

Kate sounded close to tears, and Emma's conscience pricked; after such an upset, she should have texted before now. But then, Kate hadn't either.

'My parents-in-law are here for a few days, so it's been busy. Is everything okay?'

'Not really. I was wondering if you had time to meet up this week? I'm worried about Alan.'

'Marie and Euan are going home after lunch tomorrow. How about getting together in the afternoon? Shall I come to the library?'

'Jo's on in the library tomorrow – do you want to come here? It's 10 Lavender Avenue. Around two?'

'Make it half past. See you then.' Emma ended the call and went back to the dishwasher.

She held her tongue about the veggie patch until they were sitting round the table having lunch. The gardening team had gone off in their van, so all was peaceful in the garden. Emma waved a forkful of broccoli and spoke brightly. 'We'll have home-grown next year. I'm glad you're doing the veggie patch, Luke.'

Luke met her eyes, then looked away.

She raised her eyebrows, gave him her best stare. If he didn't have an ulterior motive for digging the veggie patch, why had he gone so red? He'd been happy enough not to help until she'd decided to grow the veggies exactly where he'd buried his oily old clothes. Marie and Euan were pink too, staring at their plates as if they were watching a film, and Emma gave up on finding out more about the veggie plot. It was time to change the subject.

The afternoon turned dull, and Emma helped Marie settle Euan on the sofa after lunch and left them leafing through a photo album Marie had found upstairs. The photos were from Luke's days at uni, and Marie was poring over them, a little smile on her face. Emma smiled too. This was a good distraction, thank goodness. They had more albums upstairs; she would bring them down and they could have a nostalgic wallow through the past.

Luke was outside with the gardening team, so she fetched the box herself. The top album held old photos of Luke's schooldays, and Marie chuckled. 'Look, love, there's the first Parents' Day we went to in York. I was so nervous, but we had a lovely time, didn't we?'

Emma leafed through one of the other albums. The photos here were even older. She stopped at a group of youngsters sitting in the playground for their class photo, a fraught-looking teacher grinning frantically beside them. Luke was in the front row; where was Alan? Someone – probably Marie – had pencilled in names under the photo – yes, Alan Johnson, there he was at the back beside Mark Peterson, the butcher's son. And a Sid Holland was beside them. Hm, Sid was the name of the schoolmate Luke had mentioned in connection with the anonymous letter. She might be able to find him online. Emma left Marie and Euan leafing through the albums, and went for her laptop.

Sid Holland in property featured nowhere, but twelve-year-old Sid Holland came up in an old report in a local paper. He was one of the gymnastics team who were entering a county competition the following year – that must be the same competition Kate had spoken of in the pub last Friday. Emma read the report quickly and examined the photo beside it, but it was pretty grainy. Apart from listing the boys, including Alan and Mark, and praising their trainer, Ryan James, this told her nothing. There was a later article giving the results of the competition, but it told her nothing new apart from who had won which medals. Emma saved the articles to show Luke later.

Euan reached for his stick and heaved himself up. 'There's the sun again. I'll go back outside and watch the workmen for a bit.'

'Yes – show me what you're planning for the garden, Emma.' Marie followed Euan to the door.

They installed Euan at the side with a grandstand view of the patio builders, then Emma and Marie wandered down the path.

'I want the veggie patch there, handy for the back door.' Emma waved her hand towards the area where she'd started digging.

'That's where we had ours, years ago,' said Marie. 'Promise you'll let Luke dig it for you, Emma. The soil's so heavy there. We grassed ours over after – after Luke went to school in York.' She glanced over to Luke, who was helping lay the slabs, and hurried on a few steps.

Emma stared after her. Luke starting a different school was an odd kind of connection to make to grassing over the veggie patch. The two things couldn't possibly have anything to do with each other. Not for the first time in the last couple of weeks, Emma gave up trying to make sense of past events. She led Marie on to the proposed fruit tree site, then opened the shed to show off the new wellies and gardening gloves she'd bought.

Marie stepped into the shed. 'We left this in a state, didn't we? I'm so sorry.'

'That doesn't matter. It's a shed. I've used a lot of the things already, and – Marie?'

The older woman was clutching her cheeks, her mouth open in a silent gasp and her gaze fixed on the old clothes Emma had dug up, still sitting on the shelf.

Emma blinked. 'I uncovered those one day while I was digging. Luke said he'd buried them after a prank. I don't know why he hasn't chucked them out.'

Marie was breathing hard, but she answered casually enough. 'What a rascal he was in those days, always up to something. Shall we go and see how the patio's getting on? The digger's stopped again.' She spun round and left the shed without waiting for an answer.

Of course, Euan insisted on going to the Black Bull for dinner. His old local. Emma cursed Luke and Alan for the scene there. Would they be allowed in? But Euan was so enthusiastic, and Luke was saying nothing. Which was a bit odd too, but with her parents-in-law listening in, there was nothing Emma could do about it.

The car park at the pub was nearly empty, which hopefully meant not many people were having dinner inside. Euan led the way in, and Emma at the rear almost laughed at the barman's expression when he saw them. He greeted Euan –

obviously a well-known guest – and Marie very kindly, though, and made a 'behave yourself' kind of face at Luke, who nodded back. The barman led them over to a table at the far end, away from the crowd at the bar.

Dinner was a lovely steak and kidney pie, supplied by the local butcher, according to the menu, and peas. Emma refused dessert, and sat back with her coffee, a rare treat now that she was pregnant. The pub was busier now, and – oops. Alan appeared through the main door with a couple of others, and they went to lean on the bar. Emma watched as they ordered their beer, and oh, how sad this was. The men were all laughing and chatting with the barman, who didn't seem to blame Alan at all for Friday's disturbance. Thankfully, Luke had his back to the bar, so he didn't have to watch the little scene. Alan was so lively, so normal with these men, yet with Luke… She would have to find out what had happened back then. Luke was a lovely guy and he couldn't possibly have been so mean to Alan that it warranted a freeze-off all these years later. Emma sipped her coffee. Men were hopeless, but if she and Kate could patch things up between their husbands, life in Ralton Bridge would be so much better for them all.

CHAPTER 13

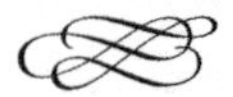

LUKE, AGED 12

THE ATMOSPHERE AT SCHOOL WAS WEIRD, NOW. IT WAS GUY Fawkes night on Saturday, but none of Luke's friends were talking about getting hold of fireworks to light on the way home from school, or making a Guy like they usually did. According to Alan and Sid, that was just for kids, though some of the other boys in the class were doing it anyway. The ones who didn't go to the gym club.

Luke clutched his book on the table, ready to stuff it into his rucksack as soon as the bell rang and Mr Aitken stopped blabbering on about the class outing to see *A Midsummer Night's Dream* in York next March. As if anyone wanted to sit through a whole Shakespeare play. The bell interrupted the English teacher in mid-flow, and Mark shot to his feet and headed for the door straightaway, but Mr Aitken came down on him like a ton of bricks.

'Mark, you need to revise your attitude. This insolence

you've picked up recently won't do, you know, and it definitely won't get you through any exams. Now sit down until we're finished.'

Mark sat, but he took his time about it, swaggering back to his chair like he owned the place, and Luke sighed. Mark was always going all OTT nowadays. You'd think he'd learn that the teachers wouldn't stand for it.

Luke was one of the first out when Mr Aitken eventually let them go, and he stood in the playground with Noel while they waited for Alan and the others. It was good Noel had come to Ralton Bridge because he'd joined the Chess Club, though he'd never come back to the gym club after that first evening. Luke couldn't blame him.

'Want to come round to mine for a game of chess tomorrow night?' Noel rootled around in his rucksack for his gloves.

Luke grimaced. Wouldn't he just, but the idea was a non-starter. 'Can't. Gym club, remember? You still not coming?'

'Not my thing, man. All that shoving you into position.'

Luke sighed. Lucky Noel. He'd managed to stop before his mum had forked out for a load of gym gear for him. He squinted at the fair-haired boy beside him. Noel's face was blank as he stared up to the hills beyond school, where darkness was already inching down green sloping fields.

Alan came out with Mark and Jon and Danny. They stood for a few minutes muttering together before Mark and Danny set off for the side gate, and Alan stomped across to Luke and Noel.

Luke walked backwards up the hill to talk to the other two. 'What were you lot yakking about so long?'

Alan stuffed his hands into his jacket pockets. He shrugged.

'Mark's getting one of those new Game Boys and a load of games for it. You know, the new Super Mario one, and Pokémon.'

Noel's face fell a mile and a half. 'I'd kill for one of those, but we can't afford that kind of stuff now Mum and Dad have split up. Did Mark have a birthday?'

'Nah. He's been doing jobs for Ryan after school.' Alan nudged Luke. 'Wouldn't mind another go with your Game Boy, huh?'

Luke nodded, but his gut was leaping up and down telling him something was off here. Ryan in the showers, and... and Mark's bag on the changing room floor. And now Mark was doing jobs for Ryan. 'You reckon that's okay? About Mark doing jobs for Ryan?'

Alan shrugged. 'I'd do jobs if I was getting money for them, wouldn't you? Ryan's a bit – intense, but he's a great trainer and he's rolling in it. Have you seen his car?'

Noel was staring as if they'd both just grown horns, but they'd arrived at his place now and he gave them the usual high five and disappeared inside without saying another word.

Luke shoved his hands into his pockets. 'What d'you really think? About Ryan?'

Alan gave him a shove. 'I think I want to be a gymnast, that's what. You don't have to like your coach, Luke, you only have to let him coach you. I'm good at this, and I'll do whatever it takes to be better.'

Luke heaved a sigh, and they trudged along in silence. It was true. Alan was way the best at most of the gymnastic stuff. Did that mean Ryan didn't have to shove him around so much now? And none of the others had said anything about Ryan pushing them into position, so it must be all right. Luke gave up. Alan collected his bike from Luke's shed – he biked down in the morning when his dad was too busy to drive him – and set off home, and Luke went inside.

And hallelujah, a note from Mum on the kitchen table. *Dad home early so we've gone to Tesco's. Back before tea.* Brilliant. Luke grabbed the remote and settled down on the sofa to watch *Space Quadrant Omega* in peace and quiet.

He pulled a face as the episode started. Some of the space station crew had zoomed off to a planet for a kind of holiday, and were skipping around in the sunshine with scantily clad humanoid aliens. Luke preferred the episodes filmed on the space station, when the crew had to ward off attacks from hostile alien spaceships. Today it was all getting a bit lovey-dovey. He watched glumly as Lieutenant Bren wandered off with Commander Kaley. They disappeared into what looked like a Roman bath, and the scene shifted to a couple of aliens plotting something dastardly. Thank goodness. The thought of what Bren and Kaley might be doing in there was making Luke feel – funny.

He closed his eyes. What wouldn't he give to exorcise the picture of Ryan in the shower from his head?

A car door slammed outside, and half a minute later Mum and Dad were in the hallway.

Dad put his head into the living room, chuckling. 'Ah, you've seized the moment. I'll just put those pots in the shed, Marie.' He vanished, and the back door banged shut.

Mum had gone into the kitchen. 'We bought some of that chocolate spread for you, darling. And guess what else we found?'

'What?' Luke screwed up his nose at the TV. Was it worthwhile trying to watch the rest of this?

Mum appeared in the doorway, waving a packet of something in one hand. 'Remember the star-shaped macaroni we had in—' She broke off and strode past him while Luke gaped.

Two seconds later she'd grabbed the remote, and Luke cringed when he saw what was on the TV screen. Oh, no, it was Bren and Kaley again and they were locked in each other's arms, all steamy and...

'I won't have you watching this rubbish, Luke! It's – indecent!'

Mum's face had gone all red. Luke sagged into the sofa while she slapped the remote back down on the coffee table, then stalked across the room and started fussing over the budgie. The subject was evidently closed. Luke slumped into the sofa. No more *Space Station Omega,* then. Maybe he could watch it at Alan's.

HE WAS UPSTAIRS AGAIN DOING his homework after tea – when no one had mentioned *Space Station Omega* or anything like it – when Dad put his head around the door.

'All right, Luke? He strolled over to the bookshelf and pulled out a couple of books.

Luke shuffled in his chair. 'Uh-huh.' What did Dad want?

'Ah!' Dad was leafing through Luke's biology book. 'Your Mum told me about that programme, son. I know you learn all about the birds and bees at school, but, ah, if you ever need to talk about anything, um...'

Now Dad had gone red. Luke ducked his head. 'It's fine, thanks.'

Dad snapped the book shut and replaced it on the shelf. 'Excellent! Time enough for a good chat when you're a year or two older, eh?' He scooted back to the door, then turned. 'Luke – don't upset your mum with things like that. Okay?'

Luke listened as his feet clattered down the stairs. Wow. They'd almost had a frank discussion there. Nice one, Dad.

Mum's voice floated up the stairs. 'Luke darling – there's a programme about gymnastics on BBC 2. Come and watch it. You might pick up some tips.'

Yuck. But better not start another argument. Luke ran downstairs and plonked down beside Mum on the sofa. The programme was about training kids in what used to be Czechoslovakia, and he blinked at the TV as a girl swung around on the asymmetric bars. No point telling Mum that boys didn't do these bars. The girl was very good, mind you, and she didn't look much older than he was. She took off into the air after her last swoop and landed almost perfectly, arms outstretched and a big happy smile on her face. The moment she hit the ground her coach grabbed her, pulling her straight and then rubbing her back while they grinned at each other. Luke screwed up his face. It seemed all gymnastic coaches were like that, and even Mum was smiling and nodding. It wasn't logical, though, was it? Luke sank further into the sofa.

His stomach lurched the way it did every time he thought about Ryan's hands shoving his shoulders and his tummy and his bum into position. But Noel must have seen exactly what Ryan had done and he'd never mentioned it, so he couldn't have thought anything of it, because Noel was the kind of person who'd ask you straight if he wanted to know something.

Luke fixed his eyes on the set, determinedly pushing the

uncomfortable thoughts away as the next girl started her routine on the bars, her coach on one side waiting to help with the landing. Maybe he was all wrong about it being weird.

Mark must have done a lot of jobs for Ryan to earn a Game Boy…

CHAPTER 14

WEDNESDAY, 12TH MAY

Having gardeners in meant everyone in the house was awake bright and early; the noise these guys were making would have wakened the dead, never mind a light sleeper. Emma rolled out of bed at seven-thirty and trailed downstairs to join Luke in the kitchen. He'd taken the morning off work today too, and for some reason this was making Emma uneasy. Was he trying to make sure she didn't grill his parents about his childhood friendship with Alan? But that couldn't be right; Luke had been outside helping the gardeners most of the time yesterday. Of course, it wasn't impossible that Marie and Euan would know what had happened between Luke and Alan back in the day, but… Emma shook her head. Asking the older couple behind Luke's back would be prying, and she wasn't going to do that.

Luke took his coffee over to the French doors. 'They should get the biggest part finished today. I'll take Mum and Dad back to York after lunch, and then I have a late meeting tonight. I won't be home much before eight.' He vanished outside to join the gardening team.

That was why he'd taken the morning off, then. She shouldn't be so suspicious. Emma laid the table for Marie and Euan's breakfast, then stood at the window watching the patio team at work. A call came from above, and she went to help Euan downstairs. He was shaky on the stairs, and going down was more painful than going up, apparently. Emma kept a firm hand under his arm as they inched down. Getting older wasn't for wimps, and why on earth hadn't she and Luke been more in touch with Marie and Euan this past year, when things had deteriorated for Euan? Emma frowned as an odd thought struck her. Luke *had* been in touch with his parents, but more often than not, he'd organised his visits to Ralton Bridge when she was busy doing something else. Had that been deliberate on his part, and if so, why? A little support was all it had taken to have Marie looking ten years younger. Miserably, Emma put the kettle on. Not much of a daughter-in-law, was she? Well, she could change that.

She sat down to chat while Marie and Euan ate. 'How did you two meet, then?'

Marie's mug clattered down on the table. 'Oh, that was a long time ago. I left Skye and came over to the mainland the moment I was old enough. Euan had a job in Aberdeen in those days, teaching music.' She descended into her cornflakes.

'What was your work back then, Marie?' Emma stirred more milk into her mug to cover the pause in the conversation. Was she imagining the awkwardness here? Marie was pink, and Euan was concentrating on his toast as if his life depended on it.

'I did secretarial work. Then later we moved to Glasgow, and from there to Ralton Bridge.'

Euan must have chewed his last mouthful fifty times. Something was definitely off.

Emma filled the silence. 'And now York.'

'Yes. I do hope we can stay there for good.'

'No reason why not.' Emma sipped her tea, pondering. She still didn't know much about Marie and Euan's early lives. 'How long have you been married, actually?' The couple hadn't celebrated a wedding anniversary since she'd known them, but then, most people didn't make a big deal of the more ordinary ones.

Marie reached across and squeezed Euan's wrist on the table. 'Forever and a day,' she said, her voice trembling. 'And not nearly long enough.'

Euan put his hand on hers, nodding silently, his eyes bright.

Aw, bless them both. A huge lump rose in Emma's throat as an unexpected tear ran down one cheek. Would she and Luke still be so in love when they were waiting for the birth of their first grandchild?

Marie jumped up. 'Emma, are you all right, dear? Let me clear away. Euan, on you go outside and watch the gardeners. Emma should be resting.' She was bundling him out before Emma could draw breath to reassure her.

'Marie, I'm fine, honestly. You mustn't worry. I've had all my checks and pills and what have you. There's no reason I wouldn't be fine – you're all taking care of me so well.'

'I'm sorry. I know I panic about it. It's just—' Marie dabbed her eyes with the tea towel.

Emma pricked up her ears. 'Just—?'

Marie dropped back into her chair, her eyes full. 'We lost

one once, a few months into the pregnancy. It was years before Luke was born – to tell you the truth it was a day or two before we were married, and it was such a shock. Then we had to wait so long for Luke to come along afterwards.' Tears spilled over, and Marie pulled out a tissue.

Oh my God. Emma bit her lip. That explained everything, and now she was going to have to be equally frank, and very careful how she did it, too.

She slid her chair round the table and took Marie's hand. 'I'm so sorry. You must have been devastated, and I know what it's like because I lost one too, years ago. But please don't worry, Marie. That problem was right at the very start of the pregnancy, and the doctor says it's perfectly okay this time.' A white lie was excusable here, wasn't it? All the assurances so far had come from the midwife, but a doctor would sound more reassuring to poor Marie, whose eyes were as round as saucers now.

Emma hugged the older woman. 'We'll see this baby at the scan very soon now. Come on. I'll help you pack, and then you can relax for the rest of the morning.'

EMMA PULLED the zip around the suitcase Marie had filled, then wheeled it out to the landing.

Marie closed the wardrobe door. 'Thank you so much for having us to stay, Emma love, and for all your help. It's made all the difference.'

Emma turned round in the doorway. 'I'll miss the pair of you.'

It was true. With Marie and Euan gone and Luke at work, it would be back to home alone for her and the baby, and Emma wasn't relishing the prospect. She was still a stranger in Ralton Bridge, and she was rattling around alone in the house most of the time. Which reminded her…

'By the way, I saw Mrs Alderson's gorgeous fireplace the other day. Was the one you boarded up anything like that? I'd love one like Mrs Alderson has.'

Marie's head was shaking vigorously. 'There was one in the second bedroom, but it was very shabby. Nothing at all like May Alderson's. And for goodness sake, Emma dear, don't start opening up chimney breasts. A woman in the village told me a while ago they'd opened theirs and found it had asbestos in it. That's not what you want with a baby in the house.' She squeaked to a halt and glared at Emma, breathing heavily.

Emma swallowed her surprise. Possible asbestos in what would be the baby's room eventually was surely the best reason of all to have the chimney breast professionally opened and renovated. Or was she missing something? She didn't know much about asbestos, and Marie would hit the roof in a minute if she wasn't careful. Yet again, it was time to change the subject.

OUTSIDE, the gardeners had done a good morning's work and gone for lunch. Luke was putting steaks on the grill. 'Ready for the last, um, not supper – the last lunch, Mum?' He winked at his father.

'Luke!' Marie wagged a finger at him, but she was laughing, and so was Euan.

Emma ferried the rest of the lunch things out to the table, which they'd set up on the unfinished patio. The section furthest from the house still needed a row of slabs, and then there was the edging to do. But enough was done for her to appreciate the beauty of the slate. They'd made the right choice. The patio was a huge improvement to their new home, and it would be interesting to see Kate's home this afternoon too, the newbuild Emma had thought she and Luke might buy, once upon a time. She poured them all iced tea while Luke dished out steaks.

Euan raised his glass. 'You're a good lad, Luke. Thanks for everything you've done for us, son – we couldn't have managed without you. And thank you Emma, too, of course.'

They all clinked, Emma trying not to mind about being tagged on as an afterthought. Luke had gone pink – were those tears in his eyes? She'd only once seen him so emotional over a thank you, and that was at their wedding, when Marie had said something rather similar to Euan's little speech a moment ago. The three Carters didn't have the same easy, huggy relationship she had with Oma and Opa, but they had the same love. Did she and Dad? Not really, but she was going to change that, wasn't she?

Conversation went back to normal while they ate, then Marie and Euan had a second coffee on the patio while Emma helped Luke clear the plates into the kitchen.

He grabbed his car key from the table and waved it at her. 'I'll whizz out and get petrol. If I fill the tank on the way back to York, Dad'll insist on paying for it. You know what he's like.' He jogged off into the hallway and out the front door.

Emma stacked plates into the dishwasher, then started back to the patio for the glasses. Marie's voice brought her to a sudden stop as she stepped through the back door.

'I wish Luke had been able to have those slabs all the way across here. It would have given him peace of mind.'

Emma jerked back, still around the corner from the garden table.

Euan's reply was almost inaudible. 'I know, dear. But there's nothing we can do. It'll be all right, don't worry.'

'You should have told me about it, Euan.'

'For God's sake, Marie – you wouldn't have coped. I had to keep it to myself, you must see that.'

'I think we should tell Luke.'

Euan's hand slapped on the table. 'We tell no one, hear? No one will find out, don't worry.' His sigh was so loud Emma could hear it. 'You know, sometimes I wish we'd all just stayed put.'

Emma hovered, but nothing more was said, and she retreated into the kitchen, questions buzzing around in her head. 'Peace of mind'? What had Euan kept to himself? And what did the size of the patio have to do with the house swap? And as wide patios were apparently on everyone's wish list except hers, why had Luke stopped that happening? He'd blamed Mrs Alderson's quince tree for the change of plan. Emma went over to the window to stare at it. It wasn't a big tree, and they'd already decided it was far enough away from the border.

And now Luke was going to dig the veggie patch for her. A cold shiver ran down Emma's spine.

CHAPTER 15

THE AFTERNOON WAS SUNNY AND WARM, PERFECT WEATHER TO bike to the Vale to visit Kate. Emma pushed her bike to the top of the hill then freewheeled down the other side. Four or five kids were sailing little boats on the pond, watched by their mums. Maybe one day she'd sit on one of those benches, chatting to the other mums while the little ones splashed around in the sunshine. It was an idyllic thought, though for some reason it felt unreal, today. Emma came to the edge of the old village, and biked on through the scenery – open fields in the foreground, the vibrant yellow of oilseed rape on her left, and sheep to her right contrasting nicely with their grassy meadow. Beyond the rape fields lay the alternating red and grey roofs of the Vale. Perfect little starter homes. Seen from here, you'd think it was a separate village, and part of Emma, quite a substantial part, actually, wished they were living there and not in the 'old' Ralton Bridge.

The streets in the Vale were all named after plants, and young lime trees were planted at intervals along the wide pavements. The houses were semis, each with a patch of grass at the front and identical garages, the same white-painted wooden fencing all the way along the street. Today, a group of little kids were shouting to each other, riding their bikes and scooters around the deserted streets, watched by a couple of older women – their grandmothers? It was suburbia out of a film, and it all looked very cosy and friendly.

Emma was parking her bike in front of the garage at 10 Lavender Avenue when Kate opened the front door.

'Come in. I'm glad you could come. I'm working at home today, so this is perfect.'

Emma followed her through to the living area, similar to their own but smaller. The kitchen area was at the street end, while bifolding doors on the opposite wall opened onto a small patio and a very manageable garden. She accepted a glass of iced tea, and they went to sit outside.

'Do you have another job, apart from the library?'

'I do some bookkeeping and secretarial work for a couple of small businesses. When we moved here the idea was to start a family, and I wanted to stay flexible. There's no baby in sight, though, and oh, Emma, I'm really worried about Alan.'

'What's up?' Emma put one hand on her middle before snatching it away again. Poor Kate. Seeing her sitting here happily pregnant must be hard.

'After that scene at the pub – and I still have no idea what it was about but it was *so* not Alan. He's usually so upbeat and enthusiastic about everything. I asked him to explain, but he said it was all in the past and he didn't want to talk about it.' Kate stared into the middle distance before continuing. 'Then on Monday morning I went into the study upstairs and found him there clutching a letter. He nearly jumped out of his skin, then he started ranting away about filthy scum as if it was my fault, then he ripped the letter up and flushed it down the loo. He still won't talk to me about it.'

Emma sat frozen in her seat. 'Did you see what was in it? We've had a couple of anonymous letters, saying stuff like "stop digging or else". Did yours come by post?'

Kate's eyes widened. 'I don't know what was in it and I don't know how it came, either. I just assumed by post. It was a normal sheet of paper in a plain white envelope.'

'Same as ours. There's something weird going on, Kate, and I reckon it's to do with whatever happened when they were kids. Luke thought it might be an old schoolmate trying to threaten us, and once he mentioned a prank at Alan's dad's farm that had gone wrong, too. I think they should tell us about it, especially with anonymous letters arriving.'

Kate pressed her fingertips together. 'Let's go through what we know. That night at the pub. We were talking about school and the guys being older than me, and I said I remembered Alan because of the gymnastics competition, and we talked about the nativity play.'

Emma closed her eyes to picture the scene. 'And then you and I went to the loo, and when we came back, they were arguing.'

'Yes. About something being someone's fault. They were blaming each other.'

'And the barman said something about it not being their fault.' Emma tried to remember the man's exact words, then gave up. Was this really about a playground scuffle? 'So I guess the barman knows what it was?'

Kate sniffed. 'We could go and talk to him.'

'That would go down well over our respective dinner

tables. We should ask Luke and Alan again. Is there nothing more you remember from back in the day?'

'I've been thinking, of course, but I was nine, so my memories are hazy. It must be a guy rivalry thing. Maybe Luke tried to do Alan out of his prize at the gymnastics competition.'

Kate was half-laughing, but Emma couldn't join in. 'Doubt it. Let's ask them again, and if we have no joy, we can look online too. We might find more about the competition, or if something else happened in the village around that time.'

Kate poured more iced tea. 'Okay. We can phone if we find anything.'

It was after five when Emma started the ride back home, feeling that she'd put down a tiny root in Ralton Bridge today. Spending an afternoon with her new friend made the village feel more like home, even if they were having problems getting the guys on board.

The road was busier now with people driving home from work. Ralton Bridge – or the Vale, at least – was a real commuter kind of place, handy for Harrogate as well as York, and not too far from Leeds, too. Emma arrived back in the old village and dismounted for the hill, glancing into the butcher's as she pushed her bike past. The shop was empty, and the hill was as steep as ever. She trudged on. Maybe one day she'd have enough muscles to actually ride up here, though with the baby growing daily, it wasn't going to be soon... but here she was at the top. Now for the freewheel back down Brook Lane.

She was enjoying the wind in her hair when a silver-grey car shot out of – had that been their driveway, or Mrs Alderson's? He was gunning his car up the hill and hogging the middle of the road, too. What the—? Emma steered as close to the side as she could get for parked cars. The grey car revved on its way uphill, then did a little swerve towards her as it passed. She wobbled frantically then jerked to a halt, falling against a Mini parked by the roadside. Shit, she'd have been down on the ground if there hadn't been a car parked here. Emma twisted round to glare, but whoever it was had vanished over the brow of the hill. Wanker.

She set off again, her heart thudding anew as a horn blared behind her. A quick glance back – hell no, was this the same car? He was way too close; he was right behind her – shit! If he touched her bike, she'd be down on the road with those wheels rolling over her before she had time to take breath. Panic seared through Emma's gut. Home was still twenty yards away…

The engine behind her revved again, and she skidded into the driveway and stumbled off her bike as the silver-grey car screamed past and vanished round the corner, heading out of Ralton Bridge and leaving the street deserted. Jeez, that had been way too close for comfort.

Panting, Emma stared down the empty road. For a few moments she could only stand there, clutching the handlebars while her heart rate steadied. That wasn't just some idiot in a hurry being careless; that had been deliberate. Whoever it was, he'd been trying to scare her, and God help her, he'd succeeded. If she'd landed under that car, it would have been the end for her and the baby. If only she'd seen who was driving.

Still shaking, Emma left her bike at the side of the house and rummaged for her keys. What should she do now? It would be hours before Luke was back from his meeting.

The stench hit her as soon as she opened the front door. One hand slapped up to cover her nose as she took half a step inside, retching and tripping over an open plastic bag on the doormat spilling – oh my God, dog poo – all over the mat and onto the hallway floor. Emma stood still, her stomach heaving.

IT WAS ten past eight when Luke's key turned in the lock.

'Where's the doormat? And what's that smell?'

Emma had spent the past two hours trying to get rid of it, but the stench was still burning in her nose. The wrecked doormat was in the bin outside, and she'd taken the plastic bag to the nearest litter bin and shoved it in there, but all the disinfectant she'd scrubbed over the hallway floor had failed to get rid of the smell. She was lighting scented candles all over the place when Luke arrived. But the dog poo was the least of what she had to tell him.

'Luke, I think I was attacked. He was out to get me!'

'*What*? Who? What happened?' He grabbed her shoulders, then pulled her in for a hug.

Emma shook free. If she let him be nice to her, she'd dissolve into a blubbing mess, and he had to know what had happened before they could tackle it. In a few sentences, she explained about the bike ride down the hill and the silver-grey car.

'It looked like every other car on the road, and God knows who was driving. Luke, I don't think we should stay here. We don't know what they'll do next.'

Luke's face was a picture of anger and disgust. He put an arm around her and pulled her over to the kitchen table. 'You've had a shock. I'll make tea.'

'Tea? That's not going to help!' Her voice rose, quivering,

and she winced. This was how Marie sounded when she was uptight about something.

'It'll help you calm down. This isn't good for the baby.' He busied around the kitchen, and Emma slumped in her chair and massaged her middle. The thought that she might have transmitted all that panic to her child was the worst part of the whole horrible thing.

Luke slid a mug across the table, then sat down opposite. 'I'll deal with this, Emmy. I know someone in the police, a guy I was at school with. He'll give us some unofficial advice, but the dog poo thing could have been kids being mean. The car could be, too. You get stupid idiots everywhere, and we don't want to encourage pranksters.'

He stomped off up the garden with his phone, leaving Emma sitting with her mouth open. Encourage pranksters? What was he *talking* about? And for God's sake, did he really think that two different people had been responsible? No way. The driver of the car must have left that dog poo – she'd seen him emerge from one of the driveways. He must have been overjoyed when he saw her coming down the hill; talk about being in the wrong place at the wrong time – she'd walked into that one. Emma trailed over to the window and watched as Luke tapped, then held the phone to his ear. A friend in the police wasn't impossible, but Luke had never mentioned him before… She sipped her tea as he paced around the garden, gesticulating with his free hand as he spoke into his phone. Who was he talking to?

CHAPTER 16

LUKE, AGED 12

It was surprising how quickly you got fit. Luke thrust his shoulders back as he jogged steadily down Alan's dad's hay barn. Who'd have thought that not even ten weeks after starting Ryan's programme, he'd be able to run for twenty minutes without a walking break? Running had turned into the good part about all this. The gym club, with the smelly, sweaty atmosphere in the changing rooms, and Ryan with his bloody 'all boys together' thing and his fake smile as he grabbed you after a jump or steadied you doing a balance exercise – that was the bad part.

Then there was the thing with Mark. None of the others seemed to think it was odd that Mark was doing jobs for Ryan... but none of them knew about that evening when Ryan had been in the boys' showers and Mark's bag had still been there. Of course, maybe Mark had simply forgotten it, and gone back for it later, like Luke had with his shoes. It was the only possible explanation. Luke's stomach lurched.

Alan jogged past, his face serious, and Luke sighed. Something else he'd never have guessed was that Alan would turn from a normal, chatty kid into a serious gymnast who spent every spare minute perfecting his handstands and doing stretches. Ryan had started a special gymnastics programme for boys with potential, and Alan was in it, along with Mark and Sid and a couple of others. They were going in for a gym competition at the beginning of March, and they'd even had their picture in the local paper last week. Luke sniffed. The special group had an extra session on Tuesdays after school, and oh boy, was he glad he didn't have to go to that. Trying to stay clear of Ryan during the Friday class was enough, and the stupid thing was, Alan hated Ryan too, but he was still dead keen to get on at gymnastics. Ryan was a brilliant coach, according to Alan and Mark, and it didn't seem to matter to them how he got his results. It was all just wrong, but Alan had gold medals dangling in front of him like donkeys had carrots.

The timer beeped, and Luke slowed down into his cool-off walk. When he was finished, he did his stretches then sat on a hay bale swigging orange juice while Alan did his then came to sit beside him.

'Friday tomorrow.'

'Yup.' There was nothing more to be said. Luke grabbed his towel and stood up to go. He was stuck. Mum and Dad wouldn't let him stop going to the gym club, and Alan would go mad if anyone even tried to stop him.

. . .

THE FOLLOWING NIGHT, Ryan called the group together at the start of the session.

'Before we get going, I want to tell you about a special afternoon session we're planning to kick-start training after the Christmas holidays. It'll be on the first Saturday in January from two until five, here and up in the woods if the weather's suitable. No cost, of course. You can let me know by next week if you're interested.'

'You going?' Luke nudged Alan while some of the others were talking to Ryan.

'We have to, in the special group. You? Would be good if you did.'

Alan wasn't looking at him, and Luke stared. His friend wasn't usually one for being soppy.

'Sure.' It was out before he'd put his brain in gear. Brilliant. Now he had gymnastics all bloody afternoon on a Saturday to look forward to. Happy New Year.

The class started, and oh, joy – Luke was allocated to a group of good runners to train up and down the corridors with Harry and Jason for the first half of the evening, while Ryan and the gymnasts remained in the gym. Luke pulled a face at Alan, who stuck his tongue out then joined Jon and Mark and the others in Ryan's group.

Running with Harry was always great, and Luke would happily have spent the rest of the gym class in the corridors, but all too soon it was half-time. He went into the changing room to refill his water bottle, then wandered over to a little group of boys huddled in one corner.

Jon was talking. 'I don't see what we can do about it. No one would believe us. All the parents think the sun shines out of Ryan's backside.'

Ryan's steamy bum that night slid into Luke's head, and he clutched the front of his T-shirt. He squinted round the other boys – Sid and Alan looked as if they were about to start crying. Fear slammed into Luke's middle.

Mark's face was set in a scowl. 'For God's sake, just chill. It's nothing. Are you all babies?'

Jon cuffed Mark's head. 'Like him fingering you, do you?'

Luke couldn't stop his gasp. Ryan's hands all over the place as he grabbed you after a jump… *'fingering you'*? Oh God. Fear rolled through Luke's middle. It was the thought he'd pushed away all this time, not allowing himself to even think it, and now the others were bloody talking about it. Out loud, so it was real.

Mark sniffed. 'What does it matter? He gives me—' He shuffled his feet and lowered his voice, '—cash. I'm saving for a computer now.'

Luke closed his mouth. He wasn't the only one gasping now. First a Game Boy, now a computer! Ryan must be giving Mark serious money.

Alan stepped back. 'Cash? He doesn't give me cash. What the shit do you let him do?'

Mark glared. 'For God's sake, man, it's not like he's chopping my fingers off or anything. And you are not to tell one sodding soul, okay? Or I'll kill you.' He swaggered off into the gym.

Alan stopped Jon from following Mark. 'Leave him. He's weird. And he's right, too – we can't do anything about it.'

Luke found his voice. 'What happened, exactly?'

For a moment no one replied, then Alan muttered in Luke's ear.

'Touchy-feely was on overtime tonight.'

Luke stared at the floor. The red and black tiled lino was ancient and cracked. He hated this; he hated even thinking about it, but it was happening. He knew what touchy-feely meant. That jump he'd done back near the start, when Noel had been watching… Ryan hadn't touched him again, but the fear was always there, unacknowledged but heavy in the bottom of Luke's gut. And Alan and the others who did extra gymnastics – Ryan was a lot more physical about pulling them into position, wasn't he? This was all, all wrong.

Jon was scowling. 'Why does he give Mark cash and not the rest of us?'

Nods and mutters came from a couple of boys at this, but Sid gave Jon a shove. 'Use your brain, dummy. It won't just be a few fingers here and there that Mark gets.'

Luke scuffed his feet on the lino. He wasn't even going to start thinking about what that might mean. Someone had to fix this, and none of them could. 'This isn't right. You – we have to tell someone. Your dad, Alan? He's collecting us, isn't he?'

Jon stuck his face right up to Luke, and he stepped back. 'How many times? They wouldn't believe it. You'd only make everything worse, ninny.'

Ryan's whistle sounded in the gym.

Mum was waiting at home to hear how the class had gone, alone because Dad had gone next door to help Mrs Alderson with her boiler. Luke seized his chance.

'I think I'd like a running club better than gymnastics.' He frowned up at her from his place at the kitchen table.

She poured milk for his hot choc into a pan and stood watching it heat. 'Maybe you can do that next year.'

Luke slumped in his chair. She hadn't even asked why. 'Ryan's always shoving us into position when we jump – that's what I don't like. I wish I'd never started gym club.'

She poured the milk into his frog mug and added chocolate powder. 'Here you are, love, but listen. Your dad wouldn't hear of you giving up the gym club so soon after it started. That would be a real waste of all the kit we've got you, and you'll have outgrown it by next summer. And I think it's a good thing for you to get fit. Like your dad says, there are bigger boys around who might pick on the smaller ones. No one's going to pick on someone who's fit and strong with plenty of muscles, are they?'

She smiled, but the discussion was over. Luke sipped his drink. It was no use; he was stuck with the gym club and bloody Ryan till summer. Yuck, yuck, yuck. Luke lifted his mug and turned to go up to his room. His father came in as he started up the stairs, but all Luke said was 'Fine' when Dad asked how the gym club had gone. Luke stomped on up the stairs, then stopped halfway when he heard Mum.

'He doesn't enjoy it, Euan. We could let him stop after Christmas. He can go on with the running and get fit without going to a class.'

A chair scraped on the floor as Dad sat down. 'It would look a bit off if he stopped just like that, don't you think? You haven't met Ryan, but he's a great one for team spirit and he wouldn't let Luke leave without asking questions. This'll do the boy good. We don't want to cause a fuss and make ourselves conspicuous, do we?'

Mum made an agreeing murmur, and Luke nearly choked. What was more important, his happiness or not being conspicuous? He fled upstairs and slammed his bedroom door. It was pathetic; Mum and Dad were always so worried about what people thought. They were always saying how important it was to do the right thing and be good, but… What *was* the right thing to do about the gym club? Luke abandoned the hot choc on the chest of drawers and flung himself onto the bed.

CHAPTER 17

THURSDAY, 13TH MAY

EMMA CAME DOWNSTAIRS SNIFFING THE MORNING AFTER THE dog poo incident, but all you could smell this morning was disinfectant and sandalwood candles. Luke had made breakfast for her, and she sat down to warm toast with honey, orange juice and Earl Grey.

'Feeling better?' He was leaning on the worktop, sipping espresso.

Emma crashed her mug down, and tea slopped onto the table. 'That sounds as if you think the whole thing was down to my overactive imagination.'

He stepped forward and kissed the top of her head. 'I don't. It was a horrible thing to happen. But a hysterical reaction is just what these idiots want, isn't it? Let's not give them the satisfaction.'

Emma jerked away. Now he was accusing her of being hysterical, and from the comfort of her kitchen, it did seem unbelievable that someone had shoved dog poo through the door and then tried to ram her. But it had happened, and the fact that Luke was behaving like this now was – shocking. All he'd said when he came back in last night was 'Sorted'. It wasn't enough, but Emma had been too sick of the whole stupid business to press him about it.

As soon as he left for work, she wandered outside. The gardeners had finished now, and Emma nodded grimly. No matter what was going on here, this shape of patio was definitely best. She stopped at the mess on the side border. This was supposed to be her veggie patch, once Luke dug it, but did she really want to grow veggies in a patch that had seen a hidden bag of clothes and heaven knows what else? Marie had been shocked when she'd spotted those clothes in the shed. And both Marie and Euan had been sorry the patio wouldn't cover the veggie patch, and they'd talked about some kind of secret, too. Emma sank down on an elderly garden chair for a think. So Marie and Euan, and Luke and Alan, and the barman, and very possibly the butcher and his wife and their son, all knew about something that had happened twenty-odd years ago, and it was still spooking them today.

And someone had tried to knock her off her bike yesterday. Emma took a deep, shaky breath. This was getting Just. Too. Scary. She needed to talk to Kate again.

Her friend answered on the first ring, and Emma started straight in. 'Did Luke call Alan last night? About half eight?'

'Someone did – was that Luke? Alan was mad as hell afterwards, wouldn't speak to me all evening.'

'Wait until you hear this.' In a few sentences, Emma described the car attack and the bag of dog poo.

'Oh my God. But Alan had nothing to do with that. I

drove to the farm to collect him straight after you left yesterday, and we were both there with a sick sheep until seven, when his dad got home from the market. What the hell's going on?'

'More to the point, what went on back in the day to cause all this now? We're not getting anywhere with the guys, so let's do some searching online. I'll send you a Zoom invite and we can have a look together, huh?'

Emma went inside and opened her laptop. Two minutes later they were looking at the articles she'd found before.

'Not much there. But let's see what else we can find.' Kate clicked around and pulled up more newspaper articles, this time about the school nativity play, which had apparently been a yearly thing. One report was about the play Kate was in with the incontinent donkey episode, and with a couple of photos, too. Was one of those children Luke? Impossible to tell on the grainy old images.

Emma put the gym club articles on the screen again. 'Let's have another look at these. I still think it's more likely to be something to do with that gym club.' She leaned in towards her laptop screen. There was the photo she'd seen before: a clutch of young boys and a couple of older ones, and Ryan James. Ryan James with... Emma's hair stood on end.

'Kate – look at that second photo and tell me I'm not seeing things.'

Taken by itself, no one would have thought twice about the photo. She hadn't, the first time she'd seen it. But in the context of something horrible having happened... Was she imagining this? A group of boys, Ryan James' hand on one lad's shoulder, three of his fingers trailing under the child's T-shirt. And the expression on that child's face – dear God, that couldn't be right. But why not? Bad things happened, even in cosy English villages.

Kate's voice was low. 'Shit.'

It was a relief that Kate saw it too. Emma pressed a hand to her chest. 'What we need is someone who was around back then to talk to us about this, and none of them are. Talking, I mean.'

There was silence for a few seconds, then Kate gave a half-hysterical giggle. 'You're right, and I don't know why I didn't think of it before. I can ask my grandmother, the one I stayed with while I was here as a kid. She'll be ninety-five next birthday, but she's sharp as you like. She might remember something, and she's nothing if not talkative. She lives in a care home in Glenfield.'

'Wow. Why don't we visit her together?'

'I'll give her a ring now, and let you know.'

Kate left the Zoom session, and Emma leaned back in the sofa. Good, they were doing something, and hopefully Kate's grandmother would be able to help. Emma pressed cold fingers against her mouth. Hopefully, too, it was nothing like what she and Kate were afraid of. Child abuse? In Ralton Bridge? Surely not… Yet the strange and suffocating silence around whatever had gone on would fit in with abuse. Emma passed a hand across her middle.

JUST OVER AN HOUR LATER, a car horn parped outside, and Emma grabbed her bag and ran. Kate's grandmother had agreed to see them that day, so they'd soon know if her memories would help them clear things up.

Kate slowed down as they caught up with a tractor on the

road to Glenfield. 'Is it okay if we sit with Granny for a while, then take her out for lunch? That's what I usually do. She's good company, though her legs have given up on her, she says.'

'Sure. I wish my grandparents lived closer.' The thought of what Oma and Opa would think if they knew what was going on here was – horrific. Longing for one of Oma's super-hugs flooded through Emma. Hopefully, she and Kate would get this sorted now, then she could tell Oma and Opa when everything was okay again. The scan was on Monday, and Oma was definitely expecting a call after that.

The North Moor Lodge was a generous, three-story Georgian building set in a huge garden, and Emma gazed out appreciatively as Kate drove along to the visitors' car park at the far side. If you weren't able to live in your own home, this was a pretty nice alternative.

Inside, they took the lift to the third floor, where Sheila's room was. Kate knocked and went straight in, pulling Emma behind her. A slim, white-haired old lady was sitting with a book on a two-seater sofa, and Kate hugged her fondly before introducing Emma.

Sheila took Emma's hand and held it. 'It's lovely to meet you, dear. How do you like Ralton Bridge?'

Clear blue eyes in a sweet, lined face were gazing into her own, and Emma swallowed. The sense of something infinitely precious missing in her daily life was almost overwhelming. Why, oh why did she have to live in a different country to the people who'd loved her the longest? She replied to Sheila's question, gazing around. The room had a hospital bed at the far end, but the two-seater sofa and an armchair were arranged by the window, which looked out over lovely countryside. Emma took the armchair while Kate settled down on the sofa, gripping Sheila's hand. A carer arrived with three cups of tea, and conversation was general for a while. Then Sheila put her cup down and turned to Kate.

'What was it you wanted to ask me, dear? It sounded rather mysterious.'

Kate shot Emma a glance. 'Emma's husband was at school with Alan, and the two of them have a silly feud going on about something that happened back in the time I was staying with you. We think it's to do with a gymnastics club. I don't remember it, but it's making Alan and Luke miserable. They won't talk about it, and we'd like to understand more. Do you remember anything, Granny?'

Sheila sat perfectly still, her expression giving nothing away. Emma's heart began to race. This was neither a 'no idea' nor an 'oh, it was nothing' response.

'Granny?'

Sheila clasped her hands on her lap, her head bent. 'I do remember it, but I don't know the details. The trainer was sent away, I think, or dismissed. No one said why, but when you look at some of the things that have come out in the news these past few years, I do wonder.'

Nausea surged in Emma's stomach. This was heading straight towards child sexual abuse, the thought she'd barely allowed herself to think because it was the worst thought ever, and how could they even start talking about it with this lovely ninety-five-year-old lady? Had Luke been abused? Had Alan? No, no. Luke would have said. Wouldn't he?

Kate had no qualms about calling it by its name. 'Oh no, Granny. Do you think Ryan James was a paedophile? How many children were involved?'

'Kate, darling – I don't know. It was all kept very quiet, and you weren't directly involved, thankfully. Plenty of people were curious, but others managed to quell any gossip about it, and in time, I suppose, nobody liked to say anything more about it.'

Kate's voice was shaking with indignation. 'I can't believe everyone just brushed child abuse under the carpet and forgot about it. The children who were abused – okay, *allegedly* abused – must still be traumatised. Why aren't at least some of them coming forward now? That guy might have gone on to target heaven knows how many more kids. And imagine if he's still doing it.'

Emma crossed her arms over her front. Was there any way they could be wrong about this? It seemed to have been hushed up very effectively, but no matter what those kids were doing nowadays, surely *all* the parents back then wouldn't have agreed to stay silent? She cleared her throat. 'Do you think we could be wrong here? Ryan James could just have been a terrible trainer, or put the kids in danger in some other way.'

Kate gave her a look. 'If that was all, there'd be no reason for Alan and Luke not to talk about it. I think we can be sure what happened, and you hear all the time how hard it is for victims to come forward.'

Sheila picked up Kate's hand again. 'I'm afraid you're right.'

Emma bowed her head. This was dire. Luke and Alan were trying hard to put whatever had happened behind them and get on with their lives, and if she and Kate carried on asking questions about it, that would be impossible. But was it ever right to ignore something as massive as child abuse, even if the victims wanted you to?

Sheila was dabbing her eyes with a cotton hankie, and tears rushed into Emma's eyes too. This lady was almost a century old, and they were making her think about something totally nauseating. And what about Marie and Euan – Marie had been pretty jumpy a couple of times, hadn't she? And that secret they'd spoken of… But *surely*…? She would need to talk frankly to Marie about this, but this wasn't the day, with Euan's operation this afternoon.

Emma cleared her throat. 'I don't get it. What reason would any parent have to cover up child sexual abuse?'

Kate nodded. 'Bang on. That's what we need to find out.'

'My darlings, be careful. It's easy to make a bad situation worse.' Sheila twisted round and pointed to a sideboard on the back wall. 'Fetch the album of your year with us, Kate. We might find something helpful in one of the snaps.'

Kate complied, and Emma perched on the arm of the sofa to see the photos. Kate had been a pretty child with long dark hair and a mischievous expression, and they leafed through a year of her life as an eight- and nine-year-old. Only a handful of photos showed any older children, notably the ones of the nativity play, but none included Luke or Alan. Kate replaced the album and came back to give her grandmother a cuddle.

'Let's leave the past where it is, Granny, and get a wheelchair for you. A walk in the park and a lovely pub lunch in town is what we need.'

Emma kept up her end of the conversation as they strolled past rose beds and a rock garden then lunched in the Bell and Whistle, where Sheila was greeted fondly. They left the old lady back at the home at three o'clock without another word having been said about the men and Ryan James.

Kate reversed out of their parking space, her mouth drooping. 'What now?'

'We talk to Luke and Alan again. Carefully, like Sheila said. Then we compare notes, and then – what more *can* we do?'

Go to the police was the logical answer, but that was what Luke didn't want. Yorkshire was picture-perfect as they drove out of Glenfield, all sunshine and woolly sheep and hills and vales, but Emma's eyes were closed to the beauty. Something dark, dark was hovering over them all, and she didn't want to think about it.

CHAPTER 18

LUKE, AGED 12

'YOU HAVE TO TELL YOUR DAD. IT'S WRONG, WHAT RYAN'S doing.' Luke could barely look at Alan.

They were in Alan's bedroom the following Thursday after school. Apparently, Ryan had spent most of the special group session on Tuesday coaching Mark, but Alan had come in for 'quite a lot of poking around' too. That meant Ryan had been touching him in the wrong places, though Alan never said anything detailed about it. None of the others had, either. It wasn't the kind of thing you just talked about.

'What if my dad goes ballistic?' Alan picked up a Batman comic from his bedside table and began to tear strips of paper from the cover.

Luke shrugged. 'He'll still know what to do. I mean, if it's okay for a coach to touch you, or not.' Was it okay? 'Tell him, Alan. It would be better if we knew what he thought.'

Alan froze for long seconds, then he tossed the comic onto his bed. 'P'raps. But you're coming with me.'

Luke shivered. Blimey. Alan must be really fed up – or else he was scared. Luke traipsed behind his friend as they headed downstairs. The worst part of all this was what he didn't know – what Ryan had been doing in the showers, for instance.

Alan barged into the kitchen, where his mum was stirring something in a bowl. 'Where's Dad?'

'In the stable. Wrap up, it's cold out.'

Luke's gut churned as he followed Alan across to the stable where Keith was whistling through his teeth and filling the hay racks for Max and Poppy, Alan's old pony and the elderly mare who was the only other horse here now. He stopped whistling when they went in, and passed Alan a bucket.

'Want to get fresh water for these two?'

'Yup. Dad, I need to ask you something.'

Luke had to fight to stop his legs shaking. Telling Keith was like a test. If he said what Ryan had done was okay, then – then the world was a dangerous place.

But it wasn't okay… If he kept thinking that, it would be true, wouldn't it, and Keith would help them. Luke leaned on the stall door as Alan mumbled an account of Tuesday's vaulting lesson. He didn't make it sound like a big deal, but Keith's eyes widened, then he looked away, not focussing on anything. A moment later he turned back to Alan, and it was as if he had a curtain over the real expression on his face.

'Show me where he touched you.'

Alan's hands circled around his front, and over his bum.

'Did he say anything?'

'He was talking about core strength and how you needed to stabilise your pelvis to be a gymnast.'

'But you didn't like it.'

It wasn't a question, and Alan didn't answer. Keith stared into space for a moment, then jerked back to Alan.

'He probably didn't mean anything by it, son, but I'll come in with you tomorrow and have a word.'

'Okay.' Alan trudged off with the water bucket, and Luke followed him into the yard.

Outside, Alan held the bucket under the tap and hissed at Luke. 'I hope you haven't started something we're all going to regret, Luke Carter. You were the one who wanted to tell Dad, and Ryan's going to be mad, isn't he?'

SLEEPING WAS HARD THAT NIGHT. Luke tossed and turned, eventually getting up at six because he couldn't lie still any longer. In one way, it was a relief that Alan's dad knew about what Ryan was doing, but right beside that was the feeling that they'd done something wrong, telling on Ryan. Luke's stomach was in knots, and choking down enough breakfast to keep Mum off his back made it worse.

School had never been so endless, and Mark getting into trouble for fidgeting around in three classes straight after each other made things even worse. He was doing more and more stuff like that now, and it got right up the teachers' noses every time. At last it was four o'clock, and Luke dived home to get his kit ready. If only, only he could stay at home and watch Mum's stupid soap on TV and just blob. But Alan wouldn't hear of him ducking out now. Luke choked down his fish fingers at tea time, then Mum started fussing around because she'd forgotten to iron his gym gear, and it was all Luke could do not to yell at her that he was the only one whose bloody T-shirts and shorts were ironed and he hated gym club more than he'd ever hated anything.

As soon as Keith's car pulled up outside, Luke grabbed his half-ironed T-shirt off the ironing board and was off, escaping Mum's wails of dismay, but what was coming would be a whole lot worse. This couldn't go well no matter what Keith said to Ryan. Luke got into the back seat, hugging his sports bag on his lap. Roll on next summer when there'd be no more gym club for him, you could bet on that.

There was silence in the car all the way to Glenfield Secondary, where Keith told Luke and Alan to wait in the corridor while he had a word with Ryan in the gym. They were early; none of the other boys were here yet. Harry came out of the staff changing room while they were standing around, and gave Luke a grin on his way past.

'How's it going, kid?'

Luke's mouth was dry. 'Okay. I ran for thirty-five minutes with no walking breaks this week.'

'Good on you. See you in a bit.'

Harry pushed through the gym door, and Luke stole a glance at Alan, but his friend was hunched up, both hands deep in his pockets. Half a minute later Ryan and Keith came out of the gym, talking. At least they weren't fighting, though neither was smiling, either. Luke shifted closer to Alan.

Ryan came right up to them. 'Hey, lads. Alan, I'm sorry you were uncomfortable last time. I didn't realise. Thing is, with vaulting, you learn the landing much quicker if there's someone there to shove you into place. Your dad and I have agreed it might be better if we withdrew you from the vault at the competition in March. That way, you wouldn't be under such time pressure to be perfect in training.'

Keith was nodding, but horror was streaming out of Alan all the way through to Luke beside him.

'No! Dad. I want to do it. I want to be a gymnast – I can learn it in time. It's okay – I'm sorry!'

Keith's eyes narrowed. 'Best not, son.'

'Please, Dad!'

Keith stood still, then Ryan clapped Luke's shoulder and Luke nearly died of shock.

'How about if Luke helps Alan land tonight? It only needs a bit more practice.'

Alan tugged at his father's sleeve. 'Yes – Luke'll help, won't you, Luke?'

Luke cringed. There was literally no way out of this. He nodded dumbly.

'All right.' Keith's sigh nearly blew them all away, but he gripped Alan's shoulder and gave it a little shake. 'I'll stay and watch.'

The other boys all gawped at them when Luke went up to the vault area with Alan after warm-up, but no one made stupid remarks, which could have been because Keith was sitting at the side looking like he was about to hand them all the death penalty. Luke took up position, ready to shove when Alan landed. But help wasn't needed.

'Did it!' Alan high-fived Luke, then trotted back to the starting mat for another run-up.

Ryan's eyes were boring into Luke like something electric. Every time he glanced the coach's way, Ryan was either staring at them, or just turning away. In the end, most of Alan's jumps were fine, then in the second half he had to practise his floor routine. Luke went to join Harry and the other runners in the corridors, but Keith beckoned him over on his way out.

'Reckon we've sorted it, eh? He's pretty damn good, my lad, isn't he?' Keith was chuckling away again, and Luke nodded. His dad never said anything like that.

The session ended with Ryan encouraging everyone to do as much practice as they needed over the Christmas holidays.

'We'll start the New Year with the special training afternoon the first Saturday in January, lads. I looked at the long-range forecast, and it's high pressure all the way, so the weather should be good for a run in the woods as well as the gym prac. Have a think what you'd like to do at the end. Fish and chips in Glenfield, maybe?'

Luke glanced round. Some of the boys were nodding and grinning, but Alan, Kev, Mark, Sid and a couple of others were looking at the floor. It didn't take an expert to work out who Ryan's favourites were.

Back at the car, Alan got in the front with Keith. 'Thanks, Dad. What did Ryan say when you talked to him?'

Keith gave Alan's shoulder a pat, and Luke's heart sank like a stone. This had all been useless, hadn't it?

'He explained the technique he was using. I reckon it was all a misunderstanding. Like he said, you can't train kids without touching them, but he agreed he might have been over-enthusiastic because you're so good. None of the others have complained, have they? Ryan wants you to win, that's clear, so you do your best, huh?'

Luke leaned his head back and closed his eyes. He must have been one of the first Ryan had touched, that night at the start. And he hadn't complained. He had made this his fault too, and none of it was right.

Back in Ralton Bridge, the evening became even more

awful because Keith pulled up outside Luke house, and twisted round to Luke in the back.

'Think I'd best tell your dad what went on, lad. We want to keep him in the loop. You stay here with Alan for a bit.'

Luke nearly died all over again. He watched as the front door closed behind Keith.

Alan's eyes were glittering in the light from the streetlamp. 'Telling my dad was your shittiest idea ever, Luke Carter, but I've got a plan. How we can get back at Ryan.'

Luke froze. He wasn't going to like this, was he? 'What?'

'On the training Saturday. We'll make sure we finish with a run through the woods and a bonfire, not fish and bloody chips. We have all the Christmas holidays now to plan how to give Ryan a sausage sizzle to remember. Something to focus his mind on proper training, not...'

He turned away, and Luke slumped back in his seat. Alan was crying.

CHAPTER 19

FRIDAY, 14TH MAY

'Have you called your mum this morning?' Emma came downstairs on Friday morning to find Luke organising his briefcase on the kitchen table. He had an early meeting today, then he was planning to visit Euan after lunch, if visitors were allowed then. Yesterday's operation had gone well, but poor Marie had sounded terribly tense on the phone last night.

'Chances are she's still asleep. I'll call her from the office. Have you seen my charger?'

Oh, for heaven's sake. Emma opened her mouth to snap, then closed it again. Luke's charger was in its usual place beside the toaster on the worktop. And Marie was a lot more likely to have been up half the night worrying than still snoozing away in bed. Luke was taking his 'it's no big deal' attitude too far, and the only reason Emma could think of for this was to stop her talking to his mother.

She dropped the charger beside his briefcase and slid her mug into the coffee machine. She needed the caffeine this morning. 'Make sure you call before you head for home this afternoon, too. Marie might need some support. You know how nervous she gets.'

'I will and I do, but you're being a mother hen. Mum knows she can call me twenty-four-seven if she needs to. I'll text you when I've spoken to her, and let you know how things are, huh?'

He stuffed the charger into his jacket pocket and left her alone with her coffee. Emma glowered after him. Obviously, she wasn't supposed to call Marie too. Did Luke think this breezy acceptance that everything was fine would reassure Marie? He was wrong if he did… and he was wrong if he thought she wasn't going to call his mother, but no need to say that.

Her phone vibrated on the table. Kate.

'Emma, Alan went ballistic when I told him about talking to Granny yesterday. He's forbidden me to mention it again, but of course I can't leave it there. Did Luke say anything?'

Emma's conscience twinged. 'I'm going to tackle him about it tonight. It was his dad's op yesterday and he had to cope with his mum's nerves last night. I didn't want to start a difficult convo when he was uptight already. I'll get back to you tonight or tomorrow, huh?'

'Thanks.'

Poor Kate sounded terribly down. Guilt thudded into Emma's middle, but there was nothing more she could do for the moment.

She waited until half past nine, in case Luke was right and

Marie was still asleep, then connected to Marie and Euan's landline. Her mother-in-law took the call on the second ring.

'Hello, dear. I'm just off the phone with Luke. I haven't spoken to Euan today yet, but the nurse said he's doing very well. Of course they would say that, though, wouldn't they? I'm going to see him later on.'

Last night's nerves were gone – or at least improved – this morning. Emma chatted for a while and promised to visit at the weekend. Hopefully she'd get a chance to ask Marie about the past, too – a ladies' lunch, perhaps? A message pinged into her phone almost as soon as she ended the call, and Emma opened it with Marie's 'bye, dear' still in her ear. *Dad had good night, Mum calm, all ok.* Emma replied with a thumbs-up, and sat down to plan what she was supposed to do with the rest of the day. The washing was waiting, and she really should get on with her translation project, too. The deadline was at the end of the month and she still had five chapters to do.

The tumble dryer finished its cycle, and Emma pulled out the spare room bed things and took them upstairs. She was remaking the bed when a thought struck. This was the room where Mrs Alderson had found her Edwardian fireplace. Which wall would it be on? Emma abandoned the pillows and went to knock on walls, and yes, one did sound different. Hollow. Wow – imagine if there *was* a fireplace boarded up here. Even if it was shabby, they could have it restored, couldn't they? A look at the house plans to see if there was any mention of asbestos before they started tearing down walls would be best, though. She made a mental note to ask Mrs Alderson about it.

Luke was as good as his word. Two more messages pinged into Emma's phone over the course of the day. *Can visit Dad this afternoon* and *With Dad now, he says hello. Dr pleased with him*. So that was one less thing to worry about. And a message from Wendy in Jerusalem was cheering, too – she wanted to confirm the date of the scan, so she and Dad were remembering about it. Emma sent a few photos of Ralton Bridge, and received a couple of Dad and Wendy's new courtyard garden in exchange. All nice family stuff, which was lovely. Well done, baby.

BY HALF PAST FIVE, she had translated two more chapters and was working her way down a mug of peppermint tea when her mobile rang.

'Kate?'

The voice in Emma's ear was high-pitched and shaking. 'Oh Emma, it's Alan. He—'

A clatter came through the phone. It sounded as if Kate had dropped hers. Emma pressed her mobile to her head, straining to make sense of the incoherent half-sentences in her ear.

'Kate. Stop. Tell me slowly what's happened.'

Deep breathing came down the phone, then:

'I tried to talk to Alan about Ryan James a moment ago and he stamped upstairs to the study and he's locked the door. He's crying – he sounds hysterical but he won't talk to me and he won't open the door, either. I'm scared, Emma.'

'Oh no. Would it help if I came over?'

'Could Luke come too? I think they have to talk about whatever happened.'

'He isn't back yet. I'll leave him a note. See you soon.'

Emma hurried to the top of the hill with her bike, then freewheeled down towards the Vale. As usual, the estate was busy with children playing and parents out gardening, calling to each other over their pretty white wooden fences. Happy faces in picture-perfect suburbia, but what was going on in Kate's study? By the sound of it, Alan needed professional help. Not talking about this was doing him no good at all.

Kate opened the door just seconds after Emma rang the bell.

'He's still not talking. Nothing I say is getting through to him. I've left him to have some space, then I'll try again. Hopefully Luke'll be here by then.' She sat down on the stairs, her mascara streaked under both eyes.

Emma perched beside her. 'You think when he's calmer he'll be more open to talking about it?' It didn't sound likely, in her ears. Someone distraught enough to lock themselves into a room to cry needed human contact. Children's laughter on the street seeped into the hallway, and Emma shivered. Luke and Alan had played in Ralton Bridge as children too. What else had happened to them here?

'Let's make tea. You can take some up to Alan.' Emma pulled Kate to the kitchen end of the living room, and Kate put the kettle on. A dull thud came from upstairs, and the two women looked at each other.

Kate thrust the tea bag tin into Emma's hands. 'I'll go up and try talking to him again. You bring the tea.'

Emma searched around until she found a tray to put the mugs on, then poured boiling water over three teabags.

She rummaged in her bag for her phone, but nothing had come from Luke. That note she'd left on the kitchen table – suppose he missed it? A call or even a text would have stressed him, though, and she didn't want him gunning the car up the A19 with anger or fear or whatever affecting his driving. But he'd be on his way by now; she could compromise. *Problem at Kate's. Call me as soon as you're home.* Her thumb hovered over 'send' before she added: *Baby fine.* At least, she hoped the baby was fine. Her own heart was hammering away; this couldn't be good for either of them. Fear pricked into Emma's gut to join the apprehension about Alan.

She was dropping the teabags into the bin when loud thumps came from above, along with a yell from Kate.

'Alan! Alan!'

More bangs, and a door rattling. Emma abandoned the tray and dashed upstairs.

Four doors were spaced along the small upstairs landing, and unusually, all had locks. Kate was standing at the furthest away door. 'He's not answering. The door's still locked and he's not making a sound. What should we do?' She jammed an ear on the closed door and listened, her face tight.

Emma crept up beside her, holding her breath. Seconds passed, then Kate stood straight and shook her head, motioning for Emma to try.

The door was white-painted wood and looked sturdy. Emma stood with an ear pressed hard against it. Kate was right. The room on the other side of the door was eerily silent.

'Call him again,' she mouthed. This was awful. What were they supposed to do now?

Kate rattled the door handle. 'Alan! I'm worried! Open the door, please.'

A chill surged through Emma as the answer was yet more silence. Kate was crying piteously now; surely Alan wouldn't ignore that.

'Alan!' Kate banged on the door, sobbing loudly.

Nothing. Emma touched the door. She wasn't going to start

trying to break it down, not with the baby. 'Is there a spare key?'

Kate pressed her hands to her cheeks. 'Somewhere. But the key'll be in the lock on the other side, so that won't work. I suppose we could try, though.' She sped down the stairs two at a time.

Emma knocked on the study door. 'Alan, it's Emma. Please open the door – Kate's worried.'

Nothing. The cold twist of fear in Emma's gut tightened. If Alan was in there, he was being mighty quiet about it.

Kate stumbled back up the stairs with a key ring holding four keys. 'I don't know which is for that door.'

She went round the other doors trying the locks, and arrived at the study clutching the correct key, the silvery metal kind with a round head and long shaft. She fumbled it into the lock.

'I can't turn it. This is hopeless. Alan!' Kate thundered on the door.

'Let me try.' Emma took the key out then pushed it back into the lock, and yes, it did go right in. There was no key on the other side. She turned, but the lock was new and stiff; it had possibly never been used before today. The memory of Opa trying to unlock the cellar door at their house in Germany came to mind. 'Get a screwdriver.'

Kate ran into another room and returned with a handful of screwdrivers. Emma took the largest, pushed the shaft through the hole in the head of the key, and levered. Kate joined in, and they pulled together until the key jerked round in the lock and the door flew open.

One glance was enough. Emma leaned on the doorway, the room revolving around her, not looking after that first time, but the vision of Alan sprawled across a red rug on the wooden floor, his eyes empty and his face contorted in an agonised grimace – she would see it until the day she died. Emma wrapped her arms around her middle. She mustn't pass out, she mustn't. Baby, baby, you're safe. We're all right.

Kate dropped to her knees and crawled forward to cradle Alan's head. 'Alan! He's not breathing. Emma, help! CPR, we have to… Call an ambulance!' She started to pound on Alan's chest.

Her mobile was in the kitchen. Emma staggered over to Alan's phone on the desk, horror and yes, anger, no, fury, bubbling up inside her. Her foot kicked something as she swerved past the body on the floor – a green bottle. It rolled under the desk. Drugs? Poison? And if so, what? Emma tapped out 999. How pointless an ambulance was, and how dare Luke and Alan keep all whatever this was to themselves. Sexual abuse was the worst thing, she completely got that, and she got why people kept schtum about it, too, but she and Kate were Luke and Alan's wives, for God's sake. If Alan had talked to someone he might be – he might be alive tonight. Because he wasn't alive, was he, and—

'Ambulance service; is the patient breathing?'

Emma spoke to the emergency operator, then put the phone on speaker so that the woman could tell Kate how to do chest compressions.

The calm, anonymous voice on the phone only added to the horror. 'Count with me – one and two and three and four and one and two—'

Kate thudded up and down on Alan's chest, and his body jerked rhythmically. Emma clutched her middle, stumbling across the landing when her mobile rang out from the kitchen.

She lurched downstairs, taking her child away, away from the monstrous scene in that room.

Her mobile stopped ringing before she reached it, but a few seconds later Kate's landline blared out from across the room. Please, please let that be Luke. Please come, Luke. Where the hell was Kate's landline phone? Emma's head swivelled round until she spotted it on the shelf, half-hidden behind a framed photo of Kate and Alan at their wedding. She grabbed the receiver.

'It's Luke. Is Emma—?'

'It's me. Come quick!'

A voice at the door. 'Paramedics! We're coming in!'

'Upstairs!' Emma rushed out to the hallway, where the ambulance team were letting themselves in. They charged up, and Emma sobbed into the phone. 'Come quickly, Luke! It's Alan.'

'On my way. Are you okay?'

'Yes.' She wasn't, but she was alive.

Upstairs, Kate was crouching on the study floor, sobbing into a tissue. The woman who'd laughed about the nativity play and kissed her grandmother goodbye with love in her eyes was unrecognisable. Two green-clad paramedics, an older woman and a young man, were working on Alan. Emma knelt down and took Kate in her arms, trying hard not to hear, but the sounds the ambulance team was making couldn't be ignored. Thud thud thud thud and on and on, and still nothing from Alan – how long would they spend doing this?

She met the young man's eyes. 'Will he be all right?' Stupid question.

'We're helping him now. Do you know what he's taken?'

Emma pointed to the bottle by the desk, and he lifted it in a gloved hand. 'Are you a relative?'

'A friend. Is Alan—?'

The paramedic, who couldn't have been much more than twenty, pressed his lips together and looked away. Kate moaned, and Emma pulled her closer. What a frail, shaking creature this was now, her eyes flitting from the grim-faced paramedics to Alan on the floor.

'Let's wait in the hall, Kate, lovey.'

Kate clapped her hands over her mouth and fled into the bathroom.

Bright lights fizzed in front of Emma's eyes. Deep breaths, Em, you have to do this. The front door banged open and steps thundered up the stairs. Luke? Emma pulled herself across the landing, and oh, no, the young paramedic was following her and the older one had gone into the bathroom and was talking to Kate. They weren't working on Alan any longer. Emma collapsed into Luke's arms.

The paramedic joined them at the top of the stairs. 'I'm afraid he's gone. The police will be here soon. Do you know of any family who can come to help?'

Luke nodded, his head rubbing against Emma's. 'I'll call his dad. Come downstairs, Emmy.'

Sick to her stomach, Emma moved down the stairs, one arm around Luke and the other around her baby. Luke would know Alan's dad pretty well. She breathed steadily through her mouth while Luke lifted the landline phone, abandoned on the hall table, and connected to Alan's father.

'Keith, it's Luke Carter. You'd better get down to Alan's right now. He's in a bad way. Come quick.'

He pulled Emma close again, supporting her over to the

sofa. 'Come on, love, let's sit you down. This isn't good for the baby.'

Emma didn't have the strength to say that she wanted to go to Kate, but within five minutes Kate was sitting beside her and the younger paramedic was handing out fresh mugs of tea while his colleague took Kate's pulse.

Luke was waiting at the window. 'Here's Keith now.' He strode from the room, followed by the young paramedic.

Men's voices in the hallway vanished upstairs, and Emma gripped Kate's hand.

More banging on the door. The police had arrived.

THE NEXT HOUR WAS A BLUR. Emma sat on the sofa with Kate and the older paramedic, whose name was Pam, trying not to hear the thumps and noises upstairs, trying not to imagine what was going on up there. There was even a policeman in here with them. In case they tried to run off? More officers arrived and went upstairs, then eventually one came down with Alan's father. Kate immediately went into hysterics, and Emma gave Keith her place on the sofa. He sat there, looking at no one but rocking Kate in his arms, and that was the only positive thing about this ghastly, horrible mess. Emma sank onto one blue microfibre armchair, meeting Luke's dull eyes as he sat slumped in the other.

A different police officer came in and stood in front of the window. 'I'm very sorry for your loss, Mrs Johnson. Was there – did he leave a note?'

'No.' Kate moaned.

Keith wiped a hand over his face. 'He's always been edgy.

Depressive. And recently he's been worried about money and his future.'

Emma winced. There was no future for Alan any more, and Kate's was changed forever too.

Pam the paramedic made a significant face at the officer, and he nodded.

'We'll leave further questions until later. Do you have anywhere to go tonight, Mrs Johnson?'

'She'll come home to us in the meantime.' Keith's voice was gravelly.

Luke sat forward in his chair, his eyes bright with unshed tears. 'I'd like to take Emma home now too, please. She shouldn't be upset like this.'

Emma covered her face with both hands. He couldn't pull the pregnant card with Kate sitting there in bits and Alan dead upstairs.

The officer noted down everyone's details, then Emma swung to her feet, glad of Luke's arm around her, more glad than she could say to be allowed to leave this perfect little house, the kind she'd always wanted, hadn't she, but that was before. Luke's body was trembling against hers, and the worst thought of all was what hadn't been said. No one had mentioned Ryan James, or anything to do with the past, yet the past had everything to do with Alan's death. What could possibly have happened back then to cause a man to take his life twenty years later?

Kate was limp and silent now, her eyes deep in dark circles, giving nothing away. Emma went over to hug her friend, then took Luke's hand to go. To her surprise, Keith followed them out, walking after them all the way to the car. He waited until

Emma was in the passenger seat, then grasped Luke's shoulder and gave it a rough shake.

'Remember.'

Luke flinched, and nodded speechlessly.

And then they were driving away. Emma closed her eyes, then opened them immediately to stop seeing Alan on the floor in the room in Kate's house. She would never sleep again.

Remember what?

CHAPTER 20

LUKE, AGED 12

IT WAS THE SATURDAY TRAINING DAY. GLUMLY, LUKE TOSSED HIS sports bag onto the bed to pack. Telling Keith had made everything worse, and he couldn't get rid of the feeling that Alan and Mark were planning something way too OTT for Ryan today, but he had no idea what it was. Nobody was talking to him. Alan and Mark were best buddies now, always muttering together about the bloody Ryan plan – and blaming Luke because he'd made Alan tell his dad and Keith had believed Ryan so it hadn't worked. Mark was mad with Ryan too now, because he'd stopped giving him special 'jobs' to do after Keith had come to the gym club that night, and Mark didn't have nearly enough cash to buy a computer yet. It was all horrible. Luke shoved his trainers into the bag on top of his freshly ironed T-shirt. The one good thing was, the training day had been switched to Ralton Bridge Secondary as there was a badminton tournament on at Glenfield Sec that day, so at least he'd be able to skive off home if things got too hairy. He kicked his sports bag downstairs. It was January. He only had to hold on until summer, then he could leave the gym club for good.

Dad hadn't been at all impressed by what Keith had told him the night he'd spoken to Ryan about touching Alan. 'I don't know what to make of that, Luke, but I'm sure it was all a misunderstanding, like Keith said. Best just say nothing, hear? Imagine if Ryan's mother or his girlfriend heard talk like that – we don't want to be accused of spreading rumours that aren't true, do we?' Luke flinched at the memory. Yet again, they were being inconspicuous. Dad hadn't even asked if he was okay, but probably Keith had told him it was all about Alan.

And he wasn't okay, was he? The plan to get back at Ryan this afternoon felt more and more iffy every time Luke thought about it, which was constantly. He shrugged into his winter jacket and zipped it right up to his chin. The boys were meeting at the bus stop before training to finalise 'arrangements', and Luke's mouth went dry at the very idea. God only knew what they were going to do. Maybe he should just stay at home.

'Here are your sausages, lovey, and some chocolate to share with the others.'

Mum bustled out from the kitchen with a plastic container and a giant bar of Dairy Milk, beaming as if this was some kind of Sunday School picnic. Luke muttered his thanks to the sound of Dad's approval.

'Off you go, Luke – you don't want to be late, son. He's a good sort of bloke, that Ryan, arranging all this for you lads. You can tell he cares about kids.'

Didn't he just. Luke hurried out as soon as Alan arrived at the door.

Alan wasn't exactly looking thrilled either. 'Come on. Let's get this done.'

Luke trailed down the path after him. 'What are we doing, then?'

Alan stomped on up the hill. 'Jon's bringing a load of torches for the run, then some of us can pretend to get lost on the way back down and Ryan'll have to look for us. We can, um, hustle him around a bit, too. He'll be mega pissed off and he won't have time to touch anyone up, we'll make sure of that.'

Luke shrugged. It sounded harmless enough, and being fooled and then jostled would definitely annoy Ryan. Who wanted to have to look for a bunch of sniggering kids in the middle of a wood when it was getting dark? It was a cold, grey afternoon; it would be dark early. Would Ryan even agree to going out for a run?

The others were waiting in the bus shelter opposite the pub. You could see Jon's red head a mile off, and Mark's ruck-sack with the fluorescent green stripes was pretty noticeable too. Luke joined them and leaned against the wall to get his breath back. It wasn't the exercise that was making him breathless today; it was nerves. He was as bad as Mum.

Mark jeered at him. 'Evening, scaredy-cat.'

Jon passed him a flashlight, and Luke examined it. Jon's dad had the hardware store in the village and he always had really cool stuff like this. The flashlight had a switch to change the light to white, blue, green or red, and there was a little drawer with a compass in it at the bottom.

Luke tried to sound nonchalant. 'Was your dad okay with you borrowing these?'

Jon rolled his eyes. 'You're not half dim sometimes, Luke. He doesn't know, and he isn't going to miss a few torches for an hour or two. I made sure to take different kinds so they didn't leave a gap on the shelf.'

Mark was grinning away like he was having the best fun ever. 'We're gonna get him, huh? I've got something of my dad's that'll give stupid Ryan something to think about and no mistake.' He waved his hands about in a kind of cowboy gesture.

A gun? But he couldn't have brought a gun… could he? Luke tried hard not to pant in case anyone laughed at him. The boys were right – telling Alan's dad was all his fault. What had he started?

Alan kicked at Mark. 'Don't be so sodding stupid. What's your dad doing with a gun, anyway? What would happen if it went off accidentally and killed Ryan? Or worse still, one of us?'

Mark tossed his head. 'Who said gun? And Dad's had one for years, anyway. He's in a club and he has a permit. It's not a big deal, guys. We'll give Mister Touchy-Feely a good scare, that's all.' He made a strangling gesture with both hands round his neck, then shrieked with laughter and danced across the road.

Luke's mouth went dry all over again. Mark going all hyper on them was exactly what he'd been dreading.

Alan glared round the boys left in the bus shelter. 'Ok. Like we said – leave the talking to me at the start. That skanky loser's going to be sorry he was ever born, and we're doing this for all of us, right? We'll make sure he's still up for a run, then we'll start the plan. Jason's not coming, so all we have to do is get rid of Harry for a bit. Luke, you can do that when we start back down from the woods. Pretend to sprain your ankle or something and keep him with you. We'll all dive ahead and do the deed with Ryan.'

Luke hunched into his jacket. This was so not like Alan, and it was hard to know what was worse, being part of fooling Ryan, or telling lies to Harry. How he wished he could go home and never think of Ryan and his searching hands again, but that wasn't going to happen, was it? It would be there in his head forever. But maybe the plan wouldn't work, maybe Ryan wouldn't let them go to the woods, maybe Harry would stop them somehow.

Maybe he should never have come here today.

'COACH! It's after four. Let's get out to the woods now. Gotta make a bonfire, huh? We've brought torches, and there's one for you and Harry too!'

Alan had his best cute smile on, and the others were all grinning and nodding. Jon ran for his rucksack and handed Ryan a head torch on a bright pink band. Someone sniggered.

Ryan fingered the torch, then turned to the window. Luke didn't dare hope it had somehow started raining, and it hadn't. The clouds had cleared and it was actually a brilliant evening for running outside, not quite dark yet, crisp and cold, and the moon was nearly full, rising over the woods like the picture on a jigsaw he'd had once, with a wolf howling in front of spooky trees. Luke rubbed his tummy.

Ryan grinned and took the headlight. 'Keen, huh? Harry's not coming to the sausage sizzle, though.'

Harry pulled a face. 'Sorry, guys. Family night out – it's my mum's birthday. Have fun!' He raised a hand and trotted off.

Looks of glee were flashing from all directions, and Luke's

throat closed. With no Harry to distract, he'd be in on the main action. Was no one else worried about what was going to happen? The others were all so confident, all big smiles and innocent faces, so sure they'd get even with Ryan tonight. Ryan was lacing up his outdoor running shoes now, and Mark, Alan, Jon, Kev, Danny and Sid were all playing with their torches and making stupid comments about lighting up their lives. Come to think of it, a couple of boys hadn't come to the training day. Had someone warned them off? Luke's gut cramped, but he couldn't back out now.

Ryan led the way outside. 'Walk ten, run thirty, boys. Make sure no one runs alone when we're in the woods, huh? Stay at least two together, and we'll gather in the clearing to make our bonfire.' He stared at Mark. 'That's a big rucksack – sure you want to bring it?'

Mark nodded vehemently. 'First aid box, coach. And sticks to spear the sausages. My dad helped me make them.' More boys sniggered this time.

Ryan nodded. 'Good thinking. Luke, you lead the way. Go!'

Luke set off. Walk ten, run thirty, walk… They had to run across a field to get to the woods. He was the best runner here – how amazing was that? Changed days, as Mum would say. Homesickness for Mum and Dad and safety welled up, and Luke slowed down to let Danny stay level with him.

It was weird in the woods in the twilight. Ralton Bridge wood wasn't as steep as Glenfield wood, but the trees here were denser. The moon was shimmering above them, sometimes flickering through to the pathway and other times vanishing behind still, black branches. Eight pairs of feet crunched and pattered along the track. The trees were creepy, tall and silent, nodding gently as if they were listening to this interruption trotting up the path. Luke breathed in damp woodland, a thick, earthy smell. One day he'd come back here at night when they weren't going to get even with Ryan, and enjoy it.

'Luke! Hang on!'

Alan and Mark came up behind, and Luke glanced round. Ryan at the back was nowhere to be seen, and neither were Jon and Sid. Sid was a good runner – why was he so slow tonight? Luke's stomach dropped. Oh no. Sid and Jon were separating Ryan off. This wasn't supposed to happen yet...

Mark grabbed his elbow. 'Don't look so gormless, dum dum. Without Harry, we can start straightaway, then we'll have all the more time for the pay back. I'll hide up here. You lot go on, and notice I'm gone at the clearing, okay?'

Luke slowed to a walk, staring as Mark started up a side track. A few seconds later the other boy's torch clicked off, and darkness swallowed him.

Alan shoved Luke on. 'Come on, baby. You want to do this, don't you?'

No, he didn't, but no use saying that. Luke jogged on. Here was the clearing, eerily lit by moonlight and various torches flashing around as the boys gathered at the woodpile. You were supposed to use some, then replace them from the undergrowth before you left, and if only they'd come to sizzle sausages. Luke fought back tears of homesickness – what a baby he was.

Ryan appeared with Jon and Sid, and came to stand beside Luke and Alan. 'Well done, lads. Are we all here?'

Jon began to count in a silly voice. 'One, two, three... Hey, keep still! How can I count when you're all moving around?'

The boys laughed and jeered, dancing and weaving about

the clearing. Ryan was motionless, his brow furrowed, but Luke didn't have time to watch him because Alan grabbed his arm, pulled him onto one of the tree trunks around the fire-place, then pushed him off, whooping.

'Boys! Are we all – where's Mark?'

'Ooh – Markie's lost! I'll find him! Come on, Danny!'

Kev and Danny vanished, and Ryan shouted after them.

'Come back! We'll—'

His voice was drowned out in yells of 'Markie! Come to Ryan, sweetie-pie!'

Two more boys vanished from the clearing, and Ryan grabbed Luke's arm.

'What's going on?'

Mark appeared at the edge of the clearing. 'Somebody called me? Ooh – Ryan's got Luke. Can't have that, can we?' He charged towards Ryan, who dodged, still gripping Luke's arm.

'Boys! You're being idiots. Back to the gym. Move.'

More jeers, and Mark called out in a high voice. 'Come along, naughty boys. Back we go! We'll find Danny and Kev on the way. I think I saw them go down there.'

He pointed to a side track that led down to the river, and someone's hands wrenched Luke away from Ryan. It was all he could do to stay upright as he was bundled across the clearing to the side track. His torch clattered to the ground and was kicked aside in the rush to leave Ryan behind.

Ryan pelted after them. 'What the hell do you lot think you're doing! You'll be sorry—'

Luke's breath hitched painfully in his throat, and it had nothing to do with running and everything to do with being so bloody scared he was almost shitting himself. They were on the side track now, and the wood was closing in on them and

Alan was still dragging him along. Then Alan's fingers sprang from his arm and oh no, Mark and Alan were doubling back. Ryan was surrounded by boys and two of them – Mark and Jon – were taller than he was.

'Can't touch me! Can't touch me!' The chant started low but was soon screaming through the trees and echoing back. Luke gaped around wildly. Boys' faces, wild in the glimmering torchlight, trees seemingly joining in the dance and – oh, no, some boys had sticks, long, sturdy sticks with sharp, pointed ends to stab through sausages. Alan and Mark were poking at Ryan, jabbing him with their sticks and – Jon was joining in, and Kev, and this was getting out of hand; this was a horror trip.

Luke grabbed Sid, the one other kid whose eyes were blank with fear. 'We need help.'

'I'll go.' Sid whirled round and was gone.

'Can't touch me! Can't—'

Boys were wheeling and Ryan was jerking in the middle, spluttering and trying to catch them, but they were circling, jeering, jabbing. Blood trickled down Ryan's leg and he stood still, rubbing his thigh, and Kev and Mark shoved him from behind. Ryan dropped to his knees, crawling this way and that, but there was no escaping the jabs now. Jeering, whooping boys danced round him, poking with sticks, and Luke was dancing too, clutching the stick someone had pressed into his hand, Alan beside him gripping his other arm so hard it hurt, and no, no…

'Can't touch me! Can't touch me!' The howls were ever-louder, the wood was getting darker and darker, and Mark was fumbling in his rucksack again – shit, shit, not the gun. Luke moaned.

But it wasn't a gun in Mark's hand. It was a knife. A long, thin, butcher's knife.

'GET HIM!' Mark held up the knife, glinting in the light from his head torch. His and Ryan's were the only torches still lighting the scene – the only torches left, now. Luke pressed a shaking fist against his chest and the vibration went all the way down to his stomach. Oh God, oh God, he couldn't stop this. Big Jon and two of the others grabbed Ryan, who was twisting and struggling to get free, spitting out words Luke was forbidden to utter. The four ended up in a pile on the ground, with Mark above them making jabbing movements with the knife, swearing and moaning as if he was being tortured too.

Stop, stop. Luke opened his mouth, but nothing came out. He was going to shit himself. Sid must be back in the village by this time, but how long would it take for him to find help? Whose help, anyway?

Luke reeled back as Danny shrieked and lunged, spearing his stick into Ryan's leg. A howl rang through the wood, and Danny wrenched, then stabbed again. Ryan was curled in a ball, kicking out against the onslaught, and Kev grabbed Luke by the neck.

'We're all in this, Luke. Get him or else.'

Or else they would get him too. Luke jabbed. There was nothing else he could do. His stick met resistance and he yanked it back, bile rising in his throat and sweat dripping into his eyes.

Mark was standing there with the knife raised high in one hand. 'Now!'

The others leapt back, and someone's elbow met Luke's

nose with a crack. Blood poured over his mouth and down his throat and he spat, then he was shoved forwards and oh no no no he was falling, he was lying on top of Ryan. Ryan was writhing and panting beneath him, all hot and wet and sweaty and where had Sid got to?

Alan hauled him back, his eyes widening as he stared at Luke. Luke thudded to the ground and crawled away. His head was exploding; he couldn't stand up any longer. Mark howled like a wolf, and the dance around Ryan-on-the-ground began anew with Alan brandishing the knife now. Blood, blood was everywhere, flashing crimson as torchlight sent shocking snapshots of the scene straight into Luke's head.

He crawled over to the nearest tree and leaned against it, wiping his nose, searing pain in his head and warm wetness dripping onto his hand and—

Lights. Lights were bobbing on the track further back. Someone was coming.

'Mark! Boys! Are you all right?'

Mark's dad appeared out of the darkness, followed by Sid's dad and Sid and Keith and – and everyone's dad except Luke's. Dad hadn't come to help him.

Luke wiped the blood from his mouth as the men surrounded them, staring at Ryan on the ground and the circle of boys. The other boys all had sticks in their hands and Alan was still holding the knife and there was blood all down Ryan's front. Luke looked away, sick to his soul. Was that his blood or Ryan's? Had Alan stabbed Ryan? Had Mark? The trainer's foot was twitching on the ground but Luke couldn't see his face and he didn't want to, either. He wanted his mum.

'Kiddy fiddler.' One of the dads spat on the ground beside Ryan.

Mark's dad took the knife from Alan and dropped it on the ground at his feet. The boys huddled together close to Luke's tree. A look passed round the dads, and Luke began to shiver and hiccup, tears pouring down his cheeks. He couldn't help it, and now Alan was sniffing too and so were Jon and Sid and – everyone. Jon's dad came over with a wodge of tissues and dabbed at Luke's face, feeling his nose with soft fingers, but it still sent a shaft of pain deep into Luke's head.

'It's not broken, son. You'll live.'

The other dads were muttering in low voices over Ryan, who was still twitching. The muttered conference went on, and on, then Sid's dad came over to the boys. 'Come on, lads. I'm going back to the school with you. Someone give Luke a hand.'

Luke stumbled along the side track, Alan clinging to one elbow and Mark on his other side. Away, away… here was the main path and more moonlight, but Luke's head shrieked at every step. Down through the woods, and out. Across the field. No one spoke until they were back in the changing room, where Sid's dad took Luke into the bogs and washed the blood from his face with paper towels. He stood over them all as they changed out of their gym stuff, then he made them sit in a row. No one was saying anything, and Luke couldn't stop shaking. What had they done?

Sid's dad bobbed up and down on his toes, looking as grim as anyone had ever looked, then he stepped forward and spoke.

'Okay, lads. We're going to get out of this mess. Something Mark said to his dad earlier today made him start thinking. He phoned around, and we were actually on our way to confront Ryan James, but you beat us to it.'

Luke clutched his chest as the room swirled around his

head. *No.* It had all been for nothing. The dads had been going to stop Ryan. All the dads except... Luke bowed his head.

Sid's dad glared along the row of boys, and Luke sat straighter.

'Boys. Listen. What I'm going to say now is the most important thing you will hear all your lives.'

A little ripple went through the row of boys, and Luke forced back tears. Danny was shaking beside him, too, and Mark was hiccuping.

'We will never speak of this again. Clear? Never. Not to anyone, not one word. Not to your mums, not your dads, not to each other. If we want to go on with our lives, it's the only way. Do you understand?'

His red, angry face peered into each boy's eyes in turn, and they all nodded.

What about Ryan? It was shrieking through Luke's head, and surely everyone else was thinking the same.

Sid spoke. 'Dad? Will Ryan...?'

Luke had never felt so sick. Was Ryan even alive?

Sid's dad's mouth twitched as if he'd stubbed his toe. 'We'll deal with Ryan. As far as you're concerned, you did your gym, went running in the woods, and came back here. If anyone asks, Luke fell on the way back and bashed his nose, and that was the one thing that wasn't normal about the run. At the end, you said goodbye to Ryan and left as usual. And that is all you will say about today. Understand? Not. One. Word. More. *Ever.*'

He walked along the row of boys and shook hands with each in turn, gazing into their faces as he did so. Luke wiped away blood and tears and snot.

Sid's dad went to the door. 'Right. We're going home as a group. I'll speak to all your mums.'

The little huddle of boys trailed along the street to the butcher's, where Sid's dad rang the bell. Mark's mum opened the door, and Sid's dad stepped forward with Mark.

'Bit of an upset at the gym club, Carol, but Doug will explain when he's back. We've forbidden the boys to talk about it, so if you could wait for Doug? He won't be long. In you go, Mark. And schtum.'

Jon's house was next, then Kev's, and then it was Luke's turn. His dad answered the bell, and gawped at the group on the path. The procedure was different here. Sid's dad took Dad to the side where they muttered for several minutes while Luke stood there with Alan and Sid clutching his elbows as if they were escorting him to jail. When Dad came back, he looked like he was wearing a mask. He took Luke's arm and pulled him inside, banging the front door behind them.

'Marie! The lad's bashed his nose.' He dropped Luke's arm and walked straight down the hallway and out the back door.

Mum came out of the living room and oohed in horror, and in no time, Luke was sitting with a mug of hot chocolate in front of him and a cold cloth on his nose. Mum went next door and brought Mrs Alderson back with her. She was a nurse, and she poked at his nose and said she didn't think it was broken either, but if they were worried, they should see a doctor. Then Dad made a reappearance and started yakking on about Leeds United while Mum rummaged around in the first aid box looking for cream for Luke's nose, and the telly was blabbing in the background and the budgie was jumping up and down and chirping and this was so bloody.

Nothing was ever going to be the same again.

CHAPTER 21

SATURDAY, 15TH MAY

HALF PAST TWO IN THE MORNING. EMMA ROLLED ONTO HER other side for the millionth time and lay still, Luke's regular breathing accompanying her through yet another wakeful hour. Was he really asleep, or was he pretending because he knew she was awake and he didn't want to talk? The memory of Kate's grief and Keith's helplessness circled around in Emma's head, and she crossed both arms around the baby growing in her womb. Alan's mother – what was she feeling now? Her only child... Did Alan's mother know what had happened in the past? Emma swallowed a sob. She had to talk to Kate, but whether the other woman would be in any state to discuss what they should and shouldn't tell the police was another matter. Hot tears spilled onto Emma's cheeks. Poor, poor Kate. She must be thinking her questions about their abuse suspicion last night had been the last straw for Alan, the one that drove him to take his life, and she'd probably be right.

How could anyone deal with being the factor that caused someone they loved to commit suicide? Emma pulled the duvet under her chin, blinking at the streetlight chinking through the bedroom curtains. *Why?* Even if they were right and Alan had been abused, he'd lived with it for twenty-odd years. What had changed last night to make him take his life? Emma pressed her fingers against her eyelids. She and Kate had missed something, and that something had killed Alan. Did Luke know what it was?

Keith's 'Remember' swam into Emma's head. That had been a warning – he knew. And so did Luke.

She fell into a restless sleep shortly before dawn, and woke at eight to find herself alone in bed. The events of last night crashed through her mind and she lay for a moment, then staggered up, nausea swirling as she pulled on a bathrobe. Luke was clattering around in the kitchen, so he hadn't gone to work today – of course he hadn't – and the smell of coffee wafted towards Emma as she went downstairs. Just like any normal day, except normal days didn't exist any more. Emma dropped onto a kitchen chair, and Luke slid a mug of tea across the table to her.

'Thanks.' She sipped, not looking at anything.

He sat down opposite, and after a moment she raised her eyes. Luke was unshaven and pale, and Emma pushed her fingers through uncombed hair then leaned her head on her hand. This was so crap.

'Luke – why? Why did he do it?'

He rubbed his chin, his fingers rasping over the bristles. 'I don—'

Shocking, white-hot rage flushed through Emma, and she shoved her chair back and stood leaning over the table.

'Don't you dare say you don't know. You must know. I want to know too, and it's the least you owe me. Tell me. Please, Luke.'

Luke winced, his lips trembling, but he was nodding. Emma sat down again.

Luke's breath was coming in pants. 'Back then. Ryan James was…' His head drooped.

'Abusing some boys in your gymnastics club. We guessed that.' A huge wave of horror and pity broke over Emma. This was real. 'Oh Luke, love – were you abused too?' She reached both hands across the table and grasped one of Luke's hands.

'He touched me once, a brush of the fingers when I was landing after a jump. I didn't tell anyone. I didn't understand, at first. He did more to Alan and some of the others. And one of the other boys – Ryan gave him money for favours.'

Emma put a hand over her mouth. A twelve-year-old. How sick. But it was better to know.

'What did you do? How did it end? Somebody must have reported him, surely?'

'No. We dealt with it ourselves, us boys and some of the fathers. Not mine. Ryan's gone and he won't be back, Emmy, and believe me, that's all you need to know. We made a pact back then – we swore we would never speak of it again. I want you to swear too.'

The world reduced to Luke's face in front of her. His eyes were boring into hers.

Emma recoiled in horror. '*No!* He's dead, isn't he? Luke – talk to me!'

Summer sunshine hit the kitchen window and slanted into the room. Emma pressed her fists to her chest, barely able to breathe. The garden, the nightmare garden with the bag of clothes in the veggie patch, those stained clothes – blood stains? And the patio that Luke had wanted to cover the breadth of the garden, but then when he saw how deep the gardeners were digging, he cancelled that plan. No. Oh no. She'd been right; there must be something else still in there. But *surely* not—

'Luke. *What would I find if I dug around at the side of the garden?*'

The question came out in a whisper, and Luke grabbed both her hands. 'You'd find nothing. Leave it, Emma. You don't need to know more.' His eyes slid away from hers.

He was lying. Bile rose, and Emma dived through to the downstairs loo and vomited tea and not much else into the pan. From morning sickness to horror sickness. What had her baby's father been through; what had he done? And if she'd dug out there with more enthusiasm a week or two ago… Thank God she hadn't, but it might have been better if she had. And Luke – he had brought her and their child to live here, with a garden where – no, no, that couldn't be right. Could it?

She dragged her feet back to the kitchen. 'Luke. Can you promise me, on our baby's life, that Ryan James isn't buried in our garden?'

Silence for two, three, four beats, then he gripped both her hands, staring intently into her eyes. 'I promise on my honour, Emma – there has never been a body buried in the garden.'

The doorbell rang, and Emma craned her neck to see out of the front window. A police car was sitting in the driveway.

THE TWO OFFICERS followed Luke into the living area, and the older man spoke. 'We're tying up as many loose ends as we can about Alan Johnson's suicide. I gather from his father that you were out of touch with Alan for many years, sir, before you came back to live in Ralton Bridge?'

Emma pulled her bathrobe tighter around her and leaned back into her armchair, cuddling her middle as the two tall officers sat down on the sofa. Please, please, she mustn't be sick again. Luke leaned forward in the other armchair, forearms resting on his thighs, his expression sorrowful but calm. Emma shivered. He deserved an Oscar for this.

'That's right. We were mates as kids, but we grew apart when I went to a different secondary school, and then I moved away. Alan was edgy, always up and down, even as a boy. Do you know what he took yet?'

'It seems to have been some chemical from his father's farm, but we'll know more later. Can you think of anything that might have made him do this?'

Emma's mind was reeling. Alan had planned this enough in advance to bring home poison from the farm.

Luke was shaking his head. 'I don't really know him. We've only met a couple of times since we moved back, and he didn't mention money worries or anything.'

'And you, Mrs Carter?'

Emma's mouth went dry. This was it. Deep breath, Emma. 'Kate mentioned he'd been moody recently, depressed, but she didn't tell me about the money worries. I'm sure she never dreamed he'd do what he did.' That at least was true.

The officer was giving nothing away. 'We'll be speaking to Alan's other contacts too. Maybe someone will be able to help. If you think of anything more, let us know.'

Luke showed them out, and Emma went to make tea and

toast. Her stomach was churning madly and she had no idea if it was pregnancy-related or not.

Luke came back in and took over the toaster. 'I'll do that. You look exhausted.'

Emma pulled out a chair, her mind whirling between the dimness of the past and the awfulness of the present, and making sense of nothing. 'Who wrote those anonymous letters, Luke?'

He didn't turn round. 'I think it was Alan. He wouldn't say, but I think he might have been trying to deter us from meddling, as he saw it.'

'Kate saw him with one and thought he'd been on the receiving end too. What were we not supposed to meddle in?'

'Ryan's death.'

'Shit.' They had meddled, hadn't they? And— 'The car that nearly rammed me? And the dog poo?'

Luke shrugged. 'Please, Emma, leave it. We'll get through this.'

'We won't if you don't answer one question. How exactly did Ryan James die?' The enormity of what she'd asked was mind-boggling.

Luke got up to spread her toast when it popped up. For a moment, a knife scraping butter across toast was the only sound in the kitchen, then he handed her a plate.

'We made a pact, and I'm not breaking it. But I can tell you one thing – I don't know the answer to the question you just asked. Truly, Emma.'

Sincerity rang from every pore of his body, but he wasn't looking at her. Emma bit into her toast; she had to eat for the baby. Luke might not know for sure, but he must have an idea about what had happened to Ryan James in the end. If Ryan was dead, he'd been murdered. By a boy – a child? Or a group of enraged fathers? *Murder.* Alan's father would know the answer to that. And Euan – did he? He hadn't been part of the group of fathers who went to help their boys. Why not? Emma stared mutely at Luke, the man she loved, the father of her child.

Luke's phone, charging on the work surface, shrilled into the kitchen, and Emma jumped. She was a bag of nerves, and no wonder. And oh no, Luke was talking to Marie now – they'd have to tell his parents what had happened.

'That's good news, Mum. Give Dad my love when you visit. We can't come today, I'm afraid. Bit of a dodgy curry last night and it's going right through us.'

Emma closed her eyes. More lies. Luke chatted for a few more minutes, then ended the call and stuffed his phone into his pocket.

He went out to the hallway without saying more, but returned a minute or two later with a sheet of paper in one hand and an envelope in the other. No name on the envelope, no stamp.

'This was lying on the floor.'

His eyes met Emma's, and she snatched the letter from him. *Schtum. Or you'll be sorry.* This one was printed in a different font. Hell on earth. But one thing was clear; the writer of this letter wasn't Alan. What kind of person sent a letter like this after a man had committed suicide? The answer slotted neatly into her brain – a desperate one. The one who'd tried to knock her off her bike, that day? And now a man was dead.

'Luke. We should tell the police about this. And about the abuse.'

Luke bent down until his face was inches from hers. 'You

don't understand. Schtum. No one can ever know. Forget it, Emma. It's a secret. Forever.'

Spit landed on Emma's cheek, and she wiped it off, flinching. Luke was afraid too. Something or someone out there, in this perfect little village, must be dangerous. Emma buried her head in her arms on the table. How she hated secrets.

CHAPTER 22

THIS WAS THE WORST DAY OF HER MARRIAGE, AND ALL SHE COULD hope was she'd never have a worse one. Emma blobbed on the sofa for the rest of Saturday morning, lack of sleep making her gritty-eyed and irritable. What Alan had done yesterday was as horrific as whatever had happened in the past. How could he have done that to his poor wife? There would never be a good time to call Kate today, but she had to try. At half past twelve Emma took her phone up to her bedroom, well out of earshot of Luke, who'd been tigering around the ground floor and the garden for the past hour.

Rather to her surprise, Kate took the call. Emma lay on the bed, one arm slung over her eyes, forcing back tears as she asked if there was anything she could do. Stupid question.

Kate's voice was a low, grainy monotone. 'No. Thank you. I'm – this was my fault. If I hadn't pushed him for details, he'd never have taken things so far.'

'He was in a state already, Kate. The story was bound to come out one day.'

'But nothing did come out, did it? I should have listened to him. What happened back then doesn't matter now, but I'll always have the guilt. His mum and dad are in bits.'

'Have you spoken to the police?'

'Yes. I didn't tell them anything about… back then. Keith said that's best. There'll be an inquest, but it won't be complicated, they said. I'm going to Mum's in Manchester for a while. She's here now and she'll help me pack some stuff. This is all our fault, Emma. We should never have meddled.'

Our fault our fault our fault… The words hammered into Emma's brain. Our fault. Her fault. Death. Suicide. Inquest. Such unspeakable words, pulling her into a pit of tears and pity and self-pity and doubt and – all the bad stuff. This was a whole new worst bit, and for a moment it was too much. Emma choked back a sob. That was the thing with phone calls, though – you had to talk.

'Oh Kate. I'm so sorry about everything. Will you keep in touch?'

A long pause hung in the air before Kate spoke again. 'I'm not sure. I'm sorry too, but sorry doesn't cut it, does it?'

The connection broke, and Emma lay in an exhausted half-doze until Luke came up and told her he'd made pasta with sauce from the freezer. Emma was about to refuse, but the thought of the baby spurred her downstairs. She had to look after her child.

THE DOORBELL RANG LATER that afternoon when Emma was back on the sofa, recovering after a distressing phone call from her grandmother. Oma had noticed something was up in the first three seconds of the call, and Emma told her about Alan's suicide, but nothing else.

Luke ushered Mrs Alderson into the living room, and the older woman handed Emma a plate of crumpets.

'I thought you might like something for afternoon tea. You look exhausted, Emma. Is everything all right? I saw the police here earlier.'

Emma sank onto the sofa. Mrs Alderson wasn't the kind of person to be morbidly curious. She'd known Luke all his life, so of course she was concerned.

'An old school friend of Luke's took his own life last night. Alan Johnson. Did you know him?'

Mrs Alderson shrank back into her armchair. 'How terrible for you all. His poor family. No, I didn't know him, but he's the son of the Johnsons up on the farm north of the village, isn't he? Oh, dear.'

Emma rubbed her eyes. It was comforting, having her neighbour here. They discussed mental health and how attitudes had changed since Mrs Alderson's time in the NHS, but how that still didn't stop people becoming desperate. Luke went to put the kettle on, and Emma circled aching shoulders. Alan's death was all around, pressing her down, filling every hour.

Mrs Alderson seemed to sense Emma needed something normal to think about. 'Did you do anything about checking for a fireplace upstairs?'

Emma stared at the wall where Mrs Alderson's fireplace was now. 'One of our bedroom walls upstairs sounds hollow, so we're thinking of having it opened up to see what's underneath. Is there anything we need to be aware of? We were wondering about asbestos.'

Mrs Alderson shook her head. 'Old chimneys did sometimes have asbestos as part of the lining, but I'm sure ours didn't. You could get yours checked before you start. An expert would keep you right.'

Luke came down the room with a tea tray, and Emma gave him a sharp glance. The uppermost expression on his face now was relief. Was that because they weren't talking about Alan any longer?

He handed round cups. 'I'll get the house plans out. Then afterwards we'll get a builder onto it.'

Mrs Alderson spread butter and jam on a crumpet and slid it onto Emma's plate. 'Eat, miss. I'll look out my house plans too, and the papers I have from getting the fireplace shifted, if I still have them. These would show us if there was any asbestos there.'

THE REST of the day passed in the same unreal way, with chunks of near-normality separated by longer chunks of horror when Emma sat frozen on her sofa. Kate's mother was with her now, but what could anyone say to comfort a woman whose husband had taken the ultimate step in rejection? Emma blinked back thoughts of her own long-gone mother. She didn't often think about Mum now; the memories were scarce. How good it would be to have a mother in her life, and oh, if only she could call Dad for support like Kate had called her mum. But she had to find a way to reconnect properly with Dad first, and the person who would help most with that hadn't been born yet.

Luke made sandwiches at six and Emma choked two down,

then left him to clear up and went for a walk in the garden. She'd been blobbing inside all day.

She thrust her hands into the pockets of her jeans – there wasn't much space in here for her hands, now. Emma gave up and patted her middle. 'Scan day on Monday, baby. We'll get to see you at last. I hope we manage to sort ourselves out before then.' Not that sorting would help Alan or Kate, or change what had happened. What *had* happened?

The sight of the planned veggie patch by the back door started a new train of thought. Those clothes she'd dug up… What if it hadn't been a prank with some farm machinery that had caused the stains? Luke had lied to her earlier; she had no guarantees that he hadn't lied about the clothes, too. In fact, he could have lied about a lot of things. This pact he'd talked of – a pact of silence. One that was so strong he was even lying to his wife? Anger rose, and Emma pressed her mouth shut hard. Luke seemed to think he could get away with lying, but that was wrong, and Alan's death only made it more wrong. She strode to the shed and yanked the door open.

The bag of clothes was gone. Emma searched along all the shelves in case Luke had put it somewhere else, but the old plastic bag definitely wasn't here, and neither were the stained clothes. Blood-stained clothes? Emma pulled the piles of plant pots and sacks of earth around, but no yellow T-shirt and blue tracksuit came to light. Okay. Someone had shifted—

'Emmy? You there?'

Luke appeared in the doorway, and Emma swung round. 'Where's the bag with those old clothes I dug up?'

'Dunno. Isn't it there? It was on the shelf last time I saw it.'

He came in and searched around in much the same way Emma had, and she watched him through narrowed eyes. He seemed to be sincere in what he was doing, and it was awful, this distrust that had sprung up between them. Luke came to the end of his search and stared at her.

'They're not here.'

Emma leaned on the workbench. 'No. I didn't move them, and if you didn't either, it must have been one of your parents.'

And that could only mean that Marie had done something with the clothes. Euan with his hip hadn't ventured this far up the garden. Different expressions were chasing across Luke's face now, puzzlement and worry being uppermost. Emma waited.

'Oh – uh – maybe I did chuck them out along with those old plant pots and stuff earlier this week. Not sure now.'

Lies and more lies. Emma raised a fist to thump on the workbench, then lowered it again. This was useless. It was all useless, unless he started telling her the truth.

'Luke, what happened to you and Alan in the past was part of why he took his life. And you know what it was. Don't you think we owe it to him to deal with what went on back then?' Keith's voice echoed in Emma's head. 'Remember.' Keith was part of the pact too. Were all the fathers?

Luke turned away and blew his nose. 'It won't bring Alan back.'

'I know. But he's dead, and Ryan James is dead, and look at all the people those deaths have affected. You, and heaven knows how many others in the past. All those families, us too, and Kate. We're still feeling it. And our baby, because he or she is going to be born into a house we would never have lived in otherwise. In a village where something vile happened.'

He spun round and almost spat at her. 'A man was killed.

And it was one of us in Ralton Bridge who did it. That's murder. And twenty years later, it's still murder.'

Emma's hands moved across her middle. Oh, baby. It was so horribly logical, although she'd never voiced it, not even in her head. Nobody let a thought like 'my husband was mixed up with the murder of a man when he was twelve' become words.

'Who killed him, Luke?' She barely heard her own whisper.

Luke's lips were pressed together so hard they were colourless. Emma put a hand on his back.

'I'm with you. The man was a monster, and some people would say he deserved what he got. Please don't let this drive us apart.' That was emotional blackmail, but she didn't care, because it *was* driving them apart. Her husband had the worst kind of secret in the world; no one could live with that.

He met her eyes again, and his voice shook. 'I don't know who killed him. All of us were there and it might have been any one of us. Or one of the dads. That's the problem, don't you see? We're stuck with it because no one knows and we all have too much to lose. Even if the police had found Ryan and investigated straight away, I don't think anyone would know who killed him.'

He moved away again, and Emma followed, her brain piecing together what he'd said. Ryan had died. Been killed. So there was a body. Who did what with the body?

'Okay, he was dead. What happened to him then?'

Luke fell to his knees, bent his head to the shed floor for a long moment, then leapt back to his feet with shocking swiftness. His face was red and white in blotches. Emma stepped back.

'For God's sake, Emma. Leave. It. Be.' He fled back to the garden and vomited into the phlox.

CHAPTER 23

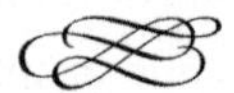

LUKE, AGED 12

THE NEXT DAY, LUKE COULDN'T BREATHE THROUGH HIS NOSE and he looked like he'd been in a boxing match and lost, but that was nothing compared to the non-stop shaking that was going on in his gut and his head. At least it was Sunday and he didn't have to go to school.

Mum fussed around at breakfast while Luke tried to eat toast and breathe through his mouth at the same time.

'We'd better keep you at home for a few days while your nose is so swollen, darling. You can put the bag of frozen peas on it again afterwards. Mrs Alderson said that'll help with the swelling.'

Luke submitted to the pea treatment, then went up to his room for some peace and quiet. This was so gross. He didn't know what had happened to Ryan, and he didn't know if Mum knew anything about it. Dad had shut himself in his study, aka the spare room, and wasn't saying anything to either of them. As secrets went, this was the crappiest ever.

Monday was a bit better because he could breathe through one side of his nose again, and Dad had gone to work. Luke sat at the dining table and did some geography, then after lunch Mum made him walk to the shops with her. He couldn't sit inside all day, apparently, but oh, yes, he could. No problem at all. He wasn't allowed to, though. He trailed uphill at Mum's side, brilliant cold sunshine mocking him every bloody step of the way. No matter where you were in this place you had to go uphill to get anywhere. Except away. Getting out of Ralton Bridge needed a whole lot less effort than going to the bloody shops did and life was so—

'Oh! The butcher's closed.' Mum stopped in front of the shop.

Luke's heart plummeted. Impossible to even think about why Mark's dad might have closed the shop. The nightmare was getting darker.

Mum tutted as she stepped forward to read the notice on the door. '*Closed until Thursday due to family circumstances.* Sounds like they've had a death, poor souls. And them struggling to keep the business going, too. This won't help.'

Luke closed his eyes. A death a death a death. And Mum was standing there peering at her shopping list and not even noticing that he was – what was he? Shitting himself, that was what, almost literally.

'We could have spaghetti for tea. Would you like that, darling? It would be nice and soft for you to eat. Spaghetti bolognese.' She swept off in the direction of the general store, and Luke followed.

And oh, he'd thought things couldn't possibly get any

worse, but Jon's mum was in the store, piling flour and eggs into her basket. And her face when she saw Luke – she knew. So Mum didn't know and everyone else's mum did.

'Hello, Marie. And Luke – your poor nose. It'll all be better in no time, though, sweetheart. Don't you worry.'

The last part was said in a significant voice, and Luke shuffled his feet on the floor. Jon's mum's cheeks were pink, and her lips were pressed together in an odd way, as if she was trying not to cry. She pulled a packet of mints from her handbag and pressed them into Luke's hand.

'Take these, darling. Your mouth must taste terrible. Isn't he brave, Marie?'

Bafflement was oozing out of every pore on Mum's face. She gave Luke's shoulder a pat.

'It isn't broken, thank goodness. He'll be fine in a day or two.' She drifted over to the shelf for a jar of bloody spaghetti sauce while Jon's mum gave Luke another pat – you'd think he was a dog – before heading for the checkout. Luke nearly started crying again. Why hadn't Dad told Mum what had happened? And he wouldn't say another thing about it to Luke, either – you could bet your life on that.

He walked home beside Mum, who was yakking away about going somewhere nice on holiday that summer. Round the bend in the road they went and the house came into view and – oh! The car was parked on the driveway. Dad was home already.

'Yes, your dad said he might be back earlier today. We can have tea soon and you can get off to bed early. Maybe you can go to school tomorrow.'

Mum went inside with the shopping, and Luke mooched round to the back garden. Dad had been digging in the vegetable patch. Luke stared at the freshly raked earth, then Dad came out of the shed, wiping his hands on his trousers.

'It'll be fine, lad. It's all taken care of, don't worry. And remember, we'll never speak of what happened. Now let's go in and see what your mum's got for tea.'

TUESDAY MORNING, just a normal school day, right? First day back after the... stop, stop. Luke crept up the hill and stood at the school gates, scanning the playground. A game of footie was going on at the far side, some of the older girls were oohing over something by the side gate, and huddles of kids were all over the place. Where was Alan? He usually called in for Luke on the way to school, but he hadn't today.

The moment he stepped into the playground, Luke was surrounded by a bunch of kids shoving their faces up to gawk at his bruises. He looked like a bloody panda bear gone wrong. He had black and purple bruises under both his eyes, and his nose was a red and squidgy mess. This morning he'd been able to breathe almost normally, though, and he was glad he'd escaped without going to the doctor. Telling lies about falling at the gym club would have been crap.

Alan and a couple of the others were leaning on the wall by the door. Luke trailed over, but they stopped talking as soon as he came close enough to hear them. Alan hunched his shoulders and slouched off.

Luke stuck his chin in the air, though his insides were bleeding. None of these boys – his *friends* – were looking pleased to see him.

'What's up?' He inched back his sleeve to get to his watch.

Another three minutes until the bell rang and he could go inside where it was safe.

A couple of the boys turned away, then Mark lurched upright and shoved his nose right up to Luke's.

'None of this would have happened if you hadn't made Alan tell his dad what Ryan was doing.'

Not a word about what had happened to Ryan. Luke stood rooted to the spot, barely able to breathe at the injustice of it all.

What *had* happened to Ryan?

His voice came out all squeaky. 'Didn't you want him stopped? And don't forget you were the one with a knife.'

Hisses from the other boys. Jon pushed Luke's chest, and shoved his face up close too. 'We. Say. Nothing.'

His breath was hot on Luke's chin, and Luke stepped back. He wasn't the bad guy here, so why were they acting like he was? The bell rang, and he swung round and went in. Mr Aitken in English tutted about his bruises and told him to make sure he caught up with what he'd missed yesterday. Then it was history and Mrs Henderson went on and on with her lesson about how World War One had started, as if that was important now, while Luke sat fighting tears. He had to find out what they'd done with Ryan on Saturday night. A sudden thought struck him – as far as he'd heard, no one in Glenfield was jumping up and down saying 'Ryan James is missing'. Was it even remotely possible Ryan was safe at home, nursing his wounds and regretting what he'd done to the boys?

At morning break, Luke searched around for Sid, the one other kid who might talk to him. After all, it was Sid who'd gone for the dads on Saturday.

'Hey.' He caught up with Sid and Noel when they were

going downstairs. They didn't look happy to see him either, but at least they didn't shove him away. He tagged on behind them as they trudged outside and over to the row of trees at the far end of the playground.

'What happened with Ryan? What did they do?' He grabbed Sid's elbow, then dropped it as the other boy ogled him as if he'd said something totally out of order.

'You know what happened. And what Mark said was right. You were the one who wanted to stop him.'

Luke nearly burst into tears. 'I *don't* know. Why are you all behaving as if it's my fault? What he was doing was wrong.'

Sid hung his head, poking a stone around with one foot, but Noel shrugged.

'I don't know what happened, but if he was—'

Sid shoved Noel away. 'Give it a rest, muppet. You're right, you don't know what happened, so shut up about it.'

Noel gave them both a filthy look and stomped across the playground. Nausea was making Luke's legs wobbly.

Sid shoved his hands into his pockets, not looking at Luke. 'Ryan was taken into the butcher's and he won't be walking out again any time soon. Understand? And you heard what my dad told us. Schtum, dum-dum.'

Luke swallowed bile. Ryan was dead, that much was clear. But what—?

The bell rang, and the kids started streaming back to the door.

'Luke! Unless you are completely conversant with your French irregular verbs, I suggest you come into the classroom and sit down.' Miss Carmichael was chivvying the stragglers into the French class. She wasn't smiling, but she stopped Luke on his way past.

'Are you all right? You don't look well.'

'I'm fine, thanks.' His automatic answering machine took over, and Luke slid into his seat. The others were coping, so he had to, too.

The school day was never-ending, but Luke sat tight because he didn't know what else to do. No one except Noel spoke to him at lunchtime, and in biology they were doing genetics and it was more like bloody maths than biology and all Luke wanted was for it to end. At long last the bell rang. Home, he could go home now. Mum might be clueless, but at least she wasn't out to get him.

Mark and Alan were standing at the gate when Luke crossed the playground, and he felt a jolt of fear. He was their *friend*, so why did they look so threatening? Was something else going on now?

They said nothing as they plodded away from the crowds at the gates. Then Mark stopped and wheeled round until his face was right in front of Luke's. He'd been doing that a lot recently.

'I hear you've been asking what happened to Ryan, pretty boy.'

His voice was soft, and a shiver ran through Luke. The other boy's mouth twitched upwards, and Luke stepped back. What was funny about this?

'Listen, Luke. My Dad's been making Ryan into parcels. We're all getting one to hide, every family. But schtum, dummy.'

He tapped the side of his nose and marched away the way they'd come.

Luke gaped at Alan. 'What—?'

'Schtum.' Alan stamped off.

Luke trailed after him. Ryan in parcels? How could—? Luke retched.

Noel ran up to join him and began yakking about homework, but Luke couldn't reply. If he'd opened his mouth, he'd have emptied his stomach there and then. Noel must have seen something was wrong, because he walked right past his aunt's gate and took Luke all the way home. He even rang the bell.

'Luke isn't very well, Mrs Carter.'

'Oh, dear, we should have kept you off for another day after all, darling. Thank you for bringing him home, Noel, that was kind. In you come, Luke.'

Ten minutes later he was on the sofa with a rug over him and a mug of disgusting camomile tea in his hands, and Mum was rootling in the cupboard for bloody chocolate biscuits to cheer him up. By the time Dad arrived, though, Luke didn't feel sick any more, as long as he was careful not to think about Ryan in parcels.

Dad stuck his head into the living room, gave Luke a thumbs up and joined Mum in the kitchen, closing the door behind him. The murmur of voices went on for a long time, but Luke couldn't hear what they were saying. And he didn't want to, either.

The phone rang on the table beside the sofa, and Luke picked it up.

'Hey, Luke, just the man!'

Bloody hell, it was Harry. Luke's throat went dry. The older boy had never phoned him before. What did Harry know? Luke said 'Hey' back, and waited, his heart thumping.

Harry sounded like nothing had happened. 'Luke, I don't know if you've heard, but Ryan's had to go away for a bit.'

Luke clutched at his neck with the hand that wasn't holding the phone. 'Oh?' He cleared his throat to disguise the squeak.

'He phoned on Sunday morning. I didn't speak to him, but Mum said he's on his way to Canada. Someone in his family's ill, or something. There'll be no gym club for a bit, but Mum's thinking of starting something for kids who like running. Would you be interested?'

Luke nearly dropped the phone. What was Harry *on* about? Ryan hadn't phoned anyone on Sunday morning, had he? This must be another plan he wasn't in on.

He forced his mind back to Harry. 'Ah, yes, I would. I've got a bashed nose at the moment so I'll have to wait a week or two, though.'

'Great. I'll tell Mum to put you on the list. Good luck with the nose.'

Luke replaced the phone on its base and sat back. Okay. Ryan was in Canada.

Dad came in with Mum skittering after him, and they sat down on the two armchairs, looking like the judge and jury in a courtroom. Nausea rose again and Luke breathed through his mouth. Had Dad been given his parcel yet? Oh God oh God, he had, hadn't he? That would be what he'd been doing yesterday afternoon – you could just bet Dad would do something as lame as bury a chunk of a bloody body in the vegetable patch. It was like one of Mum's bloody Agatha Christie books. Oh God… He mustn't be sick; he mustn't be sick… Luke forced himself to look at Mum and Dad. Both were wearing odd, tight smiles.

'Luke. Your mum and I have been thinking about what, um, happened, and this is what we've planned. No school for you until you're properly better. You and Mum are going to York tomorrow, and you'll stay overnight. You deserve a treat after – everything. When you come back on Thursday, there'll be a surprise waiting for you here.'

A surprise? How old did they think he was? Luke nodded, and Dad switched on the six o'clock news.

'There's been a lot of unpleasantness recently. Nothing we need to worry about now, though. I'm dealing with it. Don't worry.'

Unpleasantness? Luke sat staring at the telly as Mount Etna spewed all over the screen. Well, sure, murder was unpleasant…

CHAPTER 24

SUNDAY, 16TH MAY

THE HOUSE WAS SILENT WHEN EMMA WENT DOWNSTAIRS THE morning after Luke's outburst in the garden. They'd spent the evening in separate chairs in front of an animal documentary, nursing bruised souls in silence. Together, yet apart, and what a train crash their lives had turned into.

A note was propped against the fruit bowl in the middle of the kitchen table. *Gone for a run xx.* Emma crushed the paper in her hand. A run? Luke hadn't gone running all the time she'd known him. What had brought this on? Or was it another lie? But it gave her the chance to go and see Kate without Luke trying to stop her. It might be easier to talk in person – if Kate was still here, of course. She might not be. Emma lifted her phone – but no, she didn't want to give Kate the chance to refuse a visit.

Five minutes' drive brought her to the farm, where the deserted yard was slick with mud after last night's rain. Emma rang the bell, and the door opened almost immediately. Keith didn't look pleased to see her, speaking before she opened her mouth.

'Kate's not here. She went to Manchester yesterday with her mum. They'll be back at the house next week sometime. She's putting it on the market.'

He stood in the doorway, his once-ruddy face an unbecoming yellow, and Emma's heart ached for him. If ever a man was suffering, it was Keith. He'd been an adult, back then. He'd known what had happened to Ryan – maybe he'd even been the instigator of the pact of silence? And now he was living through what silence had done.

She put a hand on his arm. 'How are you? And your wife? This is dreadful for you.'

He shook her hand off, glaring. 'Nothing to be done about it, is there? The inquest's next Thursday, and then we can organise the funeral. We want to be alone now.'

The door closed in her face, and Emma took a step back, stung. But he was grieving, of course he was.

The church clock was chiming for the morning service when Emma turned into the driveway at home, and Luke was still out. The entire bruising episode of going to the farm had lasted less than half an hour. She was about to make a cup of tea – and oh, how she was looking forward to unlimited coffee when the baby was here – when Luke arrived back, sweating hard.

He came into the kitchen and poured a glass of water down his throat.

Emma passed him a towel. 'I went to the farm to see Kate, but she's gone back to Manchester already.'

Luke crashed his glass down on the worktop. 'I told you to

leave this alone! You don't know what you're dealing with!'

'So why don't you tell me?' Yesterday's argument wasn't over, apparently, and neither were Luke's evasions.

Desperate eyes met Emma's, and she lowered her voice. 'Luke. Let's go. Leave Ralton Bridge, and leave the problems in the past where they belong.' That would only work if he told her what the problems were, though.

Luke was shaking his head. 'No. We have to sit this out. Leave it to me, Emma. Ryan James was the worst kind of scum, but we tell no one what happened to him. Okay? Now, we behave as normal. We'll visit Dad this afternoon, and not one word – do you hear?' He wheeled round and went upstairs. The shower in the ensuite started, and Emma slumped into her chair, loneliness mingling with fear in her gut. She was alone here. Telling no one what happened to Ryan James would be easy, because all she knew was that he'd been killed. By whom? Alan? That might explain the suicide. Or – surely not Luke? But that couldn't be. Luke wasn't capable of murder. No. But his behaviour now was inexcusable.

The beep of the landline phone interrupted the scary thoughts, and Emma dragged her feet up the room to answer it. This would be Marie, and actually, a visit to York wasn't the worst idea. Anything was better than staying home. She lifted the phone, but the voice in her ear was Mrs Alderson's.

'I've found our house plans, Emma, and the estimates and receipts from having the fireplace moved. There's no mention of asbestos, so you should be safe enough. How are you, dear? This must be hard for you both.'

Emma sat down on the sofa. 'It is, but we'll get through it. We're going down to York to see Marie and Euan today. Euan's doing well after his operation.'

She chatted for a few more minutes, then rang off. Her parents-in-law were going to be horrified about Alan, and of course it was kinder to wait until Euan was discharged before telling them. Problem was, she wasn't sure if she could act that well.

THE CLINIC WAS near the town centre, a long and elegant Victorian terrace, recently renovated by the looks of it. Inside, it didn't look like a hospital, but the usual hospital smell was wafting around the corridors, although there was none of the hustle and bustle and queueing and noise Emma had experienced on the few occasions she'd visited someone in an NHS place. Money equalled peace and quiet, apparently.

Luke gripped her arm as they went upstairs. 'We say nothing, remember?'

'I know. This is hardly the place, anyway.'

Euan was in a two-bed room, propped up in bed with a cage lifting the blankets from his leg. His roommate wasn't there, but Marie was sitting by his bed. She rushed across the room to fetch chairs for Luke and Emma, and the next few minutes were taken up with hellos and health enquiries.

Marie returned to her place and gripped Euan's hand. 'I can't believe how well he's doing – aren't you, love? He's been up walking with a frame already, and it'll be home on Wednesday if everything goes well.'

The pair beamed at each other, and a lump rose in Emma's throat. Would she and Luke be like that in thirty years? Unexpected loneliness stabbed in. What was wrong with her today? She wasn't even alone in her body, never mind her life.

Luke handed over the book he'd brought for his father, and

Euan pointed out his crutches in the corner.

'The physio's promoting me to these tomorrow. They're being very careful with me, after the problems last time.'

Marie was full of chat about Euan's treatment, but Emma allowed the tales of hospital life to wash over her head. They were such a couple, those two, finishing each other's sentences half the time, Marie still clinging to Euan's hand. It was hard not to compare it to the way she and Luke were with each other. But maybe you couldn't compare a long and happy marriage with one as young as theirs, and people were all different, weren't they?

The conversation turned to Ralton Bridge, and Luke started talking about the new benches round the village green.

Euan shifted in bed. 'We had some good times there, didn't we, Marie? Ralton Bridge is a great little place. We were sorry to leave, but I suppose it was for the best.'

Marie patted his hand, her eyes sombre. 'Luke will look after everything, love.'

Emma choked back a comment. They chatted for another half hour, then Emma poked Luke when his parents weren't watching. Time to leave the lovebirds to it. A vague plan formed in her head as they were pulling on jackets, and she took Marie's arm while Luke was saying goodbye to his dad.

'Marie – I have my scan tomorrow morning in Glenfield. Luke'll be going on to work afterwards, so why don't I drive up to York with him and collect you? We can go for lunch somewhere, just the two of us.'

Marie beamed. 'That would be lovely. Then you can tell me the latest about the baby!'

Emma smiled back. Disapproval was radiating from Luke, but there was nothing he could do to stop her, was there?

CHAPTER 25

MONDAY, 17TH MAY

'SEE YOU TONIGHT, THEN.' EMMA SLAMMED THE CAR DOOR SHUT and watched as Luke drove away. She turned towards their old flat, pressing her handbag with the precious first photos of the baby against her chest and barely glancing at the breathtaking gothic towers of York Minster to her left. She'd seen the little blob on the ultrasound screen kick and move around inside her, and it was perfect. For the duration of the scan that morning she had shut out the world and allowed today to be the happiest day, the best day she'd had for weeks, the best moments since that first positive pregnancy test. Luke was thrilled too, and oh, what a long time it seemed since they'd been a normal happy couple. Emma hadn't wanted it to end, but of course it did.

And here she was, walking on earth again, and having lunch with Marie was going to bring all the horror and uncertainty in her life right now back to centre stage.

Marie had the door open as soon as Emma rang the bell, and the usual 'this flat was once my home' feeling swept over her.

'Hello, Emma dear – did everything go all right?'

Emma produced the three photos she'd been given, and wow, this was lovely too – standing here with Marie, drooling together over the baby.

'I'm going to make copies, so I'll send you some.' And oh, to be able to drool with Oma too. But they would do it on Skype. Oma was good at technology.

Emma sank down on the sofa, watching Marie pore over the photos, and heck, she was going to have to be careful here. Not telling her parents-in-law about Alan's death until Euan was discharged meant that any questions she asked Marie about the past would need to be very carefully phrased. Marie was all too good at reading people's body language when there was something wrong, too, and – oh dear. Emma caught sight of a newspaper sitting on a pile of things waiting to go to the clinic that afternoon. But even the local paper for Glenfield and Ralton Bridge had reported the death without naming Alan, so it was unlikely to be in the *Observer*.

They spent an hour shifting furniture and rugs to make the flat safer for Euan on his crutches, and Emma looked around nostalgically. She would live in York again like a shot, given the chance.

'Living on the one level is such an advantage.' Marie gave Emma a rather shamefaced smile. 'You know, back then, I thought you'd been pushy about the house, but being in York is so much better for us. And of course we understand now, with the baby coming.'

Emma smiled vaguely, her mind whirling. Pushy about the

house? Who'd been pushy? Hadn't the two older Carters concocted the plan in the first place? Uneasiness wormed through Emma's gut. That evening when Luke had dropped the bombshell on her, pretty much where she was standing now, actually – what had he said? 'We're swapping houses with Mum and Dad. They're desperate.' According to him, it had all been connected to the hip operation and Euan's age. It was a sound enough idea – very sensible, in fact – but Marie's remark was making Emma think that the original push might have come from Luke. But that couldn't be right. He hadn't known about the baby when he and his parents made the house swap decision.

She cleared her throat. 'Had you ever considered selling up before?'

Silence. Marie was gazing earnestly at the now rugless floor, and Emma waited. Was it such a difficult question?

Marie glanced up again, her eyes wide. 'No, not really. We couldn't leave the house. I mean – it was our home.'

A jagged thought zipped into Emma's head. Who had Marie meant with 'I thought *you'd* been pushy'? She went into the bathroom to wash her hands and think. She'd taken the remark to mean her and Luke, but what if Marie was under the impression that the removal was all her darling pushy daughter-in-law's idea? Could Luke have been trying to get his parents out of the house, and done it by vilifying his wife? Surely not. And why would Luke do that, anyway? Emma pressed her fingers to flaring cheeks. Paranoia was striking again, and there was too much she didn't know here. It was time to go for lunch.

. . .

EMMA TOOK Marie's arm as they ambled through town to Betty's, the famous tea room. She had to find out whose idea the house swap had been, as well as the reason behind the move. Was it really Euan's op and the fact that he was getting older, or was it something to do with the house? Or the garden? The worst thought was that something else was buried out there. But Luke had sworn it wasn't Ryan James' body, so it wasn't. Yet – there was his behaviour over the patio, and Marie and Euan had been very quick to agree about appropriateness of a wide patio. The patio they didn't have, now. Emma shivered. What were they all afraid of? Think, Emma. Ryan James was dead. Killed by an unknown someone in Ralton Bridge. And Luke didn't know, or wasn't saying, what had happened to the body. That was what she had to find out.

The waitress showed them to their table, and Emma ordered a glass of prosecco for Marie and grape and elderflower juice for herself. They clinked glasses when the drinks arrived, and Emma grasped her courage and smiled at her mother-in-law.

'I'm glad you're loving York as much as I love Ralton Bridge.' Emma crossed her fingers under the table.

Marie sipped her prosecco, her cheeks pink with pleasure. 'I'm glad you're happy there, and this is lovely. Thank you, Emma dear.'

Emma smiled back. 'My pleasure. Tell me, who do I have to thank for the house swap idea?' Too bad if Luke had told his parents it was all her idea.

Marie sipped again. 'It happened when Luke drove his dad to the doctor's that time he was staying with us in March. They had it all worked out when they came home again. I wasn't keen at first, but Luke was very persuasive. He was so sure it was best for us, and he said it was what you wanted too. And Euan was all for it, with his bad hip.'

Emma blinked. Hm. Luke *had* been economical with the truth. 'It must have been a wrench to leave Ralton Bridge. You'd been there forever.'

'It was, but Euan and I talked it over and decided Luke was right. We want him to have a good life, you know, after everything that happened when he was young. We had to keep the house, you see. It was Luke's future at stake.'

Emma sat back as the waitress brought their kedgeree and refilled Marie's glass. She'd been right. The move *was* connected to what happened when Luke was a child. Marie chatted away about food while they ate, but when they were sitting with coffee in front of them, Emma swung the conversation back to her investigation.

'Marie—' She put a hand on the older woman's arm. 'What did happen when Luke was young? He never speaks of his school days, but I know there was a problem with a gymnastics group, wasn't there?'

Marie sighed, her eyes unfocussed. She put a hand on top of Emma's and squeezed. 'The trainer wasn't a nice man, dear, if you know what I mean. In the end, the menfolk dealt with him; to this day I'm not sure how, exactly. The boys were all quite shaken. We must leave it in the past, Emma. That's where it belongs.'

The word gave a nauseating jerk, and Emma had to make a conscious effort not to clap her hands over her mouth. Marie knew. At least – she knew something. 'Not a nice man' meant only one thing, and why, oh why, had it all been 'left in the past where it belonged'? Okay, it was the kind of thing her mother-in-law's Highland Free Church upbringing might not allow her to think about, never mind have a frank conversation about, especially in the middle of lunch in a genteel little tea room. But back in the day – why had no one gone to the police then? Before it got to the point of Ryan James being killed. By someone. Emma took a sip of her grape and elder, her head reeling. What did Marie know about that part?

'The trainer was Ryan James, wasn't he?'

'That's right.'

How did a nervous woman like Marie manage to be so calm about it? Of course, it was possible she didn't know the whole story either. Emma continued carefully. 'But this Ryan, if he was, um, into underage boys, why did no one involve the police?'

Marie went sheet-white and shook her head. Emma winced. She'd gone too far. She wouldn't get more out of Marie today, that was sure.

'I'm sorry, Marie. I misunderstood.' Emma signalled to the waitress, and rummaged for her purse. 'My treat, remember? Shall we head over to visit Euan?'

THE TRAIN JOURNEY home gave Emma time to think. A chat with Luke would be the next step, and heaven only knew if he would talk about it. All this was driving a huge wedge right down the middle of their marriage, and if they were to survive as a couple, Luke was going to have to tell her what had happened.

Home again, she sat down for an hour on her laptop, finished her translation project and heaved a sigh of relief. She'd leave it for a day or two and then re-read it to make sure all was as it should be, then send it to the publisher to be proof-read. Job done. Now, half-four might be a good time to call Kate and see how she was doing, and it might not be an easy call.

She was right about that.

'Emma, please leave me alone. I don't want to think about you or Ralton Bridge now. Alan would still be alive if we'd never met, and I'll never get past that.'

The connection broke before Emma had said a word. She slammed her phone down on the sofa and burst into tears. Kate had stopped short of 'this is all your fault', but that was what she'd meant. And that was wrong.

She was banging about in the kitchen when Luke arrived home. He went straight to the photos of the baby on the coffee table, and stood there with a big grin on his face. Emma lost the last scrap of control she had.

'That scan was the one good part of the day, and it's ruined now. Why did you want to move here? And don't tell me it was your dad's hip, because it wasn't. It's to do with whatever you're not telling me about Ryan James' death. I hate this, Luke, and just know I'm within half a millimetre of packing my bags and going back to York. With the baby.'

Luke dropped the photo, his face white. 'Emma, no. You know why we're here. The house, and—'

'All I know about this bloody house is there's some secret attached to it – it's like the house is blackmailing you into living in it. What is it that's keeping you here, Luke? If I'm to stay here too, I'm going to need a bloody good answer right now.'

Wow. She'd never yelled at him like that. Emma waited, her eyes fixed on his.

He swallowed. Then a hoarse whisper. 'There's a – a parcel of Ryan here.'

'*What?* What do you mean?'

His head dropped until his chin was nearly on his chest, and he leaned both hands on the kitchen table, his face almost grey now. 'They made him into parcels. We all had to hide one.'

Emma clutched her stomach, fighting the rising bile. Calm, Emmy, look after the baby. She took a few careful breaths through her mouth, and the nausea subsided. Who? – why? – where? were all waiting for answers. For the moment, she pushed the horrific mental picture to one side and concentrated on the most important thing.

'Where is this parcel hidden?' The moment she spoke, she knew. 'It's where I wanted to dig the veggie patch, isn't it?'

A silent nod from Luke.

'Why? And who killed him?'

'We were all there with sticks, prodding and jabbing at him. And Mark – he had a knife. He and Alan both used the knife. But… Ryan was alive when we left him with the dads. I think. But I don't know…' He closed his eyes, his face agonised.

Emma clapped her hands to her face. Oh my God. *Alan.* She'd chatted to him, clinked glasses with him, she'd made friends with his wife – and Kate hadn't known either. Children… and they'd killed their tormentor.

'But why hide it? Why did no one tell the police? Ryan James was the criminal.'

He blinked at her. 'The dads decided that. It was to save us from becoming a media sensation.'

Emma gazed out to the garden, her thoughts reeling. Right, wrong, true, false – but he was telling the truth now, that was clear. Again, the most important thing should be dealt with first.

'Come on. We're digging.' She pushed him out the back door.

He gave a start, then strode towards the shed. Emma bent over the original ex-veggie patch. Luke returned with the spade for him and the fork for her, and two pairs of gardening gloves. Emma pulled hers on thankfully. What would they do when – if – they found the parcel of Ryan?

Half an hour of heavy work by Luke and assistance from Emma followed, then they looked at each other. Luke's face was blank with astonishment. 'It's not here.'

Emma leaned on the fork. 'Are you sure we've dug in the right place?'

His head swivelled right and left as he stared at the corner of the house, then the rectangle of dug-over ground. 'Positive. Mum and Dad bought the bulk of their veg at the market, with the patch here for radishes and a few beans and things. We've covered way more than her little plot.'

'So...'

The word dangled in the air as they gaped at the earth they'd turned over. Luke broke the silence.

'I guess Dad shifted it.'

'For heaven's sake, Luke – would he really shift a parcel of another human being, once he had it buried in the first place?'

Luke shrugged.

Emma took the tools back to the shed without saying more. She would have to think about this.

CHAPTER 26

WEDNESDAY, 19TH MAY

EMMA PRESSED THE REMOTE, AND THE TV SCREEN WENT BLANK. For the hundredth time that evening, she flipped her phone open to find no new message from Luke. What on earth was going on? Euan had been discharged that afternoon, and the arrangement was that Luke would drive him home from the clinic, have dinner with his parents and check everything was okay at the flat for them, and tell them as gently as possible about Alan. And come home. But now it was nearly eleven, and still no sign of him.

Emma took her empty mug to the dishwasher. The past couple of days hadn't been easy, with Luke being tight-lipped about the non-appearance of a parcel of Ryan in the garden. It had been all Emma could do not to throttle him, but as he said, she knew as much as he did now, and as they couldn't exactly barge into the clinic and interrogate Euan, there was nothing to be done except wait until he was discharged. Which had happened seven hours ago, so Luke and his parents had had the chance to talk the whole thing through ten times now. And if Marie and Euan had been so upset about Alan that Luke didn't want to leave them, surely he'd have let her know?

There was no further news about Alan's death, either. Emma had gone to the butcher's that afternoon and been served by Mark, who said nothing at all except the bare necessities. How macabre it was, looking at a man who, as a child, had killed a man, assisted by other children. Or another child. Alan. How many villagers went into that shop to buy their meat, knowing that Mark was a killer, knowing what had happened to Ryan James? Was that death the reason behind Mark's morose blankness, or did it have more to do with the fact that the shop was losing money by staying open but he couldn't move away because of the secret of Ryan James?

Luke's key in the door came when Emma was reading in bed, and she put her book down, relief washing through her. He came straight upstairs, exhaustion written all over his face. Pity speared into Emma.

'How did it go? Is Euan okay at home?' She stopped there, though she had a million other questions queued up for answers.

'It was tough. I had to sit with them for ages, then I helped Dad to bed. I'm bushed, Emmy, and I have an early meeting in the morning. We'll talk tomorrow night, huh? There's nothing urgent needs saying.' He vanished into the ensuite.

EMMA JERKED AWAKE the following morning to find Luke tiptoeing from the room, briefcase in hand.

'Sorry, did I wake you? I'm off now. See you tonight.' He stepped over to peck her cheek, and was gone.

Emma pulled on her robe and went downstairs. She'd slept well, in spite of all the angst yesterday evening. Maybe she should go to bed late more often. She made tea and toast and took them through to the coffee table. With any luck, their talk tonight would clear the air enough to show them a way forward, a way to put the past to rest, though she couldn't imagine what that would be. She would spend the day checking her translation; that would fill the time until Luke came home.

Twenty minutes later she closed the laptop again. It wasn't fair, checking something with half her brain disengaged. How were Marie and Euan feeling today? Elated to have the op behind them, and gutted about Alan, and what a state Marie would be in, even though Luke hadn't planned to mention the missing parcel of Ryan yet. A death was enough bad news for one day.

Emma's conscience pricked. She should call them; it wasn't fair to leave Luke to help his parents deal with such big and distressing issues alone. She'd get dressed first, though.

The idea came when she was pulling on her baggiest jeans. Awkward conversations were always ten times worse on the phone – she would go to York and visit Marie and Euan. That way, she'd be right on hand with her support. The bus to Glenfield left in twenty minutes. Emma grabbed her bag.

MARIE CAME TO THE DOOR, her face lighting up when she saw Emma.

'Hello, dear, what a lovely surprise! Come in. Euan, Emma's here to see you!'

Emma's heart sank like a stone. Hell's teeth. Hadn't Luke told his parents about Alan? In two minutes, she was sitting on Marie's sofa with a glass of orange juice in one hand, having refused a share of Euan's footstool. He looked well, and Marie was in her element, rushing around taking care of them both. Emma sipped her juice, uneasiness spreading through her. Had Luke had any kind of conversation with his parents yesterday? And if not – why not? She was going to have to tell them about Alan at the very least, and Marie was going to have kittens. But what else could she do? They had to know, and keeping it from them any longer wasn't really an option, was it? What had Luke been thinking? Emma took a deep breath and started.

She was right about the kittens. Marie burst into tears, rocking back and forwards on her chair, her head buried in her hands. Euan was pale, white-knuckling the crutch propped at the side of his chair.

'What have the police said?' His voice was a whisper.

Emma went to perch on the arm of Marie's chair, rubbing the thin back. 'That it's clearly suicide. There's to be an inquest, but they say it'll be a formality.' She cleared her throat. 'Alan had money worries, his dad said.'

Euan sighed. 'It'll be all right, lass. Don't worry.'

Emma said nothing. That remark was for Marie, and it wasn't about Alan's suicide, was it? They – or Euan at least – must know what had happened to Ryan in the end, because how else could Euan tell his wife it would be all right? But this was where she was going to shut right up and talk to Luke before saying another word about it to his parents. She went to fetch Marie a glass of water.

'I'm sorry to bring such bad news. Alan must have been desperate. It's so sad.'

Marie's teeth chattered on the glass. 'I'm going to choose a nice charity and make a donation in his memory.'

'That's a lovely idea.'

They sat in silence for a moment, then Emma pulled out the prints of the baby she'd made for them, and the talk went on to her plans for giving birth. The colour returned to Euan's cheeks as Marie calmed down, and the conversation became positively upbeat as they discussed all the places they could take the baby to when it was older. Luke had enjoyed coming to York as a child, apparently. It was as if Alan and his untimely death had never been mentioned.

Emma's feeling of unreality deepened when Euan suggested lunch at a restaurant around the corner from the flat, but Marie was nodding away. They set out, Euan looking pretty confident on his crutches.

The restaurant was old-fashioned and dim, with wooden panelling on the walls and mock paraffin lamps on the tables. Emma ordered avocado with bacon on toast, and sat back while the waiter took Marie and Euan's orders. Now for a nice neutral conversation.

She smiled across the table. 'I was talking to Mrs Alderson about her fireplace again. They found no asbestos, so I'm going to get someone in to look at ours next week, if possible. Even if the fireplace is old and battered, it might be salvageable.'

And dear heavens, her parents-in-law were back to white, horrified faces. Marie gripped her arm so hard Emma had to prise the older woman's hand away. What was going on now?

Marie's sibilant whisper hissed across to the nearby tables.

'Emma, leave the fireplace. It's safely covered now. Please, it's not worth the risk. Asbestos is a – a killer, you know.'

People were staring. Emma patted the hand she was still holding. 'Don't worry, Marie. We won't do anything dangerous, I promise.'

'Euan, you must have a word with Luke.' Marie's eyes were wild.

Emma swallowed her indignation. Obviously, Luke had more say than she did about what happened to the fireplace. But she should keep the peace here, get things back to what passed for normal in this family, for as long as they were out in public, anyway.

She forced a smile. 'Yes, that's the best idea. We'll leave it to the men, huh, Marie?' Oma would have killed her for that remark if she'd been here.

The food arrived, and Euan started talking about his new hip and the holiday plans they were making. Emma ate her avocado, nodding in all the right places while her brain whizzed off in a direction of its own. Opening the fireplace was another big no-no, and if Mrs Alderson was right, asbestos had nothing to do with it. Emma's skin crawled, and she pushed her plate away. The parcel of Ryan that wasn't in the garden where Luke thought it was... Could it be that the boarded-up fireplace in her spare room held – a body part? Or an entire body – a skeleton now? But no, there was no reason on earth why Euan would have agreed to anyone hiding a murder victim in his house, and anyway, it would have smelled. None of this was adding up.

The rest of lunch passed peacefully, and Emma went for a stroll around the Minster with Marie, leaving Euan at home to rest his leg. Emma chatted about this and that as they walked, then went back to the flat for coffee. Best not to bring any more awkward subjects up until she'd talked to Luke. Or at least tried to talk to him. What had he thought he was doing, not telling his parents about Alan?

But her mother-in-law had other ideas. When it was time for Emma to go for the train, Marie left Euan in his chair and came right out to the communal hallway with Emma, closing the flat door behind her.

'Emma.'

Marie moved in front of her, barring the way to the front door. Emma recoiled at the terrified eyes just inches from her own, like those of an animal caught in the headlights and seconds from death.

'You must promise, Emma, never, ever to speak about what happened with Alan. About his death, and – back then. Not to the police, not to anyone. If you do, it'll be the end for us. For Euan and me. We'll be the victims. Promise, Emma.'

Wiry fingers were digging into Emma's arm all over again. What was this about? *Was* Ryan James in her spare room? And what *would* happen if a body from twenty years ago was found behind the fireplace? Emma swallowed the nausea.

'Marie, I promise I'd never put you and Euan in any danger. Never.'

The fingers slackened around her arm, and Marie stepped back, her eyes not shifting from Emma's. Then she pushed past without another word, and the flat door clicked shut behind her.

Shaken, Emma started out for the station, trying frantically and unsuccessfully to get her thoughts in some kind of order. Even disregarding the murder aspect, there didn't seem to be any reason why Marie would think that she and Euan would be the victims if it all came out.

It wasn't until she was on the train on her way home again that a couple of possible reasons for Euan hiding Ryan's body whammed into Emma's head. One couldn't be true because Luke would know if he alone had killed the man, and he'd said that hadn't happened. But if Euan thought his son was guilty… Or had Euan somehow been blackmailed into hiding a body? And if so, why?

IT WAS a repetition of last night, except this time, she didn't know where Luke was. Six o'clock came, then seven, and no car slid into the driveway. Emma tried to phone Luke, but her call went unanswered and the message she sent remained unread. Eight o'clock, nine, ten. Nothing. Nausea, anger and fear churned around in Emma's gut, not to mention helplessness – what could she do? She couldn't report him missing already, and calling his parents wasn't an option either. If Luke was holed up in a pub nursing his sorrows and avoiding talking to her, well, damn him to hell. That would be the end for them.

Emma went up to bed, and lay wide awake for several hours before dropping into an uneasy sleep, dozing fitfully until a bird outside woke her at seven. Luke's side of the bed was cold and empty.

CHAPTER 27

LUKE, AGED 12

JANUARY WAS A STUPID MONTH TO GO AWAY FOR A FEW DAYS. Luke sat opposite Mum in the train to York on Wednesday morning, his breath fogging the window beside him and people sneezing their germs all over the place. You'd think Mum would want to keep him safe at home for a bit. Everyone was staring at his face, which now had yellow patches to contrast with the blue and purple. Dad wasn't even going to work today. He had put them on the train at Glenfield, saying, 'Have a good time, you two,' as if this was a normal trip and not getting them out of the way while he dealt with whatever, and it was something to do with Ryan, you could bet on that. Luke wound both arms round his front and leaned his forehead on cold glass.

'Nearly there.' Mum fussed around getting the tickets out and making Luke zip his jacket all the way up. They arrived at the station exit, where Mum immediately bundled him into a taxi.

'Accident and Emergency, please.' Mum sat back in the cab while Luke gawped at her.

'Why are we going there?'

'To have your nose looked at properly. Not another word, Luke. We should have gone right at the start.'

So why hadn't they? Luke stared out of the window as the cab crossed the river. It was because they were being inconspicuous, that was why, and A&E at York Hospital was definitely more anonymous than Doctor McGarry at the surgery in Ralton Bridge. Did Dad know about this, or was Mum doing something off her own bat for a change? Going against the flow, Mum? Ooh, dangerous.

They had to sit for an hour and a half in a smelly waiting room with loads of coughing people, but at least he fitted right in with all the blood and bandages on display there, and everyone was nice to him. At last, they were called into a cubicle, and a nurse came to look at his nose.

Mum leapt into speech, talking too fast and twisting her gloves on her lap.

'It happened on Saturday night, but it didn't look too bad at first. My neighbour's a nurse and she said it wasn't broken, but then we saw all the yellow this morning and I thought we'd better check.'

The nurse was young and pretty, and her hands were light on Luke's face. 'I think you're probably at peak bruising now.'

He relaxed, but then the dreaded question came.

'Tell me exactly how this happened, Luke?'

'I – someone banged into me and some of us fell, and I don't know if I banged my nose on the gym floor or if it was someone's elbow or what.' Most of that was true, apart from the bit about the gym floor, but he had to say that because Mum had already said it too.

The nurse straightened up. 'I think it's fine, but we'll get the doctor to have a look.'

The doctor arrived, and poked about a lot harder than the nurse had, then said he didn't think it was broken but they'd get an X-Ray just to be sure. The queue at X-Ray went all the way down the corridor, and it was all a total waste of time because everyone had been right and nothing was broken. The doctor was sniffy with Mum about waiting so long to get it checked, and she was all pink and bothered as they left. Another taxi took them to the hotel, where Luke had a room of his own instead of a bed in Mum's room.

Mum heaved her weekend bag onto her bed and unzipped it. 'Do you want to have a rest, darling? No? All right, let's go for a stroll round The Shambles before we have lunch, and afterwards there's something I want to show you. I'll come and get you in ten minutes.'

Luke took his rucksack through to his own room. This was actually okay. Better than staying at home, anyway. The picture of bloody Ryan in the woods loomed in his head yet again, and he squashed it back. Schtum. Mum and Dad were taking care of it.

What was Dad doing?

THE SOMETHING MUM wanted to show him turned out to be a school. They took a bus across town, and walked along a leafy street parallel to the river.

'Your dad and I have talked it over a lot since – for the past two days, Luke, and we both feel a change of school would be best for you. Your dad's called the head teacher here, and he's confident they'll have a place for you after Easter. Dad being a teacher helps, of course, even though he doesn't teach here.'

Luke gaped through a high iron fence at the school, a three-storey grey stone building with a patch of grass in front. Mum sounded quite matter-of-fact about it all. Did she know everything, or had Dad fed her a prettied-up version of the truth? A change of school wouldn't undo what had happened.

'Is it a private school?' Going to school with a load of posh kids might be worse than going to school with Mark and having Ryan's ghost in his face all the time.

'Yes, but it's not like Eton, or Harrow. We'll manage. And it's not a boarding school. You can drive here with Dad in the morning, or get the train. We have an interview in three weeks.'

Which would give his nose time to look normal again. Nice one, Mum. Luke nodded slowly. Mum's voice was higher than usual but it was firm, too, and something was telling him he wasn't going to have much of a say in this. But maybe a new school would be okay. Except – would he be able to go to Harry's mum's running club?

They walked past the school, and by the time they were back on the other side of the river and Mum was making noises about afternoon tea, Luke was almost looking forward to his new school. Keeping schtum about what had happened at Ralton Bridge would be easy here, and he'd have different things to think about.

Mum was definitely trying to get him onside about the school, because she let him order two cakes then gave him a goofy grin while they were waiting for the waitress to bring her coffee and his hot choc.

'You're a good boy, Luke.'

Luke barely managed to meet her eyes. Dad definitely hadn't told her everything.

The next day, his nose was hardly hurting at all and Luke was almost back to his usual self – or he would have been if only he could forget he'd ever heard of the gym club. They went to the Viking Centre in the morning, then Mum dragged him round a museum in the afternoon, full of prehistoric vacuum cleaners and stuff she remembered from being a kid on Skye, but it was interesting in a weird way. Luke was sorry to leave York when they went for the four o'clock train.

Dad was waiting in the car outside the station at Glenfield. 'All aboard! You're looking better, lad! And wait until you see your room!'

Mum plonked down in the passenger seat and gave Dad the same sniffy look the A&E doctor had given her. 'We paid a visit to the hospital to make sure his nose isn't broken.'

Dad raised his eyebrows at her. 'Did you now? And what did they say, Luke?'

'Not broken. It'll be fine in a few weeks. They gave me better painkillers.'

'Painkillers and *anti-inflammatories,* Euan.'

'All right, all right. As long as he's okay.'

'They said we should have had it checked immediately.'

Luke almost laughed. Mum was milking this; it was like watching tennis. Better change the subject. He leaned forward in the back seat. 'We saw the school, Dad. Looks great.'

Dad gave him a big grin. 'We'll practise for that interview later on, huh? Don't worry, I know the music teacher there and a couple of the others too. I'm sure we'll get you a place. They're sending the prospectus.'

The rest of the drive home was taken up with Mum telling Dad about the vacuum cleaner museum. Luke went straight in and up to his room and – wow! The hated yellow walls were gone. At least, the walls were still there but they were white now, and the ancient old fireplace on the back wall had been closed off. The paint smelled awful but the effect was actually pretty cool.

Dad had followed him upstairs. 'The white's the base coat. We'll go to the DIY place tomorrow and you can choose your colours, two different ones if you want, and you and I can roller it on. You can sleep in the spare room in the meantime. How's that?'

'Brilliant.' It was, too, so why did he feel like crying?

Luke wandered across the room to the window. You could see for miles and miles across the valley, fields and trees everywhere. It all looked so normal, as if nothing ever happened here. He started to move away, but oh, no. Luke clapped both hands to his mouth, and pain seared through his nose. He stared at the garden below. Part of the vegetable patch was newly dug up, a dark square of fresh earth that contrasted horribly with the winter-neglected look of the rest of the plot. Dad had been digging again, why? As if he didn't know…

Dad cleared his throat and hugged Luke to his chest, jerking him away from the window.

'Come on. Dinner time. Nothing to see down there, is there?'

. . .

THEY STARTED PAINTING Luke's walls the following afternoon. He'd decided on orange for two walls, but he was still thinking about the other two so they didn't buy paint for them yet. Luke rollered the top coat onto the walls. It was called 'Caribbean Sunset', but it really just looked orange. Dad did the tricky bits, and it was more fun than Luke had expected. They covered the floor near the wall with a big dust sheet so drips didn't matter, and Dad put on the radio on the chest of drawers. Luke got to choose what station they listened to, and Dad didn't complain once about loud music. He even allowed Luke up on the ladder to do the bit near the ceiling.

'Looking good, son.'

Dad stepped back to see it better, and Luke pulled the ladder a couple of feet to the left. The two walls were almost done, all except a thin strip beside the door.

'You finish there, then we'll let it dry before doing another coat. I'll see what your mum's up to.'

Dad's feet clattered downstairs. Luke swapped the big roller for the small one to do the bit between the door and the wall, and set to work, rollering from ceiling to floor to avoid having drips running down already-rollered bits. There! Now to–

A muffled exclamation from his mother in the living room had Luke pricking his ears up. He waited until she and Dad were talking again, then crept down half the stairs and sat listening.

'–simply carry on as if everything's normal!'

That was Mum's worst voice, the high shaky one. Luke could picture her wringing her hands as she spoke. Dad was his usual unflappable old-fashioned self.

'It'll pass, Marie. Sensations always do.'

'This isn't a sensation, Euan. A man is dead!'

Luke's breath caught in his throat. Was this the first she'd heard of that part?

'And we have to deal with the consequences. That means carrying on. And keeping our heads down.'

Mum was in floods, and Luke's heart thundered in his chest. Consequences? Heads down?

'It's not the fact that he was killed that terrifies me, Euan. It's *why*.'

Huh? It was obvious why Ryan was killed, and at least he wouldn't be doing the same things to other kids now. Why was it so terrifying now he was dead? Muffled sobs were coming from the living room, and Luke's throat closed. He had done this.

'Marie. It's not the same thing at all. All we have to do is keep a low profile, and believe me, the past won't catch up with us. It doesn't matter.'

Huh? Luke gripped the wooden banister. What past? And what wasn't the same thing?

'It does matter, and a lot of people will think it was exactly the same. It was illegal, Euan. They'd come after us.'

'Which is why we need to keep a low profile and carry on. Come on, love. Luke will be down in a few minutes, and you don't want him to see you so upset. Let's get his lunch on, shall we?'

Luke crept back upstairs and closed the bathroom door loudly. What did all that mean? Had Mum or Dad done something wrong, way back whenever? That was what it sounded like, but they so weren't the kind of people who went around breaking the law. What could possibly have happened that was making Mum so scared now? He would have to find out, somehow. And what did it have to do with Ryan's death?

He thundered downstairs and called from the hallway. 'What's for lunch?'

'Vegetable quiche. Is that okay?'

Mum didn't sound as if anything was different – except she didn't often ask him if the lunch menu was okay.

'Yum.' Now he was the one acting weird, because you didn't get much yukkier than bloody vegetable quiche. Luke went into the kitchen, where Dad was washing lettuce and Mum was laying the table.

And all through lunch it was as if they were actors in a film of their lives, Dad trying to be jokey and jolly and Mum trying to get Luke to eat more salad, and Luke trying to look as if everything was all right. Nothing was said about doing something illegal, and nothing was said about Ryan, either. It was like a – a parody, that was the word. A parody of their normal life.

CHAPTER 28

FRIDAY, 21ST MAY

Fear snaked through Emma as she grabbed her mobile from the bedside table. Late home was one thing, not home at all was quite another. Luke wouldn't scare her like this, so something must have happened. Her fingers were shaking so much she could barely flip the phone case open. No missed calls, no new messages. Shit, shit, shit.

She tapped, and listened as the call rang through to voicemail. 'Luke, I'm worried. Call me as soon as you get this. Please.' She sent a message too, then sat clutching her phone. What did people do when their partner didn't come home? Should she worry Marie and Euan already? The police? Were you supposed to call 999, or go to your local police station? Where was her local police station, actually? And the loneliest feeling in the world: there was no one, no one at all in this awful village that she could turn to for help and advice.

Downstairs, with peppermint tea churning around inside

her, realisation dawned. The stretch of road from York to Glenfield was busy; the road from Glenfield to Ralton Bridge was well travelled. If Luke had been involved in an accident on his way home, she'd have been informed by now. So that meant he was staying away deliberately, unless someone had kidnapped him, which was just so melodramatic she wasn't even going to consider it. Emma sagged over the kitchen table. Someone shoving dog poo through the letter box and trying to knock her off her bike was pretty melodramatic too, wasn't it? But Luke's behaviour over the past week gave her enough reason to think he could be avoiding confrontation and avoiding having to tell her the truth about what had happened to Ryan James, too. The story about those parcels wasn't ringing true, somehow. Who would make a man into parcels? Doug the butcher's face swam in front of her eyes. No, *no*... Get a grip, Emma – find out how to report someone missing.

The internet provided her with terse details. You didn't have to wait twenty-four hours before going to the police, and you could phone or go to a police station. However, you were supposed to ask people who might know the missing person's whereabouts first, and in Luke's case, that meant scaring Marie and Euan into the middle of next week all over again.

Emma drummed her fingers on the table. She could go into Luke's email account; she knew his password. But that was such a breach of trust... On the other hand, what he was doing to her with this entire 'let's move to Ralton Bridge' project wasn't great either. She made fresh tea while she was thinking about it, and yes, she was hoping he'd rush in with an out-of-battery phone, saying, 'Sorry, sorry, I crashed on Mike's sofa and...'

She'd do it. Emma sat down again and negotiated her way

into Luke's email account. Work emails, emails from two or three friends but nothing that helped now; a couple of removal-related ones that Euan had sent on for Luke to deal with. There was nothing you'd call personal here, but that could be a guy thing.

Or maybe Luke kept his personal stuff in a different account. After the disclosures of the past few weeks, anything was possible.

Outside, it was a beautiful sunny day complete with blue skies and the odd powder puff cloud, and Emma swallowed. She wouldn't panic yet. She would walk into the village, go to the library where there were advice leaflets on everything, find out where the nearest police station was, and yes, she could do that online, but... Waiting here at home was doing her head in.

Ralton Bridge was waking up as she walked up the hill. The barman at the Black Bull was outside wiping the tables and chairs there, and he nodded as she passed. Further on, kids were milling around in the two school playgrounds, waiting for the bell to ring, and the shriek of young voices filled the air. Friday, yay. The last school day before the weekend. Tears filled Emma's eyes, and she laid a hand on her tiny bump as she hurried on.

Carol the butcher's wife was in front of the shop, pulling a squeegee on a long pole down the window. She stopped as Emma drew level. 'Morning, love! Oh my – are you–?'

Her eyes widened as she stared at Emma's middle, and Emma snatched her hand away from her bump. What an idiot she was, calling attention to her pregnancy like that.

She nodded. 'Early days.'

A little smile flashed over Carol's face. 'It's a special time, isn't it? Don't worry, I won't spread it around.' Her face returned to her usual sombre folds. 'Terrible about Alan Johnson, wasn't it? That poor girl… Mark was – we were all–' She glanced into the shop, where Mark, behind the counter, was staring out at them.

Emma struggled to find something to say. 'It's dreadful. I'm glad Kate's gone back to Manchester with her mother.' What *had* Mark thought, when he heard about Alan? But it was definitely time to change the subject, and there was something Carol could help her with.

Emma waved a hand at the shop window. 'Do you still chop up cows and pigs on the premises, like in the old days?'

The older woman smiled grimly. 'No, not any more. My father-in-law used to, but that all stopped in the early nineties. It isn't worthwhile for small businesses like ours. The meat comes ready-butchered from Glenfield.'

'So it's still local meat?' Best if Carol thought that was the point behind her question.

'Absolutely. Everything we sell here would have grazed on the fields we see every day. It's a high-quality product. What we need is more customers to appreciate it.'

Carol was still gazing at her, and Emma tried to look businesslike and busy. 'I'm off to the library to gather info about services in the region, you know, Citizens Advice and police and so on. Everything seems so scattered, online.'

'The library's your best bet, love. Or the Post Office in Glenfield.'

Emma thanked her and hurried on without looking to see if Mark was still staring. She checked her phone outside the library in case she'd missed something from Luke, but there was nothing, and the signal here was shaky too. Oh, glory.

A strange woman was at the desk in the library, dealing

with an elderly man, and Emma swung the circular stand of leaflets round. The nearest police station was in Glenfield, who'd have guessed, and it was time to do something more concrete. Emma stuffed a couple of leaflets into her bag and hurried back up the hill, glad that Carol was nowhere to be seen. She would call Luke's friends and see if they knew more than she did about his disappearance, and if she had no joy with that, she'd be on the first bus to Glenfield. Reporting her husband missing was definitely something she'd rather do in person.

'AND HE'S NEVER DONE anything like this before? Any reason he might go off now?' The young police officer at Glenfield Police Station was reassuringly calm, and the tension in Emma's middle eased slightly. She was doing something official now. She'd called eight of Luke's friends before leaving home, saying she needed to get hold of him but he wasn't answering his phone and did they know... No one did, so she called Marie, told her a lie about Luke's phone, and listened to a story about Euan's first mobile that he was never fully in control of. Unless Marie was made of Oscar material, Luke wasn't there either.

Now, with the police officer waiting, she cleared her throat. She couldn't explain Luke's possible reasons for not coming home without revealing what was going on, and she didn't want to do that. Yet.

'Never. We've – he's had some problems recently, family stuff, and a friend died last week. He hasn't been himself, and I'm worried.' Heck, that sounded as if she thought he might be a danger to himself.

'And he's been missing since yesterday, you said. Did he go to work?'

Emma stared. That was a very good question, and one she should have thought of too. 'He left home at the usual time, but – I'll check.' A quick call revealed that Luke had left work at four-thirty yesterday afternoon but hadn't appeared that morning.

Emma relayed this to the officer at the desk, and he nodded, his eyes creasing sympathetically.

'Right, love. Tell you what. I'll take his details, but he hasn't been gone long and from what you say, he could just be wanting some quiet time? Most people aren't really missing, but of course it's worrying for the families no matter what. If he hasn't appeared by, say, six tonight, give me a call and we'll start searching. Now, I'll need a photo, and…'

Emma supplied the necessary details and a photo from her phone, and took the card he slid across the desk. PC Jon Baker, and a mobile number. Good. But how horrible – she'd come to the end of what she could do.

She was in the bus rattling back to Ralton Bridge when an idea sprang into Emma's mind. She could do something – she could open that fireplace.

It was one thing saying she would open the fireplace. Doing it was going to be quite another. Emma stood in the second bedroom, tapping the wall opposite the bed. They hadn't decorated in here yet, so she could crack the fireplace open without having to worry about the wallpaper. But how to go about it? She opened her laptop and tapped 'how to open a fireplace' into the search engine.

Golly, you could learn about everything on the web. *Do your research,* said the first website she went into. Box ticked and thank you, Mrs Alderson. *Break through the plaster.* Right. Tools. That was the first thing. There was a toolbox in the hall cupboard, and the things in the shed. And she'd need dust sheets, too. Emma searched around, then gathered her finds in the second bedroom: an axe and a mallet from the shed, the toolbox, plus a shovel and Euan's old gardening gloves, which were thicker than her own. She fetched the dustsheets they'd inherited from Marie and Euan, and arranged them on the floor in the spare room, then bundled the bed things into the smallest bedroom and shoved the bed as far as possible from the chimney wall. There weren't enough dust sheets to cover the furniture as well as the floor, so she fetched a few sheets from the airing cupboard too.

She was ready. Go, Emma, and fingers crossed Mrs Alderson was right about no asbestos. Hm – the chimney might be dusty and sooty inside, though, so maybe a face mask would be a good idea. They had some with the painting stuff under the stairs.

Preparations complete, Emma tapped around with the mallet, then hefted it and struck the wall, which splintered. Plywood, excellent. An old, dusty smell wafted into the room. Another couple of blows shifted some more wood, and Emma stared at the gaping hole that had appeared in the wall. Wow. Demolition work wasn't as hard as you'd think. She stepped back until the dust settled, then chopped about with the axe before pulling a large section of plywood free. More dust billowed from the chimney, dropping onto the dustsheets as grey and black specks. Emma crept forward to see into the hole.

First of all, there *was* an Edwardian fireplace there. Not as ornate as Mrs A's, but still a handsome piece, if marked and shabby. And in the bottom lay a mess of dirt and debris and – what was that?

Emma leaned into the hole, her heart thudding. As well as soot and dust, a depressing little collection of bird skeletons and a couple of stray half bricks that might have come from the walls of the chimney were all lying in the fireplace. And right at the back lay a ball of dirty, yellowed newspaper, about the size of a football. Emma's breath caught in her throat. Was this the parcel of Ryan? There was one way to find out, but was she ready to do it?

She raked around with the shovel, making yet more dust fly around. Nothing more came to light, and a bucket for all this junk would be a good idea. And a break, while she thought about what to do about that newspaper ball. She dropped the shovel and clattered downstairs.

By the time she came back, after a drink and a check of her phone – nothing – the dust had settled. And no matter what that ball was, she would have to deal with it, either by opening it herself or taking it to someone else – the police? – to open. Emma pulled on her mask and gardening gloves again.

She gave the ball a little push with the shovel. Hard to say how heavy it was. And actually – how many families were involved in this parcel of Ryan cover-up? Five? Six? No way was there one-sixth of an adult man in this parcel. Which meant – what? It meant she was going to open it right now, that was what.

CHAPTER 29

EMMA STRAIGHTENED UP FOR A BREATHER, THEN LEANED RIGHT into the hole in the wall, grasped the ball of newspaper and deposited it swiftly onto the dustsheet, where it rocked and then settled. It wasn't heavy – a couple of kilos, no more. Breathing fast, she crouched beside the parcel, her face hot in the mask and sweat gathering on her brow. The paper – it was an old *Daily Mail*, by the looks of it – was crinkled as if it had been wet at some point, and there was a patch stained darker than the rest. Clumsy in the gardening gloves, Emma lifted the ball again. Surely this couldn't contain bones? She gave it a shake, and something rattled inside. A dried-up kidney? And how macabre that she was even thinking that, because it wouldn't have happened. Would it? There was no saying until she opened this ball, and the sooner she did, the sooner the suspense and the horror of not knowing would be over. She stood up and grabbed the axe.

One good whack had the axe head buried in the newspaper ball, then she held the ball steady with one hand and twisted the axe with the other. What was she going to find in here? If it was a chunk of a man she would be sick; her stomach was heaving at the mere thought. She peered into the ball. And this wasn't a kidney; this had never seen the inside of anyone's skin.

Emma turned the broken ball of newspaper up, pulling the slit she'd made as wide as she could, and shook the contents onto the dust sheet. A stone. It was roughly the size of a tennis ball, the kind of thing you saw all over the place here. She'd removed heaven knows how many of them from the would-be veggie patch just a couple of weeks ago. Bloody hell, why on earth would anyone put a parcel of a stone into a chimney and board it up?

She went to sit on the bed; leaning her hands on her knees to stop them shaking. Was this the 'parcel of Ryan'? If so, someone had tricked Marie and Euan. And Luke. Euan must have hidden the newspaper ball here because he thought part of Ryan's body was inside. And all the time Luke had thought it was buried in the garden, and what Marie had thought was anyone's guess. How horrendously cruel this all was. Emma rubbed her face with her sleeve. How could she find out what really happened to Ryan James?

Slowly, she cleared up the worst of the mess she'd created, shivering as realisation struck anew. None of this was helping her find Luke. And the one person who could help her with that was Euan. She pulled out her phone, startled to see that it was nearly six o'clock. Luke had been missing for over twenty-four hours. Shouldn't the police be looking for the car now, at the very least? She should call that policeman first.

Emma rummaged in her bag for the officer's phone number. It rang several times, then connected.

'Jon Baker.'

'It's Emma Carter in Ralton Bridge. I reported my husband missing earlier today, and there's still no sign of him.'

'Okay...'

A rustling noise came down the phone, then a keyboard clacked. 'Right, love. I'm passing this on now. We've got everything we need – car number, photo and so on. If you think of anything else that's relevant, give me another call, and you're welcome to call again tomorrow to see how the search is going. If we find anything, we'll be in touch.'

Emma flopped back in the sofa, her stomach cramping. The search for Luke was on, and this was where she'd have to tell his parents, because the police would certainly be in touch with them at some point.

Marie's phone rang seven times, and Emma was about to give up when the call connected. They were probably having dinner.

'Sorry to disturb you, Marie, but I think you should know that Luke and I have had a bit of a – a disagreement, and he, well, I don't know where he's gone.'

'Oh, dear – have you tried Tom? I can't talk, Emma – I'm at the clinic with Euan. He slipped in the bathroom this afternoon and the pain in his hip's back. He's in X-Ray now.'

Emma closed her eyes. You couldn't make this up. 'Thanks, Marie. I'll call Tom. Let me know how Euan gets on, huh?'

Marie disconnected before she did, and Emma sat back again. Tom was one of the people she'd tried already. Please, please let the police find Luke – didn't they have ways to find people's cars? She lifted the card with the police officer's number to replace in her bag, then noticed something.

PC Jon Baker. Jon Baker. There was something familiar

about that name... Her stomach rumbled, and she went through to the kitchen. Eat for the baby, Emma.

A plate of soup and a banana later, Emma realised where she'd seen the name Jon Baker, and grabbed her laptop to check. There was the article she'd saved, the one from Luke's schooldays with the photo of the gymnastics team and Ryan James, and yes, Jon Baker was one of the kids. Bloody hell. Was 'her' policeman the same Jon Baker who'd been at school with Luke? And if he was, he might be all too aware of the situation now. Could she really trust him?

SATURDAY MORNING DAWNED after another sleepless night, and Emma dragged herself downstairs. The thought that the baby might be as exhausted as she was horrified her. She scrolled through her phone, but apart from a couple of junk emails, nothing new had come in. Heavy fear settled in her gut, because no message meant that something must have happened to Luke. He wouldn't, he would *not* scare her like this, not all this time, not with a baby on the way. And he wouldn't scare his parents, either. This entire situation had come about because Luke and his parents were trying to protect themselves from the past. But whatever they thought had happened back then couldn't have happened, because the parcel of Ryan – if that was what she'd found in the chimney – wasn't a parcel of a man. Nausea surged in Emma's gut. She had to talk to Euan ASAP.

She hesitated, then tapped to connect to her father-in-law. Marie had texted yesterday evening to say he'd been sent home under strict instructions to rest, but no harm had been done by his fall, thankfully.

He certainly sounded chipper enough. 'Morning, Emma. Have you and that lad of mine made up yet? Marie told me about your argument.'

'Um, not quite. I still don't know where he is. Are you okay, Euan?'

'Fine, fine. Luke'll be with Tom – hang on, Marie wants a word.'

Banging and moving about noises came down the phone, then Marie's voice, rather breathless.

'I'm in the bedroom, Emma. We're not to worry Euan. The doctor said he has to rest. I can't understand why Luke isn't getting in touch, even if his phone is broken. Have you called Tom?'

'I'll call him again today. Marie, I opened that fireplace. No asbestos, just a lot of dead birds and stones. One of them was parcelled up in newspaper.'

The connection broke. Emma shrugged. Heaven knows what the couple would make of the wrapped-up stone, but if they didn't let her know pretty soon, she'd call Euan again. And maybe a second call to Tom wasn't the worst idea. He and Luke had been friends since they were about fifteen.

A brief conversation convinced Emma that Tom genuinely didn't know where Luke was, and she slumped over the kitchen table. It was one dead end after—

A car drew up outside, and she flew to the window, her heart soaring. The car! Luke? But no. No. It was their car, yes, but Jon Baker was in the driver's seat, his face grim.

Emma ran outside. 'Where did—?'

'In the car park at Glenfield Station. We found it early this morning and took it in to be examined. Nothing was found, so here it is.'

What was she supposed to say to that? Now that the glimmer of suspicion had entered her head, it was hard to know if he was trustworthy. His expression was inscrutable, and he was standing there in his police uniform, but – how could she know?

'Oh. But – what about Luke?'

'If he got on a train, he could have been heading anywhere. Look, I know it's hard, but it really is early days.'

Emma frowned. Didn't police officers usually do things in pairs? Why had he come alone? 'Thanks. Can I drop you off anywhere?'

He shook his head, half-turning towards the street, and Emma saw that a police vehicle was sitting there.

'My colleague and I are going on to the Black Bull, to talk to the owner about a disturbance last night.' He pulled a face. 'The barman's my dad. Not sure I'm going to win this interview. Try to stay calm, Mrs Carter.'

Emma watched as the police car pulled away. His dad was the barman? She thought back to the fight between Luke and Alan in the pub, with the barman flapping his towel at them. The barman knew the secret… and he was PC Jon Baker's dad. That did nothing to increase her confidence. Emma walked right round the car, which looked exactly as it always did, and there was nothing unusual inside it, either. Okay – suppose what Jon Baker said was true. Did policemen have spare car keys? Because presumably Luke would take his key with him, but hell, of course the police would be able to start cars. Emma went back inside to think.

She paced up and down in the kitchen, hands clasped in front of her. Something had happened to Luke, and she couldn't be sure the police were helping. Who *could* she trust to help Luke? Well, Marie and Euan, but they were non-starters as far as concrete help went.

An idea slid into her head. Alan's dad. He'd sat on the sofa that awful evening, rocking Kate, comforting her. But oh, was it fair to go and bother him like this when he was grieving for his son? He hadn't wanted her visit last Sunday; he'd made that plain.

But Luke was in danger… Emma searched around for her car key, and ran outside. Thank heavens she was more mobile now.

THE FARMYARD WAS AS DESERTED as it had been a week ago. Was that normal, or was it because the family in here was grieving the loss of a son, never mind what had gone on twenty years ago? Emma pulled up beside a Land Rover parked in front of the grey stone farmhouse, and sat still. Nothing was stirring bar the wind in the trees at the side of the house, and it was hard to know if she was doing the right thing, intruding on the family's grief like this.

Again, it was Keith who came to the door. 'I told you Kate's not here.'

Emma grimaced. Quite possibly, Kate had told him that she blamed Luke's return to Ralton Bridge for Alan's death. Maybe Keith did, too.

'It's you I wanted to see. There's something I need to ask you.'

He came right out, closing the door behind him. 'My wife's asleep on the sofa. What is it?'

Emma folded her arms around her middle. She wasn't alone; Luke's child was here too.

'Luke has disappeared, and I know it has something to do with what happened to Ryan James. Please. I need to know about that.'

The corners of Keith's mouth drooped, and a muscle at the corner of his eye jumped. 'Luke shouldn't have told you.'

'He didn't. I worked it out myself.'

'Too clever by half, you are.'

He could have been talking about anything; she'd never heard such an expressionless voice. Pity pierced through Emma. Alan's dad was grieving, and he'd been grieving for a long time. Grieving the loss of a happy, innocent life for his son. Luke had said that Alan and Mark had both used the knife, so Keith would be part of the pact. What a burden to carry through the years, and now Alan was gone. Oh God. She shouldn't have come here...

Keith glanced at the open window behind him, then stomped across to a fence surrounding a field where a herd of sheep was grazing peacefully in the sunshine.

Emma followed, and they stood side by side, leaning on the fence. The Yorkshire landscape in front of them was timeless and picture perfect, green fields and sheep as far as the eye could see. How unbelievable all this was.

Keith turned sideways to look at her. He pointed to a barn at the other side of the yard. 'The lads used to practise their running in there, back then. Luke was a great one for the running, once he'd got used to it. Every second day he came, that winter, and ran up and down here, doing his intervals and timing himself with Marie's kitchen timer. He was looking forward to running a 5K event. I don't know if he ever did.'

Emma shrugged. 'I'm not sure he did. He hasn't done much running since I've known him.'

Keith glared at her. 'Ryan James was a bastard. My lad was never the same afterwards. We've lost everything, me and Sue.' He leaned forward and gazed into Emma's eyes. 'Alan always said it was down to Luke that things went as far as they did, back then.'

Emma shivered. He was deluding himself. 'That's not true. And did you never think it might be best to bring the abuse out into the open? Tell the police? The boys were victims, not criminals.'

'Aye, they were. But we made sure it would never come out, don't worry.'

'But – *why*?' What was he seeing here that she wasn't, for God's sake? Heat flushed through Emma, then she looked at the farmer. Oh no, he was crying.

'Keith? Why not?'

'Just – go. And don't come back. I wouldn't care if I never saw you or that bastard husband of yours again.' He shook his fist at her, then burst into loud sobs and turned away.

Appalled, Emma pressed clenched fists to her chest. Then she ran for the car, and gunned it down the lane back to the village.

CHAPTER 30

SATURDAY, 22ND MAY

As soon as she was out of sight of the farm, Emma pulled up and leaned back in the driver's seat, bile rising in her throat. She opened the door and spat onto the grass verge. This was going to be with her all the rest of her life. And she still didn't know where Luke was.

Back home, she cleaned her teeth and forced down a cheese sandwich for the baby. Who was there left to turn to? And the other question was – why, when Ryan's death had been completely hushed up, were Marie and Euan so worried about it? There must be something else going on, something only the parents knew about. What had Marie said? 'If you do, it'll be the end for us. For Euan and me.' That needed clearing up.

Euan answered the phone. 'Hello, love. You've missed Marie. She's at the hairdresser's.'

'It doesn't matter. Are you okay?'

'I'm fine. We've put a non-slip mat in the bathroom. Is Luke back? We had a text from him half an hour ago, but he didn't say much.'

What? Emma sat straight in sheer shock. 'What did he say?'

'It was quite short: *Am well, will talk to you soon*. I tried to call him but it went to voicemail. The text put Marie's mind at rest, anyway, so I'm glad he sent it.'

Emma's thoughts were reeling. Why hadn't Luke texted her? But now she knew he was alive. Or someone was using his phone, which was less reassuring, and neither option would help her find him. Couldn't the police locate people's phones? She was back to the question of whether or not Jon Baker was to be trusted.

Emma gripped her mobile. Had Marie told Euan she'd warned Emma off looking into the past? A direct question would be best; Euan was unlikely to go into hysterics like Marie might.

She took a deep breath. 'Euan, is there anything in the past that could harm you and Marie, as a family? Something she said when I was leaving the other day made me wonder. I wouldn't like to say the wrong thing to someone by mistake.'

Silence. Then, 'There was something, but it's nothing to do with Ralton Bridge. Don't worry about it, Emma, but leave our past where it belongs. Happiness is quickly destroyed, and sometimes you don't get it back.'

She was left listening to a dead connection. Nothing was adding up here.

A crunch of gravel on the driveway galvanised her to the front window. A car had pulled up behind theirs, and a stranger, a fair-haired man around her own age and dressed in jeans and a black sweatshirt was standing beside it, staring at the house. Emma hurried to the door as the bell rang.

She opened the door halfway. It was horrible; she didn't trust anyone now. 'Can I help you?'

'Hi. I used to know the people who lived here. I was at school with Luke Carter for a while. Are you—?'

'I'm Emma Carter. Luke's wife.'

He stretched out a hand. 'Noel Thomas. My aunt lives in Ralton Bridge, but we're helping her move to Leeds to be closer to Mum. I've come to shift furniture, basically, and I thought I'd come and see if the Carters were still around. Luke and I were quite friendly for a bit.'

Emma hesitated. Sincerity was streaming out of Noel, and in the normal way she'd have asked him straight in, but... She didn't know this man from Adam, and she couldn't remember Luke ever mentioning a Noel, either. She gaped at him, and his smile faltered.

Oh, for heaven's sake, this was ridiculous. Emma opened the door wider.

'Come in and have a cup of tea. Luke isn't here at the moment, I'm afraid.'

She led the way, and he followed her into the kitchen area. 'This is all quite different to the last time I was in here. Very nice. How are Luke's parents?'

Emma put the kettle on. 'They're in York now.' She chatted about Euan's new hip and the house swap, and Noel told her about his London home – he was a doctor, and he worked in a psychiatric unit for teenagers. He raged for a while about the lack of services that still existed today, no matter how much better people's understanding of mental health was. Emma was glad to let him talk. Eventually he ran down, and gave her a shame-faced grin.

'Sorry. My work is my hobby, as you see. Tell me about Luke – what's he doing these days?'

Emma refilled both their mugs. 'Accountancy. How old were you, when you were friends with Luke?' If he was surprised by the question, he didn't show it.

'About twelve. I was only here for a few months, and Luke went on to a different school halfway through my stay. We still saw each other after that, but not very often, and then Mum and I moved to Leeds.'

So Noel was another of the classmates in Ryan James' time. 'Do you remember Ryan James? The sports trainer?'

He screwed his mouth up. 'Awful guy. He wasn't much of a trainer – I remember how he grabbed Luke in quite the wrong place once. I never went back to the gym club after that. Then later, some of the kids had a go at him and he was more or less hounded out of town, I think. Why do you ask?'

Emma put her mug down. Interesting. Noel had been right there in the same class, and he thought Ryan James had left town alive. Where to start explaining? And how much to say? Emma came to a decision. She had to trust this man, because there was no one else.

'You'll remember Alan Johnson? He never got over what happened back then. He took his own life last week.' A few more sentences, and Noel knew everything. The clothes in the veggie plot, the parcel of Ryan in the chimney, Luke's disappearance, the lot. She finished with her visit to the farm where she'd left Keith in tears, and oh, the relief that Noel was taking her seriously.

He pushed his hair off his forehead. 'Bloody hell. This is unbelievable. I knew something had gone on, back then, but… They covered it up very successfully, didn't they? You poor thing. So now Luke's parents have heard from him, but you haven't?'

Emma nodded, and Noel tapped his fingers on his mug. 'Okay. We need to find Luke, and it sounds like the clue's in the past with Ryan James. Why did no one miss him? I never once thought he was dead, back then, you know. But I'll tell you who might know more – a bloke called Harry Stanfill. He was assistant trainer at the gym club.'

Emma went for her laptop and clicked into the telephone directory for the area. Stanfill wasn't a common name; if Harry was still local, they should be able to find him. And golly, a Harold Stanfill was living in Glenfield. Was it going to be that easy?

Of course not. Emma called the number and found herself talking to Mrs Stanfill, who turned out to be Harry's mum, so Harry and his dad must share their Christian name. Emma told the woman about Alan's death and how Luke had come back to Ralton Bridge, then asked for Harry's phone number.

The other woman was brisk and polite, but she wasn't forthcoming with her son's phone number, and Emma couldn't really blame her.

'Harry lives in Scotland now. I'll let him know you called, and he can call you back.'

'Thank you. It's, um, quite urgent. This is my mobile number, but we have a landline phone too, and we're in the phone book as Luke and Emma Carter.' She ended the call.

Noel nodded at her. 'What more do you think we could do?'

'Other people who've behaved oddly are the butcher and his family, especially Mark, and I don't know about Jon Baker, either.'

Noel frowned. 'Mark was a bit excitable back then, but he

calmed down a lot later. Jon was a nice kid. Let's try to get hold of one of them and get some straight answers.'

Emma opened her mouth to object, then closed it again when her mobile rang. It was a strange number – could it be Harry already?

It was.

'I'm Harry Stanfill, and I guess you're Luke's wife? My mother told me you'd called.'

Emma nodded at Noel and put the phone on speaker while she filled Harry in on Alan's death. 'His dad says it was money worries, but Luke and I are wondering if it had anything to do with, um, with something that happened with Ryan James, way back in the past.'

Harry's shock had the ring of complete authenticity. 'That's terrible. I wasn't aware of anything with Ryan, though. What was it?'

Emma pulled a face at Noel. Better fudge over this for the moment. 'I'm not sure. Do you know—?' She took a deep, shaky breath. 'Do you know what happened to Ryan James? He seems to have disappeared.'

'He went to Canada because someone was ill, and as far as I know he's still there.'

'Did he have family there?'

'I don't know. He grew up in care – I remember him talking about that. His mother died of Aids in the eighties, and I don't think his dad was around either. I suppose it must have been a brother or sister in Canada. He'd split up with his girlfriend a few months before he left, so I suppose there wasn't much to keep him here.'

Girlfriend? Good God. That must have been a smoke-screen. 'What happened about his job at the school?' This was where Harry would have every excuse to think she was the biggest nosy parker ever and bonkers too, but he replied readily enough.

'He was a freelancer, worked as sports trainer in different schools and clubs. Mum took over the club at Glenfield eventually, but Luke went on to a different school. I was sorry he stopped coming. How is he?'

After another chunk of fudging about Luke, Emma disconnected and turned back to Noel. Where did that leave the search for Ryan's body? They were no further forward, but someone had spread the story about going to Canada so cleverly that Ryan's disappearance had never been questioned. That someone was more than likely to be connected to his death, so it must be one of the parents. And oh, how good it felt that she wasn't alone here now.

'This is taking you away from helping your family. Thank you.'

Noel gave her a brief smile. 'No problem. I'd been hoping that Luke would have time for a good catch-up. Okay, let's recap. Ryan James is dead, and he died after that hike in the woods.'

'And Luke said it was murder. Mark had a knife and he and Alan used it, and the others had sticks.'

'And the fathers created a cover-up. We need to talk to the fathers. Let's head back to the farm first, and see if Alan's dad's still around. I remember him as a nice bloke, helpful and jolly, just the kind of dad you'd want.'

Emma stood up. Keith definitely knew something, but he wasn't going to be pleased when she rolled up again. 'I never met him until after Alan's death.'

Noel waved his car key. 'I'll drive, shall I?'

'Give me five.' Emma went upstairs for her things, and returned to find Noel tapping his phone in the hallway.

He thrust it into his pocket, his face grim. 'I'm glad Mum and I didn't stay long in Ralton Bridge, back then.'

Emma settled into the passenger seat, and they drove through the village. The aching fear for Luke was making her feel sick, though it was a huge relief to have someone to share the burden. This new-found feeling of security vanished abruptly when they pulled up outside the butcher's.

'What are we doing here?'

Noel parped the horn, and Emma gasped as Mark ran out of the shop and got into the back seat. The car sped off, and she shrank back in her seat. What was going on? Had she walked into a trap? The sickening realisation that she hadn't told Noel about the car forcing her off her bike thudded into her gut. What if that had been Mark? Mark, who'd taken a knife to a bonfire party and used it on a man?

CHAPTER 31

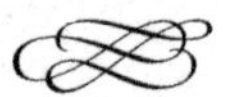

LUKE, AGED 12

THE HEAD JUDGE CAME UP TO THE MICROPHONE, AND SILENCE fell in the hall. This was it, the results of the gymnastics competition beginner categories. Would Alan win a medal? Luke, perched on a bench at the side of the hall, balled his fists. Harry on his right and Jon on his left were holding their breath too, and out on the floor where the teams were sitting, Alan was hanging onto Mark, with Debbie, Harry's mum, beside them, and they were all goggling at the judge like he was a magician about to pull something from his hat.

The judge cleared his throat. 'First of all, the vault results. Bronze medal – Alan Johnson.'

Cheers from the crowd and high fives and back slapping on the floor. Mark was hugging Alan, and Debbie was waving her arms in the air.

Harry bumped his shoulder against Luke. 'He'll be pleased with that.'

Luke settled down again. In the circumstances, Alan probably would be happy, though he'd been hoping for more. Debbie hadn't taken over the gym club until the middle of February, so they'd only had four weeks to practise after Christmas. The silver went to Sid, and gold went to someone from a different gym club, then the hall settled down to listen to the floor event results. Luke held his breath. This was the biggie for Alan.

'Bronze medal – Stuart Carr.'

Cheers and clapping, and Luke shifted to the edge of the bench. Now for silver. If Alan won this it would be great – not as great as gold, but still not the lowest medal.

'Silver medal – Mark Peterson.'

More cheers and clapping, especially in their corner. Mark waved as he went to stand on the podium, and Luke pressed a hand on his churning stomach. Had Alan won the...?

'Gold medal – Alan Johnson.'

Luke was on his feet with the others, yelling and high-fiving and almost crying as Alan ran up to stand on the highest podium, looking all hot and bothered. Debbie was one huge grin, and Keith and Sue on the other side of the hall looked like they'd won the lottery. Keith was mopping his eyes.

The hall settled down to listen to the other results, and Luke slung an arm round Alan when he came to sit beside him, two medals dangling round his neck. This was brilliant – this was how it should always have been, but, oh, God. Luke's stomach sank like a stone as that picture of Ryan on the ground in the woods slid into his head, like it did ten times a day at least. Would that ever stop? Nobody mentioned it now. Everything had gone back to normal, and Ryan's name was never mentioned. Not at school, not in the gym club, not at home. Especially not at home. Mum and Dad had probably only let him go back to the gym club because it was more inconspicuous than him not going. They always put on special happy bright voices to talk about it – and that itself was enough to trigger the thought of Ryan bleeding on the ground.

The news arrived back in Ralton Bridge before they did. A crowd of kids and parents were standing along the main street as the little cavalcade of cars returned from Glenfield. Someone had made a 'Congratulations Alan, Mark and Sid' banner on a long piece of cardboard, and Mark's dad's shop had a stand with free hot dogs on the pavement outside the shop. Luke got out of Keith's car with Alan, and they mingled around in the crowd of villagers. Luke didn't expect Mum and Dad to be here, and they weren't – they never came to things like this. The loneliest feeling in the world zipped into Luke's stomach, then out again. He bit into his hot dog, standing beside Alan as everyone came to poke at the gold medal. It wasn't really gold, of course, but it was still a totally cool thing to have. How great would it be if he got one for running, someday? Mum and Dad would have to come to that, wouldn't they?

'All sorted, eh, and all worthwhile.' Keith ruffled Alan's hair. 'I'm proud of you, son.'

Others were saying the same kind of thing, and Alan was grinning like a weirdo every time someone congratulated him. Luke stuck his hands into his pockets; he didn't have his gloves, and the Yorkshire spring sunshine was chilly. Gradually, people started wandering away, and Mark's dad came over to speak to Keith.

'Let's get all the families together, round the back of the

shop. Are we all here?' He stared round the thinning crowd. 'The Carters. I'll go for them. Back in five minutes.'

He winked at Luke, and Luke cringed. What was this about? As if he didn't know... And how ironic that Mum and Dad were so keen on being inconspicuous – ha! That had backfired nicely today, hadn't it? Having to be specially fetched for whatever Mark's dad was going to do. Luke rolled his eyes. He still didn't know what was prompting Mum and Dad's wish to remain unnoticed everywhere they went, but he'd find out one day.

Keith started shepherding people through to the yard behind the butcher's shop, and Luke kept close to Alan, Jon and Sid at one side. They were all here, all the boys who'd been on that awful run in the woods, and all their parents except – but here they were. Mark's dad came out clutching a bottle of whisky and a bottle of something else, followed by Mark's mum with a tray of glasses, and then Mum and Dad. Mum's cheeks were fiery red, and Dad just nodded brusquely and stood to the side next to Sid's dad.

'Mark, get cokes for the boys, love.'

Mark's mum started handing round glasses, and his dad filled them. The other bottle held sherry. Luke clutched the can of coke Mark chucked at him. What was coming now?

Mark's dad stood in the middle and raised his glass. 'Friends. Boys. We've had a difficult time here in Ralton Bridge. We all know what happened, but we've kept it to ourselves and we've put it behind us. And that's the way it has to stay – with us alone. To protect our boys. Today, with the lads happy again and successful, it's more important than ever that we keep our pact. Silence. Or, as the boys say, schtum. Let's stand together and raise a glass to the pact. To silence.'

He lifted his whisky in the air, and everyone else raised their drink too. Luke held his can high, showing Mum and Dad that he was a part of this, no matter what they thought of it. He glanced at them out of the corner of his eye. Dad was holding his whisky up, a stern, determined look on his face. Mum was still pink, but her glass was high too. Good. There was a moment's pause when no one said anything, then Mark's dad knocked back his whisky, and everyone else drank too. No one said cheers, or anything, but a round of hand-shaking started, and Luke found himself being hugged and back-slapped. And wonders would never cease, Mum and Dad were joining in.

Five minutes later they were all on the way home. Dad put his arm round Luke as they walked down the hill, and he was walking between Mum and Dad for the first time in oh, ages.

'Reckon that was a good thing he did, Doug Peterson.' Dad let go of Luke as they went up the path to the front door.

'Yes.' Mum fished for the key. 'I'm glad it's been – formalised. A pact of silence is exactly what we needed.'

They trooped in, and Mum and Dad went through to the kitchen. Dad's voice was low, but Luke, unpicking a knot in his shoe laces in the hall, heard every word.

'We know how to do it, lass, don't we? We've had our own pact of silence for years. We'll keep this one too.'

Luke scowled. This would be something to do with them staying inconspicuous. It was probably something stupid that only people like Mum and Dad would care about it, but look at how it had affected him too. Dad hadn't been there for him when he'd needed him most, that night. He would have to find out what this other pact was.

. . .

THE PROSPECTUS FOR ST. Stephen's High School had arrived ages ago, but Luke still pored over it nearly every day. Their interview had gone like clockwork, and he was to start in April after the holidays. It was great in one way, but... Sid and Mark and all the other kids weren't sitting at home looking at prospectuses and planning to change schools, were they? It didn't seem fair that he had to be the one to move. Did Mum and Dad think he was to blame for what happened to Ryan? Or maybe they thought they'd somehow be less conspicuous with Luke at school in York, well away from nasty memories and people who knew what had happened.

His chance to have a look through Mum and Dad's papers and stuff for clues about their other pact came the following Sunday, when Mum and Dad set off for church. There was a special springtime service on, and Mum wanted to go. She tried on Saturday night to get Luke to go too, but fortunately Dad had backed him up.

'The lad's a teenager – almost. He needs his kip at the weekends, don't you, son? And I'm sure he wouldn't enjoy coffee and cake with the Woman's Guild after the service.'

Luke made sure he stayed in bed until Mum and Dad had left on Sunday morning, but the moment the front door closed behind them he was up, peeking through the curtains as his parents headed off along the road. Now he had two hours or so to poke around in Mum and Dad's stuff, and hopefully it would be worth it. He could watch a whole load of telly in that time. Sunday morning was good for cartoons and other programmes Mum would turn up her nose at. But then, he might find something that would tell him what they were always so odd about, and if he was lucky, he'd still have time for some telly.

Mum and Dad's old papers and stuff were in a box at the back of the kitchen dresser – that was going to be the most likely place to find anything. Luke transferred a shedload of old plates and bowls to the floor beside the dresser and pulled the box out. It was surprisingly heavy, and he opened it wondering what was actually in here, but it was all papers. He settled down on the floor for a rummage.

Boring, boring and boring. Piles of papers about the house and all the work they'd had done here since time began, then papers from Mum's old job in Glasgow and from the time she'd worked in the stationery shop here in Ralton Bridge, before it closed. Nowadays she only did some typing stuff here at home, and even that was getting less and less because they didn't even have a computer. According to Mum and Dad, computers were as bad as... The picture of Ryan in the woods slid into his head again. Luke took a deep breath.

Underneath the papers about Mum's job was a mountain of stuff from Dad's job, and more tax papers and insurance certificates and so on. There was nothing here, unless all those accountancy papers were hiding something. But Dad wasn't the kind of person to cook the books; he wouldn't have the nerve. Luke lifted the last of the paperwork out, and found another box, a smaller one, in the bottom of the large one.

He eased it out and opened it. School stuff from centuries ago, and it was all Mum's. Her report card from primary school, yikes. Luke flicked through it, but she'd been boringly good at most things. The photos were more interesting, old snaps where the colour had gone funny. He turned the first one over; the date was smudged but it had been taken in Skye in nineteen-seventy something, yikes. They really had crap gear in those days – look at this one. Mum on the beach wearing shorts like dungarees with a bib at the front, and long green socks with trainers and her hair in two tails on either side of her head. And was this one Dad? Yes, it was, and he was standing on the same beach. It looked like he'd taken her photo and she'd taken his. Dad's clothes were more normal – blue jeans and a black T-shirt, so he'd been boring even when he was young. He'd had a lot more hair then, though.

Luke pulled out the rest of the photos and flipped through them. They were all Mum or Dad, with just two snaps of them together. He put them to the side and lifted a couple of post-cards – nothing interesting here either. The only other thing in the box was an envelope holding something soft.

He tipped the envelope up and two yellow blobs fell onto the table. A pair of baby bootees, but they weren't very nice; one had a holey bit in the toe. Had these been his? Poor him if they had. A little card was in with the bootees, with a picture of Mary and the baby Jesus on the front, both with halos and looking sorrowful with a large wooden cross behind them. Luke turned the card over, and there in Mum's handwriting were three words: *For my baby xxx* Yuck, how soppy.

Luke sat back, gaping at the piles of paperwork spread over the floor. Nothing here was obviously illegal, and nothing was connected to Ryan. He replaced everything, and returned the box to the dresser cupboard. What a waste of time, and he hadn't even had breakfast.

He smeared peanut butter on a piece of bread and took it through to the living room, but... he gaped at the television. He didn't want to watch telly now. Before, he'd have gone for a run this morning, but he hadn't run outside since – that time. A run would do him good, though, and he should get back into practice for the running club at the new school. He could go along the main road and then back across country; that way he wouldn't be anywhere near – don't think about it don't think don't think, just go, stupid.

He ran upstairs for his outdoor running shoes, unused since that night because he had the indoor ones for the gym club. Debbie wasn't going to start outside running until after the April holidays when the weather was better. He'd be gone by then. Luke scrabbled in the bottom of his wardrobe where he'd shoved the shoes and – bummer and shit. Squashed into the back corner of the wardrobe under all his junk were his blue tracksuit and yellow T-shirt, the things he'd been wearing that night, and they were all stiff with blood. He'd forgotten about them, and Mum must have too. He should get rid of them. But how? He couldn't exactly stick them in the bin. He stuffed the clothes into a plastic bag and stumbled downstairs. The garden. He would bury them, quick, quick. He'd just have time before Mum and Dad arrived back. Least said, soonest mended, as Mum would say.

Luke grabbed a spade from the shed and ran back to the vegetable plot. This was foul. Should he dig in the softer ground where Dad had been digging, getting the ground ready for the broad beans he wanted to try this year, and risk finding the parcel of Ryan? Don't think, don't think. Or dig somewhere else, which would be more difficult and more conspicuous? He stuck the spade into the earth Dad had already dug over, going deeper than the broad beans would need and working right at the edge of the vegetable plot. Dig, Luke, dig and hope. How could Dad even think about planting broad beans anywhere near that bloody parcel of—? Don't think don't think, just do this, Luke. Thankfully, he managed a nice deep hole without seeing a trace of – *it*. Luke stuffed the bag of clothes into the hole and covered it over, then raked the ground out carefully so that no one would notice. Sorted. Pity about the tracksuit, but if Mum asked, he'd tell her he left it at school that evening and someone had chucked it out. He still had the grey one, thankfully.

He cleaned off the spade and put it away, then went back to the house. Good job he hadn't showered this morning, or he'd be doing it again now. Okay, he had about ten more minutes before they got back. Luke checked the kitchen was tidy, and ran up to the bathroom. He was standing with water cascading down his back and tears dripping from his chin when he heard Mum's voice on the stairs.

'Come down when you're ready, Luke, love. We've brought you some cake!'

Luke towelled off, pulled on fresh clothes and went downstairs, smiling carefully. More acting. Would this ever be over? Or would Ryan still be haunting him when he was old like Mum and Dad?

CHAPTER 32

SATURDAY, 22ND MAY

EMMA'S MOUTH HAD GONE DRY – WHAT THE HELL WAS NOEL playing at? He said nothing more, driving steadily towards the farm, with Mark equally silent on the back seat.

Emma grasped her courage before it flew out of the window. 'Noel? Why is Mark here?'

Noel's face was grim. 'If what's going on now has its roots in the past, we need someone who was in the middle of it back then. Mark knows exactly what went on. We don't. Don't worry, Emma.'

But she was worried… of all the people in Ralton Bridge, he'd chosen a killer to help them. Heck. She'd taken Noel at face value – he was a doctor, for heaven's sake. Emma put a hand on her bump. You're okay, baby. We'll be okay. They were going to Keith; hopefully he would be a bit more forthcoming with the men than he'd been with her. And whatever had happened back then, Keith had tried to sort it.

The farmyard was deserted, with the Landrover gone from its parking space. Did no one work here any more? They had livestock, even if most of them were sheep, which possibly didn't need as much looking after as cows. Emma and the two men got out, and Mark strode to the door of the farmhouse and rang the bell. Silence. He hammered with one fist while Emma stood with Noel behind him.

Again, no one answered. Mark banged again, then tried the door. It opened, and he stuck his head in.

'Keith? Sue? It's Mark Peterson. Are you there?' He stood listening, then turned back to Emma and Noel, shaking his head. 'Seems to be empty. You two have a look inside – I'll search round the barn and stables.'

Emma followed Noel into the farmhouse kitchen, a big, homey room made less welcoming by a thin layer of dust over everything. She shivered. Why had Mark suddenly taken charge?

Noel headed for the dark passage leading out of the other end of the kitchen, and Emma followed. The living room behind the kitchen was cold and gave her the feeling it had been a long, long time since anyone had sat here enjoying a drink or a game of cards.

Noel shrugged. 'We'd better check upstairs.'

'Huh? Do you think Keith's hiding? Why would he...?' It was all too puzzling to work out. Emma tried again. 'Are you sure you can trust Mark?'

'Yes.' Noel turned to meet her eyes. 'He looked me up a year or two back when he was on holiday in London, and we've stayed in touch. I didn't know about his role in Ryan's death, but's a long time since he was that kid, Emma, and we don't know exactly what happened to him back then, anyway.

Everyone deserves a second chance. He told me Luke isn't at the butcher's place, and I believe him.'

Okay, but— A dull thud in the room above interrupted Emma's thoughts.

'Someone's up there.' Noel spoke softly. 'I'll have a look. You stay here.' He ran upstairs.

Emma started back to the kitchen, and thank goodness, a car was drawing up outside. That would be Keith. They might find out what was going on now.

'Keith!' Emma hurried back up the passage, then jerked to a halt as a roar filled the air and the farmer charged across the kitchen, then stopped in the doorway. His face was red and his eyes… Emma backed away. This was what someone looked like who'd gone mad with grief.

'Get out of my house!'

Emma stretched out a hand. They had to find a way to help each other. 'Keith, we need to talk.'

And oh, my God, no… Keith grabbed a stout walking stick from a stand by the kitchen door and charged towards her, brandishing it as spit flew from his mouth. Emma leapt backwards, almost falling over a small table in the narrow passage.

The farmer's face was savage. 'Talk! It's not words I need.'

Emma ducked under his left arm and sashayed into the kitchen, shoving a wooden chair in Keith's path. Not looking to see what he was doing, she fled outside. Mark was nowhere to be seen, and she sped across the muddy yard to the barn opposite, a loud crash and a howl from Keith in her ears. He'd fallen over the chair, good.

'In here, quick!' Mark was running towards her now. He grabbed Emma's hand and pulled her into the barn and behind a pile of hay bales to one side of the door. Emma crouched behind him, fighting to catch her breath.

The barn door crashed open, and she peeked round the hay bale to see Keith standing there, the stick in one hand and the other balled in a fist.

'Think you're smart, missy? You'll soon see.' He vanished into the yard, slamming the doors shut behind him. The sound of a chain rattling came, then silence. And then the roar of the Landrover.

Emma straightened up. It was like something out of a film. They'd been locked in here; what the hell did Keith think he was doing?

Mark went to try the door. It didn't budge. 'Don't worry, we'll get out.'

He marched to the other end of the barn, where a small window at chest height was letting in a few rays of sunshine. In less than a minute, he had the window open and was climbing through to jump to the ground below.

'Think you'll manage?'

Emma dragged a nearby crate to the window, and stepped up. She sat on the windowledge and swung her legs round like Mark had done, and he grabbed her arms, half-supporting her down to ground level. Emma heaved a shaky sigh. Made it.

Mark pulled her round the barn. 'Keith's lost it – he'll be back, though, and we don't know what he's gone to fetch. Let's find Noel and get out of here.'

Emma couldn't have agreed more, then she remembered the thud from upstairs. 'There's someone else in the farmhouse too.' Logically, that would be Keith's wife. Or – now that she'd seen the state the farmer was in, it was only too easy to think that the other person could be Luke. Locked in a room. Nausea rolled round Emma's gut.

There was no sound at all in the farmhouse kitchen, and dread followed the nausea through Emma's middle. What had happened to Noel? But Keith had followed her straight out, hadn't he? He hadn't had time to harm anyone.

Mark yelled. 'Noel!'

Feet pattered downstairs, then Noel appeared. 'Has he gone? We need to get him help. But there are two locked doors up there and I think we should check what's behind them first. Quick!'

The two men thundered upstairs, Emma running after them. Two locked doors… what did that mean? What – or who – had made the thud she'd heard?

Mark put a broad shoulder to the first door Noel indicated. A couple of good thumps with his body weight had the door frame split and the door wide open. Both men rushed in, then Mark wheeled round, retching.

He pushed Emma further down the landing. 'Don't go in. It's Sue. She's gone.' He leaned on the wall, breathing heavily.

Emma hesitated. 'Noel? Do you need help?' No way did she want to see another body, but oh, that poor woman.

Noel came back, his face set. 'She's been dead for a couple of hours. The key's on the inside of the door. Looks like she locked it then took something.'

Emma clapped her hands over her mouth. How alone Sue must have felt, after Alan's death. Had she taken her own life because she was unable to go on without her son? Or because her husband had gone mad with the grief of it all, having to keep that terrible secret all those years and still losing Alan? Emma's thoughts whirled. Ryan James had abused Alan and

Mark... and they had 'used the knife' in the woods... Now Alan was dead... Mental illness wasn't a scientific thing – different people had different personalities and everyone reacted differently under stress, didn't they? Who could say what had driven Sue to death? And *where was Luke?*

Noel shook Mark's shoulder. 'Get a grip, man. We have to open that other door.' He indicated the first door on the landing.

Emma's legs gave way, and she sank down, the dim landing swirling around her. No, no, no... Suppose Luke was here, behind that door. Suppose he'd been given 'something' too. But – that sound she'd heard, not half an hour ago – if the farmer's wife had been dead for a couple of hours, she hadn't made that thud.

Emma watched as Mark gave the second door the same treatment as the first. It took him four goes this time, then Noel rushed into the room.

'Emma! Come here – it's Luke. He's unconscious.'

Emma staggered across the landing. Luke was lying half on, half off a single bed in a tiny box room, his face waxy pale, but he was breathing, he was breathing. Noel bent over him, feeling Luke's pulse and pushing his eyelids up to see his eyes.

'He's been given some kind of sedative. Let's get him out of here before Keith comes back.' He pulled Luke into a semi-upright position, and he and Mark dragged the unconscious man to his feet. Emma's heart plummeted. Luke was making no effort to stand; his head lolled against Noel's neck as the two men manhandled him out of the room.

They had reached the bottom of the stairs when car noises outside filled Emma with horror. Mark slid out from under

Luke's arm. 'Emma, you help Noel get him out. I'll deal with Keith.'

Emma put her shoulder under Luke's, supporting his weight with Noel. Mark waved them into the living room. 'Stay quiet till I get Keith upstairs!' He ran back up and started banging and thumping around the landing.

Emma held her breath as Keith's heavy footsteps thundered along the hall and up the stairs, then she and Noel dragged the unconscious Luke out through the kitchen. Three petrol cannisters were sitting on the table, and a sharp, pungent smell was filling the room.

'Outside, quick.' Noel did most of the work, dragging Luke past Keith's Landrover parked outside the kitchen door. He opened the back door of his car, and together they bundled Luke inside.

Emma got in too, and slapped Luke's cheeks. 'Luke! Wake up!' He grunted.

'I'll go back and help Mark. Get in behind the wheel, Emma – if we're not out in five minutes, take Luke to a doctor.' Noel ran to the kitchen door and vanished inside.

Emma belted Luke in, then took her place in the driver's seat and touched the key in the ignition. Should she reverse round, to let them drive off more speedily? A quick getaway – how completely macabre that sounded, like a scene in one of those action films she never watched. Now she was in the middle of one. She started the engine and reversed Noel's car in a wide arc, finishing up with the car pointing towards the lane leading to the main road, and – oh my God. Now she saw it… Parked to the side of one of the outbuildings was a silvery-grey car. Keith's? Sue's? Had this been the car that had rammed her as she freewheeled down Brook Lane that day? Sick at heart, Emma turned her attention to Luke. He was silent, slumped in the seat with his eyes closed, but he was breathing okay.

Two minutes. Three, and no sign of life from the farmhouse. Come on, come *on*. Emma's breath was coming in short pants now. There was a lot of petrol in there; if anything exploded it could take the car up with it. She released the handbrake and they slid a few metres down the sloping yard.

Four minutes. She should go. Luke needed help. The kitchen door crashed open and Mark and Noel tore out and into the car, bringing a strong smell of petrol with them.

Mark slammed the passenger seat door shut. 'He's sloshing petrol around in there. Quick!'

Emma turned the key in the ignition, and they shot down the lane.

CHAPTER 33

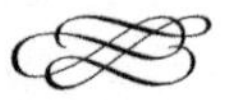

EMMA FIXED HER EYES ON THE ROAD, CONCENTRATING ON getting away as fast as she could. Not an easy task while Noel in the back was slapping Luke's cheeks as he tried to bring him round, the sound cracking through the car. Luke was grunting and groaning now – did that mean he was conscious?

'Stop, Emma! He's going to be sick.'

Emma slammed on the brakes, and they pulled up at the side of the lane. Noel opened Luke's door and supported him while he vomited on the grass at the side of the road. Emma hurried round the back of the car to help Noel, and oh, thank God, Luke's eyes were open.

She fumbled for her phone. 'Shall I call an ambulance?'

Mark had taken her place behind the wheel. 'No – we need to get back to the village first. I'll drive now.'

Emma didn't argue. She put a hand across Luke's shoulders, hugging him as tightly as she could, but a yell from Mark had her scrambling into the passenger seat.

'Get in the car! Keith's coming after us!'

Noel shoved Luke back in the rear seat and fell in after him as the car jerked forward again. Emma twisted round to see the Landrover speeding up behind them and oh no, no. Keith's face behind the wheel… murderous didn't come into it. Yorkshire countryside swam before Emma's eyes. Ryan James had done this; the pact of silence had done this. The Landrover was ramming them now, they were jerking around and swerving from side to side; she needed both hands to hold on. Mark was swearing and Luke was groaning and – another bang from behind and the car kangarooed to a halt, its front bumper jammed against a fence post. The engine cut out.

Keith stopped the Landrover beside them and stumbled onto the lane. Emma stared at the farmer, who had his stick in one hand and a gun, a pistol of some kind, in the other. Hot, shocking anger rose inside her and she forced her legs into action. They had to stop this. It wasn't only her and the three men in the car with her. Her child was here too. She had to save her child.

Moving slowly, Emma got out of the car, twisting away from Mark as he reached out to stop her. She walked up to the older man, hands spread out at her sides. 'Keith. We can't go on like this.'

His eyes were blank now, and she put a hand on his arm. Keith shook it off, then pointed his pistol at Luke in the back seat.

'It was all his fault.'

Emma met Noel's eyes, and he shook his head slightly, getting out of the car to stand a few yards away from her. She shouldn't argue with Keith. 'Keep him talking' – that was the usual advice in bad situations, wasn't it? At least Keith was still, now, though the expression on his face was ferocious.

She tried again. 'It was a long time ago, Keith.'

He turned bloodshot eyes back to her. 'Aye, it started a long time ago. But we had it sorted. Then—' He sniffed loudly. 'Then *he* came back, and now I've had to bury my lad.' Malevolent was a good word to describe his gaze as he looked at Luke now.

Emma shivered, covering her bump with one hand. Imagine burying your child; it was the worst thing any parent would ever go through. Except maybe knowing that your child had been vilely abused. She glanced back to the car. Mark was motionless in the driver's seat. He wasn't going to be any help here.

She took a deep breath. 'Keith – what Ryan James did was criminal. He – he deserved what happened.' Some people would argue with that, but Keith was nodding, his lips a thin slash across his face.

Emma went on. 'Why don't we get it sorted properly now, Keith? It won't bring Alan back, but if the police knew what happened they could…' She blinked at the farmer.

Keith's face had gone even redder, and his mouth was working again. 'The *police* – have you any idea what would happen if they knew even part of what went on here?'

He flung the stick to the ground and wiped his face on his shirt sleeve. Emma didn't speak – what could she reply to that?

Keith spat on the ground. 'Why do you think we covered it up? Huh, Miss Clever? Because telling the police back then would have been like unleashing an atomic bomb on our lads. We'd have been knocked over in the rush of the media with their cameras and their TV vans, all looking for the best sick story. We'd have been swamped by reporters and flash photography. We'd have been the village of the paedo monster and the child killers, we'd have been on the telly. And that's what will happen if you tell the police today. We'll all be able to sell our stories and our souls to the gutter press and we can open tea shops for the gutter tourists. Tell who you like, missy. It won't hurt my boy now. But if you do tell, everyone who passes by will know the evil that happened here. Worse than – than Lockerbie. Than Dunblane. Do you want that? No. If you don't keep the pact, you'll destroy an entire village.'

He swung round, climbed back into the Landrover and pulled it into a U-turn back towards the farm. Emma's legs were shaking now, and she sat down on the road, appalled. He was right, yet he was so wrong, too. But what could you do for someone whose life had been shattered?

Noel crouched beside her. 'Well done. We need to get him help, though. I'll call for emergency psychiatric assistance.' He straightened up and walked a few steps away, his phone pressed to his ear.

Emma trailed back to the car, and got in beside Luke. He was slumped in his seat, breathing heavily, his eyes closed, but he gripped her hand when she touched it.

Mark turned round, his face wretched. 'God knows what he's been going through all those years.'

Emma nodded. Did Keith even know his wife was dead? Losing Alan on top of the horrors resurfacing from the past, and then having her husband go mad enough to drug Luke and lock him up might well have pushed Sue over the edge. Now Keith was in the same state.

Noel spoke on the phone for several minutes, then came back to the car. 'They're sending – oh my God!'

One look, and Emma clapped both hands to her face. You couldn't see the farm buildings from here. What you could see was a ball of black smoke billowing skywards. By the look of things, help would arrive too late.

Mark pulled out his phone. 'I'm calling Jon. The police have to come to the right conclusion.'

Emma sat limply beside Luke as they drove back down to Ralton Bridge. Was the suffering never going to end?

BACK HOME, Luke allowed Noel to examine him, but refused point blank to go to A&E.

'I'll be okay. Just feeling a bit washed out. He must have put something in the water he gave me.' He leaned back in the sofa.

Emma sat down on the armchair, where she could see his face better. 'Luke – how did you get there? What happened?'

He pulled a face. 'I drove there on the way home from work on Thursday. I wanted to talk to him – Keith – see if we couldn't sort something out. He went to bits, though, bashed me with something and locked me in Alan's old room. I think he was afraid we'd report everything that happened back then, and Alan's name would be vilified.'

Emma felt sick. 'So – was it Alan who killed Ryan James? I thought—' She blinked at Mark in the other armchair.

He stirred, his face white. 'It was my fault. I'd taken one of Dad's butcher knives. And I started it. He was such a bugger, Ryan, you don't know what he did…' He swallowed. 'After – you know – they took Ryan back to the shop and my dad and Keith had a look at him. Dad said he had two deep stab wounds to his chest, and they'd be what killed him. I didn't stab his chest, though, I was aiming at – at a different part of his anatomy. Alan grabbed the knife from me.'

Silence fell in the room. Emma sat thinking sad, angry

thoughts about the little group of boys whose lives were never the same again. Nothing would change that. And now Alan and Sue were dead, and only God knew if Keith was still alive. She glanced at Mark, and he shook his head.

'We were kids, and we were all half-crazy, that night. I hated him so much. He knew I didn't have much – the shop was struggling even then, and I didn't really get pocket money. I felt horrible about it – it was great to have the cash, but Christ, what he did…'

He sniffed loudly, and Emma passed him a tissue, anger flooding through her. He'd been as much a child back then as Luke had.

Noel and Mark left soon afterwards to go to the police station and see what Jon had to say. Emma watched as Noel's car drove off. If Mark had his way, yet again the past wouldn't be mentioned, only Keith's grief at Alan's suicide due to 'money worries'. How achingly sad it all was.

Luke pulled himself upright and leaned towards her. 'Emma. I'm sorry. Are we going to be all right?'

Emma shook her head, then shrugged. Was 'sorry' enough? He hadn't trusted her. He'd lied to her. He'd put her life – and her baby's – in danger to keep a pact of silence made twenty years ago. The pact had been more important to Luke than his wife and child, and now that she didn't have to worry about him, that was all she could think about.

'Why did you text Euan and not me?'

His eyes widened. 'I did – at least, I tried to. The signal's crap up there. I guess you didn't get it.'

Emma thumped the arm of the sofa. 'Why did we stay here, Luke? Oh, I get now why we came. You wanted to keep the parcel of Ryan safe. But why, when you saw what was happening, didn't we leave immediately? You knew what happened back then. I didn't.'

'Don't you understand? We can't sell this place, none of us can. If even one of those parcels of Ryan is found, that would be it. It would all come out. We all had a hand in stabbing at him, you know – the rest of us had sticks, sticks with pointed ends we were supposed to sizzle sausages on.' His voice rose hysterically.

Emma shook her head. Now she was the one who knew more. 'I'm pretty sure there were no parcels of Ryan. I opened the chimney and found a parcel with a stone in it. It was just a story to buy everyone's silence.'

'Christ. So where is he?'

'I don't know, and I don't care, Luke. I suppose the butcher got rid of him somehow, so he's the one you should talk to. I guess none of the other fathers knew, except maybe Keith. And by the way, your dad had a fall and bashed his hip, and he and your mum both warned me to say nothing to anyone about anything.'

'Bloody hell. I'll call them in a bit. Emma – we have to be all right. The baby…'

Emma motioned him to stop, then went through to the kitchen to make tea. She had reported Luke missing. If she went along with this cover-up, she would have to lie to the police at some point. Was that what she wanted?

CHAPTER 34

SUNDAY, 23RD MAY

IT WAS THE FOLLOWING MORNING BEFORE THEY LEARNED WHAT had happened at the farm. Emma took her laptop and settled into an armchair after breakfast, supposedly to check though her translation but really to attempt the impossible and get her thoughts clear about what to do with the wreckage of her relationship. Luke was pale, slumped in the sofa catching up with messages on his phone, but he said he felt better and there was no reason to disbelieve that.

The landline phone rang beside the sofa, and Luke reached for it. A couple of non-committal remarks and 'uh-huhs' later, and he put the phone down and rubbed his face.

'That was Mark. Keith's dead. Word in the village is that the farmhouse has been gutted by fire, and that it probably started when he was storing petrol cannisters in the cellar. Mark says everyone's accepted this.'

Emma pictured Keith's face coming towards her in the

farmhouse yesterday, mad with rage. That poor man. All those years, Keith had carried the burden of what Alan had done as well as his own guilt, and what a huge burden of guilt that must have been. Young Alan had tried to tell him what Ryan James was doing, but Keith had allowed Ryan to stop him seeing the truth. No one would get over that. They would never know what Sue had known about it all; maybe she blamed Keith for believing Ryan. And then Alan's terrible death – had his mother seen his body? Probably. Oh God…

Emma turned to Luke. 'Was it Keith who sent those letters, then?' And forced her off her bike... and that dog poo...

Luke grimaced. 'I reckon the first two were Alan, then Keith took over. Forget the letters, Emma. That whole family's gone, now.'

Emma nodded, but she didn't have to say anything, because Luke was calling his parents. Sundays at ten was his usual time to phone them for a chat, so Marie would be nicely reassured now. Emma didn't move from her chair. Normally, she'd leave him alone for a private chat with Marie and Euan, but today – admit it, Emma, you want to hear what he's going to say to them. She squinted at Luke on the sofa while Marie's high-pitched tones squeaked unintelligibly from his phone.

Unexpected pity pierced Emma's heart as Luke replied to his mother. His upbeat tone was in direct contrast to his pale face and limp posture.

'Glad he's none the worse … Yes, I came home yesterday, it was all just a silly misunderstanding … I know, sorry … Not sure about this afternoon, I had a bit of a dodgy tum again … That would be great. I'll pop by early next week after work, shall I? Is Dad there?'

He gave Emma a grim smile and held his phone against his

chest for a moment. 'She's buying me a course of probiotics for my gut.'

By the look of him, they would do him good, too. Emma put her feet on the coffee table and closed her eyes. She hadn't been this bushed on a Sunday morning since she was a student. The tight band of pain around her forehead would be stress as well as exhaustion. She needed to look after herself, and she was bloody well going to do it. Starting today.

Luke went back to his phone call. 'Hey Dad … I know … Sorry about that … Okay, tomorrow … See you then, huh?'

His mobile clattered on the coffee table. 'Dad's not pleased. I think Mum's been pretty uptight these past few days.'

Emma opened her eyes. 'Can you blame her? Think how I felt, without even a text to let me know what you were doing.'

He still wasn't looking at her. 'I'm sorry.'

Emma sniffed. 'Does your mum know everything that happened with Ryan James?'

Luke shrugged. 'I'm not sure. Dad knows, and he's always so protective of her. I suppose he's the one who suffers when she gets uptight, and it doesn't need a murdered sports trainer to have her on edge. Look at how nervous she is about the baby.' He gazed at Emma's middle.

Emma sniffed. 'Well, I can understand that. She told me about her miscarriage. Quite a late one, too, I gathered.'

She got up to fetch a glass of orange juice and went back to her chair, then saw that Luke was staring at her as if she'd grown horns.

'What miscarriage?'

'The one she had just before they were married. Didn't you know about it?'

'No.'

Luke slumped back into the sofa, frowning silently at his knees while Emma massaged her forehead. The headache was lifting, thank goodness.

'Emma – they were married when she was sixteen.'

Emma gaped at him. It wasn't a huge deal, surely? Sixteen was young, but it wasn't as if they'd split up three months later. Luke's face flushed dark red, then he leapt to his feet and charged upstairs. Emma only just managed not to pout. He'd found his energy again and no mistake. Lucky him.

Thuds from boxes being shifted around in the smallest bedroom vibrated through the ceiling. A moment later Luke came back with a file box.

'Dad kept all the important documents here, and he gave it to me when we moved in. I opened it to look for the house plans when we were deciding about the patio, and I noticed there are photocopies of some old family certificates here, too. Give me a hand, will you?'

He started sorting papers into piles onto the coffee table, his face intent. Whatever this was, it was important. Emma swallowed her resentment and joined him on the sofa, and he passed her a heap of papers.

'What are we looking for?' She lifted a sheet about Capital Gains Tax from her pile and laid it to the other tax stuff on the table.

'Mum and Dad's marriage certificate. Here's all the mortgage stuff.' He slapped down a bundle and rootled further while Emma sorted through her own pile, which was all tax and insurance papers. What was so urgent about Marie and Euan's marriage certificate?

An exclamation came from Luke, and he waved a sheet of

A4. 'Here it is. Yes. Look. They married in Aberdeen, five days after Mum's birthday. Five days... Oh my God, Emma.'

Emma took the copy of the marriage certificate and stared at it stupidly. He was right, it was dated shortly after Marie's sixteenth birthday. Her mind was foggy today – why was all this significant? And what did it have to do with Marie's miscarriage? Emma leaned back in the sofa, her thoughts swirling. Marie'd told her the miscarriage was just days before their wedding. At – how many months pregnant?

Horror and pity flooded through Emma as everything snapped into place. 'Oh my God, Luke.'

Luke thumped a fist on the arm of the sofa, then buried his face in his hands. 'Underage sex. With a girl over ten years younger. And Dad was a teacher, remember. They'd have called it abuse and thrown the book at him.' He leaned back in the sofa, his breath coming in pants. 'This makes it all clear, why they were so keen not to get involved when a paedophile targeted us as kids, everything. They must have been bricking it.'

Emma sat numbly. 'Would it matter if it came out now?'

'I don't know. It might. Wasn't there something like this in the news a few years ago? And they try people older than Dad for war crimes.'

'That's not the same.' But they didn't know for sure, did they?

'I think the kindest thing would be to work out a way to let them think we have no idea about it. Oh Emma. That's it. Everything. It's finally over.'

He put both arms around her, and for a brief moment they clung together before Emma broke away. He was wrong. No matter what would happen with Marie and Euan, the story of the boys' fight with Ryan James would never be over. Somewhere, there was a body. Or more likely, a skeleton, after all this time. And there were still the lies Luke had told her, the information he hadn't shared with her. That was betrayal. She knew why he'd done it, but it was still hard to take.

Luke was pacing up and down now, rubbing his hands together. 'We'll need to make sure they hear the bare minimum about Alan's inquest and funeral.'

He stuffed the papers back into the box and ran back upstairs with it. A wave of exhaustion flooded over Emma. It was ridiculous, when Marie and Euan had been married all this time, to think that they might be prosecuted for loving each other in the nineteen seventies. But Luke was right; this was the best way to go. More lies, more pretending. Could she really live like this? She had a lot of thinking to do, because she was deciding for the baby, too.

She wandered around the garden while Luke fired up the grill for the steaks he'd removed from the freezer. She had two secrets now. The secret of Marie and Euan would be easy to keep because it was no one else's business, but Ryan James was different. What he'd done was wrong. But so was what had happened to him, and nothing would put it all right. Wasn't it the kind of secret someone should know about?

CHAPTER 35

IT WAS THE MOST UNREAL DAY SHE'D EVER LIVED THROUGH. Emma ate a tasteless steak for lunch, went for a lie-down on her bed but couldn't sleep, then sat at the kitchen table with a cup of tea and a comfort chocolate digestive. Luke was out for the count on the sofa, but he was breathing calmly and regularly and his colour was good. They both needed to recover emotionally as well as physically from what had happened, and while the best thing would be to talk it all through with someone, that was exactly what they couldn't do.

The doorbell shrilling through the house jerked her out of her daydream, and Emma trailed down the hall to answer it. Noel and Mark were standing there, Noel looking determined and Mark with a pale face and dark circles around his eyes.

Noel stepped inside before Emma could speak. 'We need to talk. Is Luke here?'

Emma led the way into the living area, where Luke was sitting up rubbing his face.

'Problem.' Noel sat down beside Luke and tried to take his pulse.

Luke pushed him away. 'I'm fine, don't worry. What problem?'

Mark sank into an armchair. 'We – Noel and Dad and I, and Jon Baker, went up to the farm this morning. The police have cordoned it all off, but Jon said they're not thinking anything other than an accident or a double suicide. The house is a stone shell now, nothing left at all, but part of the barn's still standing. The fire brigade got to it before it burned completely.'

Emma covered her face with both hands. The final moments of Keith's life didn't bear thinking about.

Mark continued, and Emma shivered at the disgust on his face.

'Thing is, Dad reckons Ryan James is up there somewhere. Apparently, Keith took the body away after he and Dad supposedly chopped it into parcels. Dad doesn't know what he did with it; I think he was just glad to have it off the shop premises and get the whole business with the phoney parcels done and dusted. Which leaves us with a problem. Dad's distaught.'

Emma sniffed. That she could well imagine. Doug must have lived in fear every day of his life since Ryan James died, though it was hard to dredge up much sympathy for a man who'd misled an entire village for twenty years. And it had been Doug's knife that killed Ryan. She could see where this was heading, though.

She cleared her throat. 'Who owns the farm now?'

Noel nodded. 'Exactly.'

Emma thought out loud. 'If Keith had a will, he'd have left it to Alan, and he's not likely to have changed that in the short time since Alan died. But as Alan predeceased him...' She stared from one man to the other. 'We can't possibly know.'

Luke leaned forwards. 'Emmy, you could ask Kate if she knows.'

Tears welled up in Emma's eyes, and two escaped before she choked them back. Her acrimonious split with Kate was one of the worst things about all this.

'Kate wants nothing to do with me now. She said if she and I had never met, Alan would be alive today, and she might be right. I can't call her up and ask about Keith's will.'

Mark got up and towered over Emma, his phone in one hand. 'I'll do it. She'll talk to me. I was a shepherd in the nativity play the year she was one of the sheep.'

An insane desire to laugh flashed through Emma. Village life. Oh, to be a townie again. She held up her phone to show Kate's number to Mark. He connected, then strode up the room and out into the garden.

Emma got up to make tea. What a horrible, stinking mess this all was.

They were onto their second cups before Mark came back in. He accepted the mug Emma handed him, and sat down. 'We had a good talk. I told her everything and she's horrified.' He glanced at Emma. 'I think she regrets what she said to you. Anyway, they all made wills when she and Alan were married, and she'll inherit the farm. She'll check with the lawyer, then come here tomorrow. I'll go up to the farm with her and see – what we see. If you guys want to come, I'm meeting her at three o'clock at the shop.'

Noel shook his head. 'I'm going back to London tomorrow.'

Emma thought. It would be good to see Kate again. It was

understandable that the other woman might not want to be friends now, but it would be so much better if they could come to a more satisfying goodbye this time.

She nodded at Mark. 'I'll be there.'

'We both will.' Luke turned to Noel. 'Thanks for all your help, mate.'

Noel and Mark left soon afterwards, and Luke pulled out his mobile. 'I need to talk to Dad. He should know some of this, then he can decide how much he wants to share with Mum.'

Emma listened as he filled Euan in on what had happened to the Johnson family, and their assumption that Ryan's body was somewhere at the farm. This was followed by a long, low drone while Euan spoke, though as the call wasn't on speaker, Emma couldn't hear what he was saying. Luke said 'yes' and 'okay' several times before ending the call and gazing at Emma.

'Dad had no idea that the parcel was a fake – I gather you told Mum about finding it? Anyway, Dad originally buried it in the garden but then he got suspicious that I knew about it – and I did – so he shifted it to the chimney, without telling Mum. I had no idea it was in the chimney either, and Dad only told Mum where it really was when they came here and saw the patio being made. He thought she'd freak out if she knew there was a chunk of Ryan in the chimney all those years.'

Emma blinked. 'Well – who wouldn't?'

'Quite. I think he's going to tell her Ryan was buried somewhere he'll never be found. We should leave that up to him, Emma.'

Emma sniffed. No way was she going to start talking to Luke's parents about any of this. She left Luke slumped on the sofa, and went for a walk around the garden. Would Ryan James ever be found?

KATE AND MARK were standing outside the butcher's when Emma pulled up behind Mark's white van the following day. Kate's cheeks were hollow, and her hair fell limply over her forehead, but there was a determined tilt to her chin as she came over to the car to greet Kate.

'Good you can come, both of you. I'm sorry I was rude, Emma.'

Emma joined her on the pavement. 'I'm sorry too. I guess we both need time to deal with what's happened.'

Mark held up his car key. 'Are we all going in the van, or—?'

Luke was standing on the other side of the car. 'We'll drive behind you.'

It was a dull, windy day and dark grey clouds were scudding across the sky as they arrived at the farm. Everywhere you looked, woolly white sheep were grazing on lush green grass, oblivious to all that was going on. Emma and Luke joined the other two at the blue and white police tape.

'Who's looking after the place?' Luke turned to Kate, thrusting his hands into his pockets.

'Two stockmen in the meantime.'

Kate brushed away tears, and Emma's heart went out to the woman. Imagine losing your partner and his parents, then learning that your husband had killed a man and his father had disposed of the body. Not to mention being left with a farm you'd never wanted to own.

She moved closer to Kate. 'What will you do?'

'The legal stuff will take months. I'm hoping the stockmen will take care of it for me until I can sell it.'

Mark lifted the police tape. 'Come on. Jon said it's not dangerous, but we shouldn't go into the house. Let's have a look.'

Emma followed him and Kate to the remains of the farm-house. Only the grey stone walls were standing, blackened by fire. This had been some blaze.

'Is there a cellar?' Mark peered into what had been the kitchen.

Kate shook her head.

'Right.' Mark looked at the barn. 'So, the body could be under one of the other buildings, or out on the fields. We'd never find it in the fields, but if we could dig around the outbuildings and make sure it's not there, that would be all that's necessary.'

'I am *not* going to start digging—' Emma started to talk, then broke off as Luke and Kate protested too.

Mark held up his hand. 'Chill, guys. No one's suggesting you dig. Kate, you said yourself it'll be months before you can sell the place. Let me manage it for you until then, keep an eye on the stockmen, and see to the demolition and any rebuilding you want done. If there's anything to be found here, I'll find it.'

Kate stared at the barn, then shrugged. 'We could do that, but… what would we do if you find—?' She pressed a hand to her mouth.

'I'll alert Jon Baker, and he'll make sure the right thing's done.'

Kate nodded, then turned abruptly and started back to the cars. Emma fell into step beside her and gave the other woman a quick hug.

Kate didn't hug back, but she blinked up at Emma as she opened the door of Mark's van. 'I've got your number.'

Emma watched as the van reversed round and vanished down the lane.

Luke gazed after them. 'She needs time.'

The decision had made itself. 'So do I. I'm going to Oma's, Luke, and I'll stay there for a few weeks. When I come back...'

He stood close without touching her. 'When you come back, we'll move forward. I'll put the house on the market, and find a rental in York while you're away. When you're back, we can discuss things like what and where and when.'

Emma nodded slowly, her lips pressed together. Luke had been a twelve-year-old child when this started, and none of it had been his fault. But she still needed time alone.

Luke got into the car, and Emma turned to take a last look at the ruined farmhouse. Keith's voice echoed through her head. *'Everyone who passes by will know what happened here. Worse than – than Lockerbie. Than Dunblane. Do you want that? No. If you don't keep the secret, you'll destroy an entire village.'*

Emma put the car in gear and drove off, not looking in the rear mirror. The secret was gone from their lives, and she couldn't let the past destroy their future. Mark would find a way to keep the pact they'd all made back then. Ralton Bridge was going to survive this, and so were she and Luke and their child. This was their second chance to be a family, and they should take it.

EPILOGUE

FOUR WEEKS LATER

Extract from the *Glenfield and Ralton Bridge Herald*

A SKELETONISED BODY HAS BEEN FOUND DURING DEMOLITION WORK at Fifty Acres Farm. It is believed to be the remains of a thirty-year-old man who was thought to be resident in Canada. The farm was struck by a triple tragedy recently with the deaths of Keith and Susan Johnson shortly after the suicide of their only son, Alan. The police have not yet named the body now found, but they are not looking for anyone in connection to the death.

ACKNOWLEDGMENTS

Pact of Silence wasn't an easy book to write. Thank you, so much, to everyone who helped along the way.

The usual big thanks to Debi Alper for the first structural edit and her advice, to Sue Davison for her insightful copy editing and to Jayne Mapp Design for the wonderfully spooky cover image. I'm also hugely indebted to Rebecca Collins of Hobeck Books for her advice on presenting the characters' motivation to act as they do in the book – it made such a difference to the story and how I feel about it.

Love and more thanks to Matthias and Pascal for their help, support, website management, bookkeeping and secretarial work (particularly the bits in German).

Thanks too to Rebecca, Adrian and everyone at Hobeck Books for their work both on this book and *Daria's Daughter*. I'd like to mention Lianne Walker here; she did a brilliant job narrating *Daria's Daughter* but the book was already published by the time the audio version was commissioned, so she didn't make it into the acknowledgements there.

To my writing friends Louise Mangos, Cass Grafton, Alison Baillie, Mandy James, Jill Marsh and Helen Pryke, thank you for your encouragement and for just being there through another difficult Corona year. Please stick around, ladies…

As always, to everyone on social media, where as well as friends and family there are the book groups, bloggers, other writers, everyone, thank you SO MUCH, and the same goes to all those who have read a book, left a review or sent me a message that they've enjoyed it. I really appreciate it.

Most especially – a last thank you to my lovely friend and fellow crime writer Alison Gray, who died in March 2021. This one's for Alison.

ABOUT THE AUTHOR

Linda grew up in Glasgow, Scotland, but went to work in Switzerland for a year aged twenty-two, and she has lived there ever since. Her day jobs have included working as a physiotherapist in hospitals and schools for handicapped children, teaching English in a medieval castle, and several extremely strenuous years as a full-time mum to two boys, a dog and a rapidly expanding number of guinea pigs, most of whom have now fortunately left home. After spending large chunks of the last few years moving house, she has now settled in a beautiful flat on the banks of Lake Constance in north-east Switzerland.

Her writing career began in the nineties, when she had over fifty short stories published in women's magazines before finding the love of her writing life, psychological suspense fiction. *Pact of Silence* is her eleventh book in this genre.

Linda says she finds her plot ideas in little incidents and moments in daily life – talking to a fellow wedding guest about adoptions, a Swiss documentary about fraudsters, a BBC TV programme about family trees.

For Linda it is when you start to think 'what if...', that is when the story really starts.

DARIA'S DAUGHTER

If you enjoyed *Pact of Silence,* you might like to try *Daria's Daughter* too.

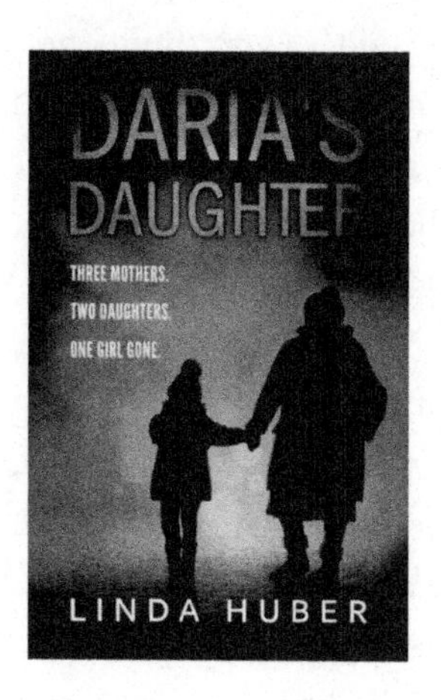

Here follows a short extract from the beginning of the novel:

DAY ONE

FRIDAY 17TH APRIL

They would miss their flight if the taxi didn't come in the next five minutes. Daria stood at her first-floor living room window, peering up the street. And oh, glory, as if there wasn't enough to worry about – the thunder that had growled in the distance for the past hour was rumbling ever louder, and look at those clouds. Her shoulders slumped as the sun vanished abruptly and fat raindrops spattered across the window, transforming the street below from Glasgow dustiness into a slick dark stripe, punctuated by blobs of hailstones that melted to join the torrents scudding along in the gutters. Daria leaned her head on the window. A spring storm when she had to get her daughter, along with everything the two of them would need over the next couple of weeks, into a taxi, out again at the airport, into the terminal building and through departures – it was exactly what she didn't need.

'Where's Daddy?' Four-year-old Evie pushed in front of Daria's legs to see outside, her pink 'ready for the taxi' jacket matching her hot little face.

Daria held out her hand. 'Come on, we'll wait downstairs. Daddy's at a conference in Stirling – remember he said bye-bye yesterday? Got your rucksack?'

Evie ran to fetch the pink elephant rucksack she'd left on the sofa. 'Daddy's in Stirling?'

They'd been through it a million times, but what did Stirling mean to a child who'd never been there? Daria dredged up a calm-Mummy smile.

'That's right. And today we're going to visit Grandma and Grandpa in Spain, and Daddy's coming to join us next week.'

Case, daughter, handbag, travel bag. Daria pulled out her compact and checked her make up. She would do. Come on, Daria, you can do this.

Downstairs, they stood in the shelter of the doorway, Evie leaning out to catch stray raindrops with her tongue while Daria fumbled for her phone. She was still scrolling down her contacts for the minicab company when a blue and white taxi screeched around the corner and pulled up by the gate. At last. Thank heavens the airport was a mere fifteen minutes away; they would make it. Daria pulled Evie's hood over her head and wheeled the case down the path to meet the taxi driver, who was standing beside his vehicle glowering at them. He heaved their case into the boot, and Daria opened the back door.

'In we get, Evie-love.' She fastened Evie's seat belt, then her own. Her daughter was a slight little thing and it was never a good feeling in a cab, when Evie had no child seat. Another reason to be thankful the airport was so near. Daria sat tapping her fingertips together as the driver organised his meter and turned on the engine. Come on, come *on*, we have to go.

The rain intensified as they crawled along to the main road and joined a column of blurry red lights as every commuter in the city headed homewards for the weekend. A band of tension tightened around Daria's head. They had less than twenty minutes now and they were inching along at a speed she could have matched on foot.

'We'll take the back road.' The driver pulled into a side street, and Daria breathed out. Traffic was flowing here, albeit slowly, but they were on their way at last. She put an arm around Evie and the little girl beamed up at her, then reached across to take Daria's hand and oh, it was so lovely, travelling with her daughter. They were picking up speed all the time; it was going to be all right. They cut round the back of the cemetery and picked up speed again. This was better.

Daria leaned over to kiss Evie's damp little forehead, then jerked back in horror as a deep horn blared and headlights from an approaching lorry swept through the cab. A single, sickening scream left Daria's soul as Evie's rucksack scratched across her forehead and the taxi skewed sideways, only to be hit from behind and flipped skywards. Her arms opened in search of her child, but she was pitched across the car, twisting in the air as metal tore around her, and–

She was flying. Daria clutched at empty air, then crashed down, rolling over and over, more screams coming from a distance. Hers? Her leg, her arm, oh please, Evie.

Silence. Stillness. Pain. Daria sank into darkness, but far, far away, something was buzzing, irritating. Find Evie, you have to find Evie. Swirling grey shapes replaced the darkness, but breathing was agony and she couldn't move her leg. Darkness was hovering; God no, she mustn't die here. A thunderclap above, and stinging rain soaked through her hair, running down her cheeks, down her neck. Far-away voices were screaming behind her, Evie's high-pitched wail the nearest.

Evie, oh baby, Mummy's here.

Daria fought to call to her child, but black pain was all around now, no, no, she was going to pass out. Her fingers splayed and met wet plastic: Evie's rucksack. Wailing sirens swooped closer as Daria fought to stay awake. Please, somebody come...

The background shouts were still too far away to help

when the choking smell of petrol reached Daria's nose. And everything went black.

WHAT THE READERS SAY

'A book I found so difficult to put down.' *****
'This gripping and emotional family drama kept me on tenterhooks from start to finish.' *****
'Brilliant, absolutely brilliant.' *****
'Kept me gripped for the entire story.' *****
'Linda Huber you are a gifted writer.' *****
'What a remarkable story.' *****
'The writing is flawless. Loved it to bits!' *****
'I was captivated from the beginning.' *****
'Can't wait for the next one!' *****

Daria's Daughter is available on Amazon as ebook or paperback.

HOBECK BOOKS – THE HOME OF GREAT STORIES

We hope you've enjoyed reading *Pact of Silence*.

Linda has written a novella *The Clarice Cliff Vase* which is available for free for subscribers to Hobeck Books.

This novella, and many other short stories and novellas, is also included in the compilation called *Crime Bites*. *Crime Bites* is also available for free to subscribers of Hobeck Books.

Crime Bites includes:

- *Echo Rock* by Robert Daws
- *Old Dogs, Old Tricks* by AB Morgan
- *The Silence of the Rabbit* by Wendy Turbin
- *Never Mind the Baubles: An Anthology of Twisted Winter Tales* by the Hobeck Team (including all the current Hobeck authors and Hobeck's two publishers)
- *The Clarice Cliff Vase* by Linda Huber
- *Here She Lies* by Kerena Swan
- *The Macnab Principle* by R.D. Nixon
- *Fatal Beginnings* by Brian Price
- *A Defining Moment* by Lin Le Versha
- *Saviour* by Jennie Ensor

Also please visit the Hobeck Books website for details of our other superb authors and their books, and if you would like to get in touch, we would love to hear from you.

Hobeck Books also presents a weekly podcast, the Hobcast,

where founders Adrian Hobart and Rebecca Collins discuss all things book related, key issues from each week, including the ups and downs of running a creative business. Each episode includes an interview with one of the people who make Hobeck possible: the editors, the authors, the cover designers. These are the people who help Hobeck bring great stories to life. Without them, Hobeck wouldn't exist. The Hobcast can be listened to from all the usual platforms but it can also be found on the Hobeck website: **www.hobeck.net/hobcast**.

ALSO BY LINDA HUBER

The Runaway

Stolen Sister

Death Wish

Baby Dear

Ward Zero

Chosen Child

The Attic Room

The Cold Cold Sea

The Paradise Trees

Daria's Daughter

Printed in Great Britain
by Amazon